She ran her hands over the corded muscles without shame, then lifted her gaze to meet his.

He was smiling, and his eyes had darkened to the color of maple syrup. The warmth she found there held her, stilling her completely.

"Hey there," he said.

"Hi."

"You're beautiful up there, you know."

"Likewise. Well. Down there. And you know. Handsome."

He chuckled and reached up to touch her cheek. "I've got an idea. How about a bit little more of that quid pro quo."

She frowned. "You want to save my life again?"

He laughed again, then tugged on the bottom of her shirt. "Nope. Yellow looks good on you, but I feel like we should even the playing field."

"Oh." Pushing through a renewed shyness, Maryse used both hands to pull off the top.

"Better?"

Brooks's eyes traveled over every inch of exposed skin before he answered. "You have no idea."

"I have *some* idea." She gave him an equally thorough onceover, then bent to kiss him once more.

* * *

Dear Reader,

Silent Rescue is a book that started with a single, imagined scene. A man watches a woman from afar. She's hurrying through the streets, her concerns and goals unknown. The woman is focused. Driven. But where is she going, and why? Is her pace the result of fear? Distress? Determination? All three? Or is the man just projecting his own worries onto the woman? Maybe he is. But then he sees the flash of a gun, and he knows his gut instinct is correct...

This is how Maryse and Brooks came to be. It's how I started to get to know them both. I discovered what a smart, dedicated mother Maryse would be. I learned that she would do anything for her daughter's safety—even risk her life and trust a man she'd just met. This one scene taught me that Brooks would have a gruff exterior but a caring heart. It showed me how his experience as a detective would mix with that kindness and help him go out of his way to rescue a child he'd never even seen. It made me want to tell their complete story. So I did.

Happy reading,

Melinda Di Lorenzo

SILENT RESCUE

Melinda Di Lorenzo

HARLEQUIN® ROMANTIC SUSPENSE

Recycling programs
for this product may
not exist in your area.

ISBN-13: 978-0-373-40216-8

Silent Rescue

Printed in U.S.A.

www.Harlequin.com

Amazon bestselling author **Melinda Di Lorenzo** writes in her spare time—at soccer practices, when she should be doing laundry and in place of sleep. She lives on the beautiful west coast of British Columbia, Canada, with her handsome husband and her noisy kids. When she's not writing, she can be found curled up with (someone else's) good book.

Books by Melinda Di Lorenzo

Harlequin Romantic Suspense

Worth the Risk
Last Chance Hero
Silent Rescue

Harlequin Intrigue

Trusting a Stranger

Harlequin Intrigue Noir

Deceptions and Desires
Pinups and Possibilities

To all the moms and dads out there who would lay everything on the line for their kids

Prologue

Six Years Ago

Maryse glanced down at her watch and cursed her inability to move quickly. Two minutes more, and she would miss the bus that would take her to the spot where she'd promised to meet her brother, Jean-Paul. Not that she was excited about whatever he had to say. Probably a request for more money or to tell her he'd been fired from his latest job. He was always in some kind of trouble—of the illegal variety, half the time—and Maryse was always the one to bail him out.

She hated the fact that he'd even talked her into coming from Seattle to Las Vegas for the week in the first place. Two days had gone by and she'd only seen him once. When he picked her up from the airport.

"Brother-sister bonding, my foot," she muttered.

She snapped up her purse from the counter, then pushed open the door. As always, the desert heat hit her like a slap in the face. The air was painfully dry. Maryse could already feel her hair wanting to bounce from its gentle waves to thick curls. She wished she'd thought to tie it back.

No time now.

With a sigh, she turned the spare key in the lock, securing her brother's basement suite. Then she paused as a

soft mewl drew her attention to the bushes to the side of
the doorstep. She peered over. A large cardboard box sat in
the shade of the prickly foliage. Had someone left a kitten
out there? Annoyed, Maryse shook her head, then moved
closer. Her brother wouldn't be thrilled if she brought some
flea-ridden beast into his place, but she couldn't leave the
poor thing outside. Even at ten in the morning, it was swel-
tering.

She reached the box, put her hand on the edge, then
gasped.

It wasn't a kitten.

"Oh, God," she said softly.

It was a baby. A newborn, swaddled in pink. Whim-
pering.

Maryse reached in to lift the child—a girl, she assumed—
and was surprised to find the blanket cool to the touch. She
glanced into the box again. One side held a diaper bag. But
the other held an ice pack. Maryse raised her head and looked
around the yard in search of whoever had cared enough to
try to keep her cool, but had been heartless enough to aban-
don the poor thing in the first place. No one was in sight.

She looked down at the infant again. A tiny black smudge
adorned the girl's cheek, and Maryse reached up to rub it
away gently. Her tiny eyes opened, and her blue, unfocused
gaze seemed to be seeking out the source of the attention.
Then the baby let out another cry, this time a little louder,
and instinct took over. With one hand, Maryse cradled the
girl, rocking her. She murmured soothing things as she used
the other hand to rifle through the bag until she found a full
bottle. The formula inside was cool, but Maryse figured that
meant it wouldn't have spoiled. And the baby was clearly
hungry. She nudged back the blanket and pressed the bottle
to the newborn's mouth. The baby immediately settled in,
sucking enthusiastically.

"Okay, sweetheart," Maryse said softly, settling to the ground.

Careful not to disturb the little one's feeding, she lifted the diaper bag and pushed it open. Inside, she found two Canadian passports, and when she thumbed open the first one, her blood went cold. Her own picture stared up at her, and the name was just as startling.

Maryse Anne LePrieur.

It was hers. But *not* hers, too. Maryse and Anne were correct. But the surname was her mother's maiden one.

She grabbed the second passport.

Camille Anne LePrieur.

And the photo was of the infant.

Feeling numb, Maryse adjusted the baby—Camille—and dug farther in the bag. Her hand found a thick envelope, and a quick look told her it was an enormous stack of cash. Her hands shook as she lifted a small, folded-up piece of paper from the front of the envelope. With dread pooling in her gut, she opened it. Her brother's familiar, untidy handwriting sprawled over the page.

Run. Far. Fast. Keep her safe. Don't trust anyone, and don't risk going to the police. Just love her like your own. She's yours now. And if they say I did it, know it's a lie.

Maryse stood quickly. And she and her belongings were gone before the first sirens even got close to her brother's house.

Chapter 1

Maryse swung open the bedroom door, a huge smile on her face. A few minutes earlier, she'd turned on the news and learned that black ice had forced her daughter's school to close for the day. She knew a lot of moms would be cursing the weather and cursing the school board and wondering what they were going to do with their kids on this extra wintery day. But Maryse was thrilled. She didn't mind the cold. She didn't mind a day off. And she didn't mind an excuse to pull out the ice skates and do loops on the pond with her daughter.

"Rise and shine, Camille!" she called to the lump of blankets on the bubble gum–pink bed.

Not that she thought the six-year-old could hear her, but because old habits die hard. And sometimes, Maryse thought if she didn't speak out loud now and again, she might lose her voice altogether.

Besides that…though she was deaf, the little girl was impossible to sneak up on. She heard everything in her own way.

You vibrate, Cami signed to her once.

Vibrate? Maryse had repeated, thinking she'd missed something.

Though Cami was a natural ASL speaker and had been taught the proper grammatical rules from the time she was small, Maryse knew her own understanding was sometimes lacking. She tended to try to translate what she wanted to say from English first, and it often mucked things up. But this particular time, she'd got it right.

Vibrate, her daughter confirmed, then giggled and added, *Like an elephant walking across the floor.*

Maryse smiled at the memory and twisted the blind slats open just enough to let in the sunshine, and with it, a puff of cold air. Because Quebec weather could be deceptive like that. The glowing orb up there in the sky looked so much like it should be warm. Like it *wanted* to provide some heat. But it was an unforgiving light instead.

For a second, the chill seemed ominous, and a shiver made Maryse wrap her arms around her own body, rubbing her palms against the comforting fuzz of her faux-angora sweater. Then she pushed off her worry and reminded herself that today was going to be a fun day.

"Nothing a jacket won't fix. Right, sweet pea?" she said as she turned back toward the bed. But the down comforter didn't move. Not an inch. "Camille?"

She stepped forward and put out a hand, wondering if her daughter was sick. But when she reached for Camille's shoulder, she found a pillow instead.

Panic didn't set in right away—the little girl was fond of pranks. And hide-and-seek.

"Very funny!" Maryse said, then gestured, too, in case her daughter was hiding somewhere she could see.

She moved around the room, peeking into the usual hiding spots. The closet. The book cubby. Under the bed, then in the tiny bathroom that adjoined the room. Empty.

She stood in the bedroom's doorway, put her hands on her hips and turned slowly, searching for her too-clever girl. Stuffed animals and knickknacks galore dominated the shelves.

"Come out, come out, wherever you are," she called, her hands moving to make the words come to life.

As Maryse turned to move her search to the rest of the house, her sock-covered foot slipped on something on the floor, and she slid across the carpet, landing on one knee. She bit back a curse—Camille always seemed to know when she let one drop—and reached out to snap up the offending object.

What the— A key card?

She frowned down at the slim piece of plastic.

Maison Blanc.

She flipped it over and found an address in Laval. The city was an hour and a half south of the tiny town, LaHache, where they lived.

"Where'd you get this one, Cami?" she murmured as she pushed herself to her feet, then set the card beside the rest of the odd little trinkets on the nearest shelf.

Collecting things was a Camille habit. Just one of the hobbies that made the kid interesting.

Maryse smiled to herself, then stepped out to scan the hallway. "Okay, kiddo. Give me a hint."

But the house stayed silent, and as she covered the scant eight hundred square feet of space, her smile began to slip.

All closets. Nope, nope and nope twice more.

Every cupboard large enough to hold a fifty-pound child. Nothing.

Concern crept in quickly.

"Camille!" Maryse called her daughter's name loudly. Useless, she knew. But she still did it again. "Cami!"

She looked in the laundry basket and up the sooty chimney. With her heart in her throat and thoughts of the sub-zero temperature outside on her mind, she eased open the only entrance to the house—a door off the living room. But all she found was the same day-old dusting of snow that had coated the patio yesterday. Impossible for Camille to have gone over it without a trace. Relief made her sag temporarily.

But where is she?

Maryse took a breath and made her way back to the bedroom, where she scanned for some hint of something she might've missed. Her eyes found the window, then stayed there. Her brain grabbed a thought and hung on to it.

That little blast of cold air...

Woodenly, she stepped closer. She gripped the blinds' rod and turned. And yes. There it was. *Evidence.* The childproof lock had been forced across the ridge at the bottom of the window, leaving a nasty groove through the metal. And when Maryse pushed the blinds aside, she could see the sliver of an opening.

Oh, God. Please, no.

Her heart thumped hard against her rib cage as she spun back to the pile of pink bedding. Then she saw it sticking out from under one of the frilly pillows: a slip of familiar notepaper dotted with fluttering butterflies.

Maryse snatched it up, her hand shaking so badly she almost couldn't read the words that were written there in large, deliberate block letters. She inhaled and forced herself to go still.

Two sentences. Two. And they were enough to take her world, stop it from spinning, then flip it in the other direction.

I TOOK WHAT YOUR BROTHER OWED ME.
CONSIDER HIS FATE A WARNING - NO POLICE.

She breathed in. She breathed out.

She fought the threatening blackness and made herself look at Camille's familiar things. The favorite stuffed bunny, one loose ear and one eye gone. The ribbon she used as a bookmark tucked into the pages of her latest read. The radio she insisted on having even though she couldn't listen to it.

And then her eyes landed on the single item in the room that she was certain she hadn't seen before.

The key card for Maison Blanc. A clue. But what did it mean she should do?

The police!

The urge to call them was instinctual. Logical, even. Or it would be under normal circumstances.

Normal.

The word was nearly laughable. There was nothing normal about this. Still. Her feet itched to move. To take her to her cell phone so she could make the "normal" choice. But there was more to consider than simply placing her daughter's fate in the hands of the police.

For one, there was the not-so-small issue of guardianship. No matter how Maryse sliced it, there was nothing legal about her parentage. Or even her identity. Sure, she had ID that had passed even strict scrutiny over the years. But this was different. This was the police, picking apart all aspects of her life. If they figured out that she was a fraud, it might influence how the case was viewed. Would they throw her in jail? Keep her from the investigation?

Of course, that was actually a small matter compared to the note and its warning. Because Cami's safety was definitely worth more than protecting her own identity, and there was no getting around what fate her brother had met. He'd died in the fire supposedly set by his own hand.

Maryse swallowed. The idea that something similar might happen to her daughter was unbearable. More than unbearable. Unthinkable.

But she was sure that every kidnapper made the same

warning about contacting the authorities. That was what they always showed in the movies, anyway. So did that mean she should just do it anyway? Was calling them worth the risk in spite of the warning? They'd already snuffed out Jean-Paul's life. Would they hesitate on making this new threat a reality, too?

And what about ransom?

Her rapidly churning thoughts paused for a moment. There was no mention of money. Was it coming later?

No. Because they already took what they wanted. Cami herself.

The thought made her want to go for the phone all over again. Because if they weren't after anything in exchange, what did she have to negotiate with? The police were surely better equipped to deal with this than she was.

Her head spun even more.

If Cami died and it was because she made the wrong call…

If Cami died and it was because she didn't make the call…

And besides all of that…would the cops even believe her story?

Probably not.

Not quick enough, anyway. It was too complicated. Too far-fetched. And the nearest police station was an hour away. In the amount of time it would take them to make their way to her, she could get halfway to Laval herself. If she hurried, she could even be there before breakfast.

Maryse exhaled, then squeezed the Maison Blanc card once more. A phone call to the hotel would be pointless. It had taken him—whoever he was—six years to find her and Cami. He wouldn't have left a clue behind. Not on purpose. He was there. He had Cami.

And Maryse was going to take her back.

* * *

Brooks Small stretched out his long legs, leaned back and attempted to bask in the sun. For about three seconds, it worked. Then a blast of crisp air cut across his face, throwing the hood of his parka down from his head to his shoulders, reminding him a little too thoroughly that it was winter.

Except it's not *winter,* growled his inner, surly self. *It's mid-April.*

Stubbornly, he reached up to snap his hood back into place, and his elbow snagged on the edge of his wicker coffee-shop chair. He heard a loud tear.

Dammit.

Pulling on every ounce of patience he had, Brooks closed his eyes, counted to twelve—because ten sure as hell wasn't going to cut it right that second—and eased the jacket away from the chair.

"You hated the coat anyway," he muttered.

It was true. Mostly because he hated everything to do with being away from his home in the ironically named town of Rain Falls, Nevada. He preferred being minutes from the bright lights of Vegas and he enjoyed the often-scorching summer days.

If he was there, now, in the good old US of A, his neighbors would be opening their pools. Not scraping the snow off their backyard ponds so they could enjoy the supposedly unseasonably cold weather.

As if this frozen city has *a season other than winter.*

He exhaled noisily, his breath frosty and visible. Brooks had heard on the radio that it was minus eighteen degrees Celsius outside today. Which translated to roughly zero degrees Fahrenheit.

Two months Brooks had been in Laval, Quebec, and he had yet to see anything but snow.

Snowy streets.

Snowy parks.

Snowy *everything*.

Like nature had whitewashed the entire city.

Don't forget the icicles, Brooks reminded himself. *Actual damned icicles, hanging from actual damned eaves.*

"*Monsieur?*"

Brooks's head snapped up at the voice, and the teenage waitress attached to the soft-spoken question jumped back. He tried to smooth out his expression, at least into something passably pleasant. He failed. It was evident in the way that the waitress continued to stand a few feet away, cowering just a little. His espresso was still in her shaking hand, and it was cooling rapidly.

Brooks inclined his head toward the demitasse cup. "*Mon café?*"

"*Oui.*"

He stifled a sigh. Usually his complete bastardization of the language of love was enough to squeeze the English out of even the most French of the French-Canadian.

Not today, apparently.

"*Mademoiselle?*" he prodded.

When she continued to stand stock-still, Brooks decided she needed a bit of motivation in a more universal language. He dug into the zippered pocket of his parka and fished out three wide gold- and silver-colored coins. He eyed them skeptically. He didn't think he'd ever get used to the things, no matter how long his banishment to Canada lasted. The damned coins seemed like toy money to Brooks, and they sure as hell didn't look like enough cash to pay for his coffee and leave a four-dollar tip on top of that.

When he set them down on the table, though, the waitress finally did snap out of her fear-daze. With something approximating a smile, she slipped the coins into her tiny apron and set Brooks's coffee—without spilling a drop, he noticed—in its place.

"*Merci,*" she said, then scurried away quickly, back into the enveloping warmth of the café.

Brooks waited until she'd disappeared before he took a sip of coffee. He knew it didn't make a ton of sense to sit outside in the freezing cold, but the ritual wasn't about reason. It was about principle. Like many cops, Brooks got into a groove and stuck to it. He didn't know if it could be classified as superstitious behavior or if it bordered on compulsive, but he did know it worked for him. He'd even argue that it made him better at his job, because sticking to a routine made it easier to spot the out-of-the-ordinary.

Every morning at home, he sat on the patio, took stock of the day, did the crossword and enjoyed an espresso. He sure as hell wasn't going to let a little thing like the temperature change that.

Yep. Principles.

Brooks had them.

He suppressed a sigh and glanced down at his watch.

It was 9:33 a.m. on a Tuesday.

In a few minutes, a gray-haired man would come by, light a cigarette, smoke it quickly, then go inside to order something in the largest cup the café offered. Shortly after that, a frazzled mother with her toddler in tow would park illegally, dash inside and come out with her personalized cup steaming. The kid would have a cookie.

Most days were like that. The same people at the same time, fully predictable. Nicely so.

Brooks noted them all, and noted the discrepancies even more.

Like right that second.

A tall, slim brunette was coming up the sidewalk on the other side of the street. She had her chin tucked into the collar of her tan duffle coat, hurrying, but trying to look like she wasn't. She kept her head still and her gaze forward, but every two or three steps, her eyes would dart first one way, then the other. Maybe the average observer wouldn't have noticed. Or maybe just assumed she was looking for a certain address. To Brooks, she looked like trouble.

Automatically, he sat up a little straighter, making more detailed mental notes.

Five foot eight, easily. Maybe five-nine.

A hundred and twenty pounds? Bulky jacket, though. Could add a few pounds to her frame.

Too thin, Brooks thought absently. *Not eating? Ill, maybe?*

Except her face had nothing sallow about it. Her skin *was* pale, but in a porcelain way rather than a sickly one. Altogether pretty, actually.

She got closer still, and Brooks fleshed out his description even more. Tight bun at the nape of her neck. Thick enough to let him know her hair would be long. A stray curl hung down over one cheek—which he could see now wasn't quite so pale, but instead, marked with a rosy glow. Likely brought on by the cold, he thought. Her lips were full and nearly crimson, and she was makeup-free.

And not just pretty, he realized. *Stand-out-in-a-crowd stunning.*

Was that why she wore her hair in that severe style? Did it have something to do with her plain skin? A mask?

She'd reached the corner across from him now, and, for a second, she just stood there, her stare seemingly fixed on the café. Then she lifted a pair of sunglasses from her pocket, placed them on her face and leaped from the sidewalk to the street. Straight into the path of a brave winter cyclist.

Brooks's heart jumped to his throat, but before he could

react—and rush in like some deranged, parka-clad hero—
the woman sidestepped lightly, lifted her hand in an apology and moved toward the café. Straight toward Brooks.

Maryse's eyes rested on the man sitting in front of the
café that neighbored the Maison Blanc.

He was dressed for the weather. But something about
him made her think he didn't belong. And even though he
looked away quickly, his gaze had been too sharp, his interest in her too pointed. Did he know something? Or was
she being paranoid?

An hour and a half in the car hadn't done her mind any
good. Try as she might to stay focused on making a plan,
her brain had insisted on swirling with dark worry, playing out every one of her worst fears.

Cami is alive, she told herself firmly.

She had to be. But the breathless, sick feeling churning
through her wouldn't rest.

From behind her deliberately dark sunglasses, Maryse
let herself study the man for another few seconds, while
pretending to look at the hotel.

Under his hood, she could just see that his hair was buzz-
cut, his face clean shaven. He had a thick build, made even
more so by the big, black coat. His face had a certain roughness, too. A fierce mouth and the strongest jaw she'd ever
seen. Powerfully handsome. That was how she would describe him. But when he lifted his eyes to her once more,
his expression softened him somehow. There was a measure of concern there. Kindness.

So, no. It's not him, she decided. *There won't be anything kind about whoever took her.*

Her gaze stayed on him for one more moment before
she moved past him—and his undeniable undercurrent of
attractiveness—and past the café toward the brass-framed

doors of the Maison Blanc. She pushed her way through, appreciating the blast of warm air that hit her as she did. It took the edge off her hours-long chill. But she didn't pull off her gloves as she strode toward the counter—she needed them to curb the urge to sign as she spoke.

Hoping she looked more confident than she felt, she approached the concierge desk. But the uniformed man behind the counter was on the phone, speaking in a hushed tone, his brows knit together with irritation. He didn't turn her way, and Maryse let out a little cough. She didn't have time to waste. So when he still didn't look up, she cleared her throat a second time.

He spun, seeming startled by her presence.

For a second, that paranoia reared its head again. She forced it back and dragged her sunglasses from her face to her head.

He set the phone down on the counter, then smiled at her. "Can I help you?"

"I hope so," Maryse replied, glad that her voice didn't shake. "I'm meeting some people—a couple of business contacts—and I think they gave me the wrong room number. The key I have won't open the door, and no one answered when I knocked."

"Which room is it supposed to be?"

"Two-twenty-eight?" She lied quickly, hoping there *was* a room 228.

She tugged the key from her coat pocket and handed it over. He took it and swiped it across the keyboard in front of him, then frowned at the screen.

"Well," he said. "That explains it. This key is for room *eight*—no two-twenty in front of it—right here on the first floor. But I'm afraid they've asked for calls to be held, and I can't issue you a new key unless the room is in your name."

"Oh." She couldn't keep the disappointment from her voice.

The concierge tapped the key card on the counter for a second, then smiled again. "You know what I *can* do for you, though? I can take you down to room eight myself and we can check if your contact is there. We'll call it a house-keeping emergency."

Maryse considered the offer. Then rejected it. She was tempted. She wanted to get to Cami. Badly. But she didn't want to endanger anyone else.

"It's okay," she said. "I'll just give them a call on my cell and leave a message."

"You sure?"

"Yes."

She slipped away from the counter and moved to the chairs in the lobby area. She perched on the edge of one of them, then pulled out her phone and pretended to dial. But she was really watching the concierge. Waiting for a distraction. And it only took a few moments. He lifted the desk phone again and started up with his hushed conversation, turning away from the lobby in the process.

Thank God.

Moving as swiftly as she dared, she eased herself up. She took another glance at the concierge, then scurried across the tiled floor to the hallway, pausing just long enough to read which direction would lead her to room eight, then hurried to the left. She stripped off her gloves now—she'd need her hands to talk to Cami—and counted off the doors in her head.

One.

Two.

Three.

And that was as far as she got. Something jabbed her in

the back, and then a click sounded from behind her, and a man's gravelly voice spoke right into her ear.

"Move," it said. "Slowly. Walk with me and act like you're having a good time. If you scream, run or try anything I think is funny, I'll make sure your daughter is the one who pays the price. Even *think* about getting the authorities involved and I'll make sure the price is extracted slowly. And not from you."

The threat was more than enough to make her obey.

Chapter 2

Brooks took a sip of his espresso—now cold—and told himself he was being ridiculous. That he had an overactive cop imagination waving flags when none were necessary.

For a second, though, he could've sworn the dark-haired woman was staring right at him. Scrutinizing him. Looking for something. Which she definitely didn't find, judging by how quickly she bolted into the hotel.

It bothered him, and he had no idea why. What was her deal? Was she actually in trouble? He wished he'd asked her.

And say what? he wondered. *Pardon me, ma'am, but are you looking for someone? Or no? Maybe hiding from someone? Yes, here in the middle of this street. No, no. Don't call the cops.*

Brooks shook his head and took another icy gulp of coffee. Canadians were friendly—that characterization had turned out to be true—but he somehow doubted that gregariousness extended to a tolerance for on-leave cops from south of the border asking nosy questions.

Still...

The sudden buzz of Brooks's cell phone jarred his attention back to the moment.

"Small," he said into the phone, his voice clipped.

There was a familiar chortle on the other end. "Now, now. Don't sell yourself short."

"Does that *never* get old for you, Masters?" he asked his longtime partner.

"Never."

"At least one of us is getting a laugh."

There was a pause. "Not enjoying your vacation?"

"It's hardly a vacation."

"Civilian life."

"Barely that, either. Isn't it, like, four in the morning there?"

Sergeant Masters let out another chuckle. "Almost seven, actually. Finishing up the night shift."

"So you thought you'd call *me*?"

"Oh, c'mon, Small. I hear the Great White North has plenty to offer."

"Like?"

"Hockey? Canadian bacon? Girls looking for a warm-blooded American to melt their igloos?"

Brooks rolled his eyes. "You've been watching too many movies, my friend."

"You're telling me there isn't one pretty girl in that entire country?"

Brooks opened his mouth, then snapped it shut again as he lifted his eyes just in time to see the brunette step out of the hotel doors. The top button of her coat had come undone, exposing her creamy throat, and she appeared oblivious to the cold air.

Yeah, he conceded silently. *At least one pretty girl.*

"You there, man?"

Brooks forced his attention back to the phone conversation. "What I'm telling you, Masters, is that there isn't one single *igloo* here—meltable or otherwise—and quite frankly, I'm a little let down."

On the other end, his partner laughed so hard he sounded like he was choking. When his amusement finally subsided, he launched into some story about their captain. But Brooks was already distracted again, the long tale fading into the background.

A man in a dark trench coat worn over a well-tailored suit was standing behind the woman. A poor-boy cap covered his head, a scarf obscured the bottom half of his face, and a pair of dark sunglasses blocked his eyes.

A tingle crept up along Brooks's spine, then settled between his shoulder blades.

He'd tuned out Masters's voice completely now, his attention focused entirely on the scene unfolding in front of him. He'd already set down his empty coffee cup. He kept his hands open and relaxed. He didn't have to work on the pose at all. Years on the job—years of waiting patiently for the right moment while looking like he *wasn't* waiting at all—bred a certain kind of readiness into a man. A second nature.

Brooks's eyes flicked to the man in the cap. Then to the brunette. Then back.

The man leaned down and put his face at an even level with her ear. Brooks watched his mouth work silently above the scarf. Though he couldn't hear a word, the intimacy of the conversation was obvious. Seconds later, the man put out his hand, palm up, and the woman reciprocated by placing her fingers in his.

A gold wedding band—on the woman's left hand, but not on the man's—caught the cold sun and glittered.

A total misread, Brooks realized.

It wasn't a criminal activity. It was an affair.

He averted his eyes, embarrassed that he'd been so caught up in the brunette's action that he'd attributed her nervousness to something dangerous, when in fact it was actually caused by something far more cliché.

You need to get back to work. For real.

"Masters," he said loudly, interrupting the unending flow of the other man's story and not caring in the least. "Did the captain say anything about when I can come home?"

The silence on the other end was a bad sign. Clearly, something *had* been said, and whatever it was...the news wasn't good.

"C'mon," his partner replied after a few weighted seconds. "Any of the guys would kill to be in your position. Paid leave in a foreign country? No collars to run down, no worrying about having some two-bit drug dealer shooting you in the—"

Brooks cut him off. "I'll take that as a *no*."

There was another pause, then a sigh. "We all know what hell you went through, Small. None of us would wish it on our worst enemies. But you lost control. A good man died."

Regret hit Brooks straight in the gut. More painful than a gunshot wound, and far more lasting, too.

He refused to let it overwhelm him. "Parler slept with my informant. He got *himself* killed. And the girl, too. The man's 'goodness' is questionable at best."

This time, the blank air went on for so long that Brooks thought momentarily that his partner might've hung up. He knew better, though. Masters was simply giving him a chance to retract his statement. To let his brain catch up to his mouth. But he wasn't going to give in to the silence.

I'm a lot of things, but I'm not a killer.

He didn't realize he'd spoken the words aloud until Masters answered him.

"I know that, man. Anyone with his lid screwed on tight knows that. But when the chief's favorite rookie winds up dead..."

The other man's voice carried on, but Brooks had tuned him out again, this time because he really didn't want to hear what Masters had to say.

His gaze drifted back toward the striking brunette, but she and her lover were gone.

Maybe to take their tryst to the next level. Maybe to—

Brooks's musings cut off as he spotted them on the corner of the road.

The girl's mouth was open in a silent cry, her body bent away from the man, who held her elbow tightly. *Too* tightly. The man lifted his other hand then and pressed it to the small of the woman's back. Something metallic glinted in the small space between them.

Brooks leaped to his feet. His thighs slammed into the table hard enough to send the espresso cup rolling off. It smashed to the ground, and his jacket snagged on the chair again, leaving him stuck.

"Small?" Masters's voice was full of concern.

"I have to go."

"C—"

Whatever his partner had been about to say was lost as Brooks clicked the hang-up button. He abandoned his jacket, dropped the phone into his pocket and took off at a run.

Because he recognized that glint for what it was.

A gun.

Without warning, the man with the gun slid an arm around Maryse and pulled her back into a darkened doorway. He clamped a hand over her mouth, pushed the weapon into her back and warned her to keep quiet as a blurred figure went running by. Even with the freezing air surrounding her, and the thick winter coat acting as a buffer, the cool metal drove into her and made her shiver.

She wanted to recoil away from it. Almost as much as she wanted to recoil away from the man wielding it. The single glance she'd stolen before he bundled up his face was enough to make her chest squeeze with fear. His eyes were dark, angry slashes. His mouth no better. A terrible, star-shaped scar covered one cheek.

Maryse closed her eyes for just a second and reined in another shiver.

What were you expecting? she chastised silently. *A kidnapper who looked like Santa Claus?*

But truthfully, it didn't matter what he looked like, any more than it mattered he had a weapon. The uncertainty of her daughter's fate and the hope that this man would lead Maryse to her were more than enough to keep her quiet.

After several long minutes, he forced her back to the sidewalk. And as he led her through the warren of streets, she swore she could feel the cool metal barrel digging a little farther into the small of her back with each step.

Hold on, she told herself. *Means to an end. This man knows where Cami is.*

She resisted an urge to ask about Camille's safety. He'd made it clear he didn't want to hear the sound of her voice. When they'd left the hotel doors, she'd uttered a single word and he'd pinched her so hard that it still smarted.

Trying to distract herself, she glanced up at the nearest building and tried to place it. But it was too late to orient herself. They'd already managed to weave through a half dozen streets that blended together.

Rue Rouge.

Rue Laurent.

Rue...who knew what?

The corners came quickly, and the buildings were piled atop one another, each looking as drearily the same as the other.

Please, she prayed silently, *just let her be okay.*

In spite of her resolve not to show any emotion, tears pricked at her eyes. It got worse when she glanced up and saw a discarded doll hanging from the edge of a balcony. Normally, that kind of thing made her smile. This time, it made her cringe. Unconsciously, she slowed to stare. And it earned her yet another sharp jab.

"Go," growled the gunman.

Maryse stumbled a little as they reached yet another corner, this one unmarked by any street sign at all. In her boot, one of her ankles twisted. Even though she tried to bite down and keep it in, a little cry escaped her lips.

Weakness, she chastised herself.

Not something she should be showing. Not if she wanted to negotiate her daughter's release. The smallest chink in the armor could jeopardize that chance. So she ignored the searing pain that shot up her leg from her twisted ankle, and she let the man behind her push her on.

But they only made it four more steps—not quite all the way across the road—when he abruptly released her arm. As he let her go, he barked out something gutturally unintelligible. For a second, she thought he'd switched to speaking in French. Puzzled, Maryse spun to face him.

Then stepped back as he flew toward her.

What the—

Her thought cut off as her mind worked, trying to make sense of what she saw.

His eyes were wide, his mouth open. A crimson drop fell from one corner of his lips. Then his body hit the ground, and she figured it out.

Not French, she realized. *And not English, either.*

The sound he'd made hadn't been words at all. Just a last utterance.

As if to confirm it, his coat flapped open, revealing an increasing pool of red, with a narrow hole in the center.

A gunshot wound.

Maryse's gut twisted, and she doubled over. The motion saved her. A bullet whizzed by, then slammed into the ground just a few feet in front of her.

With her heart in her throat, Maryse righted herself, turned and fled toward the buildings on the other side of the road. She pushed her back flat against the icy structure just as another bullet hit the cement, this time mere inches from her boots.

Sure it had come from above, her gaze flew up, searching. Was that a pinprick of red light, up in the window of the low-rise up the road? Did the curtains just flash? But everything was still now.

She hazarded a quick glance toward the fallen man. His head had rolled to one side, and his chest no longer rose up and down at all.

Cami.

Oh, God. What did this mean for her daughter? The man on the ground had been her one link to whoever had her.

The wall Maryse had been holding around her heart for the last few hours teetered. A dull ache formed in her chest as the anxiety threatened to overwhelm her. It made her sway a little on her feet. And she stumbled.

But surprisingly, she didn't fall.

Instead, a warm, strong hand closed on her elbow, steadying her. Then the hand pulled her back into the building. Out of sight. Out of the potential line of fire. It gripped her tightly. And for a paralyzing instant, Maryse's instinct wasn't fight, and it wasn't flight. It was simply to sink into the reassuringly solid touch. And the strange sensation worsened when she looked up and met a man's gaze. Hazel, flecked with gold, and full of genuine concern.

She had to force herself to pull away enough to take in a little more of his appearance. Whoever he was, he had a frame as bulky as it was tall, and if his height topped less than six foot three, Maryse would eat her wool hat. But as he pulled back a bit more and opened his mouth, it wasn't his impressive size that made her gasp. It wasn't even the fact that she finally recognized him as the man who'd been sitting outside the café near the hotel. It was the slight flash of metal at his hip.

Oh, God. This man is the shooter.

And Maryse was off as fast as her legs could take her. Three steps to the edge of the street. Another five to put her past the body lying there. Two more and—

The stranger's body slammed into hers, then twisted. The motion sent them to the ground together, and for a second, Maryse was on top. But the momentum kept them going, and they rolled. Once. Twice. And on the third time, his powerful forearms locked to her elbows and his thick thighs locked hard against her hips, pinning her to the icy concrete.

He stared down at her, his hazel eyes dark. Like it was *she* who'd done something wrong. And it made Maryse mad. All the stress of the last few hours funneled through her, found purchase in her knee, then jerked up full force. The man must've seen something in her gaze, though, because he swung sideways at the last second, and she just barely managed to graze his hip.

"Stop," he ordered, his voice full of authority.

Yeah, right.

"I'm trying to help you," he growled.

Equally unlikely. She struggled harder to free herself, flailing wildly.

"Parlez-vous anglais?" he asked in badly accented French. "I want to let you go so we can get the hell out of here."

As if to prove his point, he released her arms. She reached up to throw a fist at him, but before she could follow through, three more bullets—not quite rapid-fire, but successive enough to be thoroughly jarring—hit the building behind them.

It really wasn't him, Maryse realized.

He glared down at her, an I-told-you-so look on his face. The smugness didn't last longer than a second, though. Another shot made him jerk backward in surprise.

He let out a groan, then rolled off her and pushed to his feet. "C'mon."

Maryse only hesitated for a heartbeat. Long enough to glance down and realize the flash she'd seen at his waist hadn't been a gun—just a belt buckle. She took his outstretched hand and let him guide her away from the gruesome scene, and away from whoever was still firing on them.

And just in time. The wail of sirens cut through the air, warning them that authorities were on their way.

Chapter 3

Brooks was careful to keep their flight as casual as possible. Not just because he had a sharp, dangerous burn in his shoulder, but because he knew what the cops would be looking for. He knew what he would be looking for himself, if he was in their shoes: a couple on the run. So he hugged the buildings to stay out of sight and moved at an unsuspicious pace. He could tell that the woman—who was now gripping his hand tightly, and who still hadn't said a word—wanted to move faster. Her feet kept trying to pick up the pace, and Brooks was the one holding them back.

Why had the sound of the siren spooked her even more?

She was visibly shaken up by the impending arrival of the police, and in Brooks's experience, that usually meant trouble. And running from the scene of a crime… He shook his head. Never mind the legality of it, he knew how bad it looked.

Deal with it later, he said to himself. *When she feels safe and is calm enough to explain.*

If she ever did. She kept glancing over her shoulder, then jerking her head forward.

"If you can understand me," Brooks said softly. "Try to focus on something ahead of you instead of thinking about what's behind you. Look at the fire hydrant. Then, when we get there, pick something else. A sign or a land-mark. Anything."

He had no idea if she knew what he meant, or if it was just his tone, but she took a breath, and her frantic move-ments eased. Her pace slowed, too.

Good, Brooks thought. *Just a couple out for a leisurely stroll. In arctic temperatures.*

Which he was really starting to feel now that the adren-aline was wearing off. The only thing keeping him from being completely frozen was the closeness of the woman beside him. In his hurry to keep her safe, he'd almost for-gotten what had drawn his attention to her in the first place. Her classic, China-doll beauty. Walking beside her, hands clasped, hips bumping…it was impossible *not* to think about it. Definitely enough to warm him far more than the parka he hated. Which he was never going to get back now. Because even though they *had* come nearer to the hotel and the café—just a few streets away, in fact—he didn't want to risk returning. If someone had seen his sudden depar-ture, they might put two and two together and want to ask questions he didn't have the answers for. Yet.

He gave the woman's hand a reassuring squeeze, then directed her up a street he knew well. His own.

He let go of her hand and stopped in front of the famil-iar brick building he'd called home for the last two months, then pointed up before asking again, *"Parlez-vous anglais?"*

She stared at him for a long moment, her pretty mouth set in a line but her arms and hands moving silently. It took Brooks a moment, but as her face and hands worked, he re-alized it wasn't random. It was something he recognized. A language he knew, at least partly.

Crazy if he thinks I'm answering, she was saying. *Cra-zier still if he thinks I'm going in there with him.*

Are you deaf? he signed back—clumsily and more of

a literal translation than a true use of the language, but to the best of his ability. *Or do you just like to talk to yourself in ASL?*

Her clear blue eyes widened, and she didn't have to sign what she was thinking. She clearly hadn't expected him to recognize the gestures, let alone understand them.

I had a cousin who was deaf, he signed, then added, *Well? Anything to say?*

She sighed. "I'm not deaf."

"And you do speak English."

"Yes. *And* French. Better than you do, apparently."

He noticed that she had to hold her hands stiffly at her sides to keep from signing along with her words. Who in her life was deaf? He glanced down at her ringed finger. Her husband? Where was he, while she was out here getting shot at in the streets of Laval? And why did it bother Brooks so much that the man wasn't there to protect her?

He forced his attention back to the moment. "Do you really have time to fight about my language skills?"

"No. I don't. Speaking of which…" She turned away.

Automatically, Brooks shot out a hand to restrain her. "You can't just go running right back out there."

"I don't have a choice."

"You *do* have a choice."

She shook off his grip and glanced up at his apartment building. "*That's* not a choice."

"Listen to me," Brooks said. "Whoever called the police may have got a good look at you. If you head back into those streets, you risk being caught. If not right this second, then as soon as they start circulating your description."

"I didn't do anything wrong," she argued.

"But you *are* a witness, and I'm guessing that if you don't have time to argue with me about my pronunciation, you don't have time to give an hours-long statement to the police, either," he replied. "And even if you *do* somehow manage to elude them, I'm guessing that whoever was firing at you isn't going to just give up."

Her face crumpled, and for a second, Brooks thought she might cry. An unexpected tug of sympathy pulled at his heart, and an accompanying urge to pull her into his arms. He made himself resist, but when he spoke again, it was in a far gentler tone.

"You may not *like* the choice, but I'm all you've got." He paused, then signed the rest of what he had to say. *I saved your life. I might be able to help you again. At the very least, give me a chance to keep you alive long enough to learn your name.*

Her eyes flicked up the street, then to the apartment building, then back to Brooks. There was the tiniest sliver of hope in those baby blues.

"Ten minutes," she said.

"Guess I'll take what I can get."

He led her through the front doors, then down the hall and up the stairs to his second-floor suite. It was a small, one-bedroom deal, prefurnished and practical. Clearly intended for short-term stay.

"Sorry about the lack of luxury," he said. "Laval isn't home for me, usually."

"It's okay."

He waited for her to add something else. A personal detail about her own home—wherever it might be—but she just stood in the center of the adjoining kitchen and living room, like she wasn't sure where to go. Admittedly, it felt funny to Brooks, too, to have company. He'd been treating the apartment more like a hotel room than like a home, barely unpacking his suitcase or adding any personal touches. Of course, this was the first time he'd even been conscious of that fact.

"Sit down," Brooks suggested. "Coffee?"

"I'm fine."

He stifled a sigh. The pain in his shoulder was back with a vengeance, and it was worsening his mood. He didn't feel much like being patient, but the last thing he wanted was for her to bolt. And from the way her eyes kept twitching toward the door, he was sure she was counting the seconds until she could do it.

"You want to tell me what's going on?" he asked.

Why would I? she signed.

So I can help you, he replied.

"I doubt it's possible," she said aloud.

"Try me."

"Tell *me* something first," she said.

"Okay."

"Why did you help me?"

Brooks said the first thing that popped into his head. "Women in distress. Personal weakness."

She blinked. "That's very honest."

"I'm an honest man," he agreed. "And a bit old-fashioned, I guess."

"Not a bad combination." It was a hesitant statement—almost a question.

"I like to think it works in my favor. Most of the time."

"And you're not afraid of guns?"

"Not afraid of them? No. But I do have a healthy respect for what they're capable of doing." Unconsciously, he rolled his shoulder.

She picked up on the gesture, and as she eyed his upper arm, a little gasp escaped her lips. "You got shot!"

Brooks tipped his head down to follow her gaze. Yep. A graze only, but the blood was there, marking a thin tear across his sleeve.

"Damn," he muttered.

He automatically started to unbutton his shirt. He got three undone before he realized that she was staring at him, her bottom lip sucked nervously between her teeth. Her eyes were on the bit of chest he'd already exposed. For a second, her stare was…warm. Then she tore her gaze away and fixed on a spot on the wall.

Yeah, he said to himself as he stilled his hands. *Because undressing in front of a woman you barely know isn't normal behavior.*

"Sorry," he muttered. "Not used to having anyone around."

"No. You really should…" She trailed off and shook her head. "*I'm* sorry."

"For what?"

"God, an apology isn't enough, is it? I just have to go."

"You've barely given me five of the ten minutes you promised."

"It took *less* than five minutes of being near me for you to take a bullet for me."

"Exactly," Brooks said, managing a half smile. "You owe me."

She didn't smile back. "What?"

"I took a bullet for you. So you owe me. And all I want is a five-minute explanation. And maybe you could bandage up my arm while you give it?"

She inhaled, exhaled heavily, then nodded. "Okay. Where should I start?"

"First things first. I'm Brooks."

He stuck out a hand, and she took it. Her skin was surprisingly warm and pleasantly soft.

"Maryse," she said.

"Good. Now that that's out of the way…" He guided her to the barely used couch and pushed her into a sitting position. "I'll grab the antiseptic and the Band-Aids. And you can tell me why someone's trying to kill you."

As the big man—Brooks, he'd called himself—exited the room, Maryse watched his receding shoulders. Something about him and his calm, matter-of-fact reasoning made her comfortable.

Well, except for the bit where he started to take his shirt off. That hadn't been comfortable at all. It had been...something else entirely. Something she didn't have time to think about.

She crossed and uncrossed her legs, afraid of getting distracted. No matter how badly she wanted to take off her coat, to settle in and unburden herself, she wouldn't let it happen. Doing so—even for the promised ten minutes—seemed like a violation of her commitment to saving her daughter.

Not that I have a lead right now.

She brushed off the thought. It was almost too much to bear. She was pretty sure her only option was to go back to the hotel. To get into the room attached to that key she'd found in Cami's room. What she itched to do, though, was to call the police. Her cell phone was in her pocket, and the proper help was just three little numbers away.

But the threat made by the man who'd been gunned down in the street stuck with her. And what Brooks had said made sense, too. She *would* be tied up if the police got ahold of her. Cami's life would only matter to them as a professional interest, while to Maryse, the little girl was everything. And that wasn't even bringing in the truth of Cami's parentage and the questions *that* would bring up. And what it would risk.

But losing her is better than losing *her, isn't it?*

She put her head in her hands.

"Maryse?" Brooks's voice was soft and full of the same

concern that had seemed to dominate his gold-flecked gaze since the second she'd spotted him.

She answered without looking up. "It's my daughter."

The couch bounced under her, and a pleasant, musky scent filled her nose, and she knew Brooks had seated himself beside her.

"Your daughter?" he said back, low with worry.

"They—someone—took her. And it's just…really complicated." It sounded lame, and Maryse knew it.

But he only paused for a second before answering. "So complicated that you can't go to the police."

"Yes."

She finally looked up. Brooks was close enough to touch, and her reaction to his nearness was startling. She tingled, head to toe. Her breath wanted to catch.

Powerfully attractive.

Hadn't that been the phrase she'd initially used to describe him when she'd first spotted him? It was even more apt now.

He'd changed out of the long-sleeved dress shirt and into a tight-fitting undershirt. His shoulders took up twice as much space as hers, and his arms were no less impressive. When he held out the first-aid supplies, she had no choice but to take them. And of course, her fingers brushed his, and of course the tingling grew that much worse.

Startled by the strength of her attraction, Maryse jerked back and just about dropped the items. Trying to distract herself, she focused her attention on the wound itself. It was a small, angry line that would've looked almost like rug burn if not for the dip in the center.

"Not so bad," she told him.

"Pretty lucky, I think," he agreed. "More of a gutter wound than anything."

She opened the alcohol wipe and ran it gently over the cut, wincing even though he didn't react. "Sorry."

He waved off her apology with his free hand. "Your daughter. Was she taken from Maison Blanc?"

"No. We live north of here on a little farm. She was taken from her bedroom."

"So the hotel was…"

"A clue. A starting point. That didn't work out."

"And do you know who took her?"

Maryse shook her head and dabbed at the cut with a piece of gauze. "That's part of what makes everything so complicated. But I guess the real answer is no. I don't know who took her."

"And the man who got shot?"

"I thought he had her. He knew she'd been taken, anyway. But as far as who he was, or why he got shot… I'm lost." The last word came out in a choked-out half sob, and she barely managed to secure the bandage just below Brooks's shoulder before a real tear escaped.

Immediately, the big man adjusted on the couch to pull her closer. For a second, Maryse resisted the unexpected embrace. She didn't know him. She didn't *need* him. Except she did. Or she needed something, anyway—a release or a bit of comfort, maybe. And Brooks seemed willing to give it. So she accepted what he offered and curved her shoulder into his solid form, and she let herself cry. It lasted for less than thirty seconds, but it was exactly right for the moment. And even though she still had nothing more to go on in regards to finding Cami, when she pulled away, Maryse felt a little better. Or at least strengthened.

She wiped her eyes. "Thank you. Sorry about that."

"Nothing to be sorry for," Brooks replied easily, meeting her eyes. "I want to help you. And I think I can."

He sounded sure enough that Maryse couldn't just dismiss his offer, and she had to admit that she probably did need help. Even just in terms of how to get from point A to point B. She'd left her own car near the hotel, but would the police be looking for it? Or would the person who'd shot at her recognize the vehicle, too? And on top of that, she hadn't even figured out where point B was.

But you can't expect a stranger to take on this kind of danger. Honesty and "healthy respect" for guns aside, he doesn't know what he's getting into. You don't even know yourself.

"You said you were lost," Brooks added gently, stopping her protest before it could even start. "So at least think about my offer before you walk away."

She nodded—not in agreement of taking his help, but in her agreement to consider it. "Can I have a minute?"

"Take all the time you need."

"Is there a bathroom I could borrow?"

"Sure. Down the hall, first door on the left."

Maryse pushed to her feet and did her best to smile at him, but was sure she failed miserably. She moved quickly, stepped through the door, flicked on the light and gave herself a hard look in the mirror. Then she turned on the tap and splashed a healthy amount of crisp, cold water onto her face. It didn't ease the worried ache in her chest, but it *was* a wake-up. She realized that she'd known she was going to say yes to Brooks before she even reached the bathroom. What other choice did she have? If there was even the slightest chance that this man could help her get to Camille, she'd take it.

She took in a breath, then turned back to the door, swung it open and frowned as she spied a bedroom rather than the hall she'd just come from. A quick glance backward told her the bathroom actually had two doors rather than one.

Whoops.

Maryse moved to close the second door, then paused as a framed picture on the nightstand drew her eye. Maybe it was because of the way the light from the bathroom reflected off the pewter. Or maybe it was just plain curiosity about the only personal item on display. Either way, she found herself drawn to it. She glanced back again, then slipped into the bedroom and moved toward the photo. She picked it up. And as she did, her blood ran almost as cold as it had when she'd found Camille's empty bed.

It was a picture of Brooks, his arm linked with another man's, the two of them grinning at the camera. And in the photo, he wore a uniform. A gun. And a badge.

"He's a cop," Maryse whispered to the empty room.

Saying it aloud made it all too real. All too risky. A fact that could only endanger both her and her daughter.

She had to get out of the apartment, and she had to do it fast. She considered her options. There was the idea of just plain telling him she had to leave. He'd said he'd let her go.

Sure. But he also failed to mention that he was a police officer. Not exactly an oversight. Did he intend to turn her in?

Her heart thundered with worry, and her gaze flew around the room, the voice of the gunman from the hotel filling her head.

Not authorities. Punishment. And not for her.

"Cami," she whispered.

Her eyes found the window. Just outside, a few feet away, was the balcony. And a fire escape.

It wasn't reasonable. Or logical. But it gave her a damned fine way of getting out without an argument.

Chapter 4

As Brooks dumped the bits of leftover first-aid supplies into his kitchen trash can, the muffled sound of smashing glass made him jump.

What the hell?

It only took him a second to realize it had come from up the hall.

"Everything okay?" he called loudly.

Silence.

"Maryse?"

More quiet air.

Brooks's tickle of worry thickened. Stepping quickly, he moved from the kitchen, through the living room, and booted it straight for the bathroom.

He tapped the wood. "You there?"

He counted to five, then closed his hand on the doorknob and he turned.

Locked.

He rattled it harder. No response. Fearing the worst—and wishing he had a weapon—he turned toward the bedroom. He pushed his back to the wall and slid along it quickly. When he reached the door frame, he pushed out one foot, then waited. Nothing. He eased his body forward. Still nothing.

"Maryse?"

Continued silence greeted his softer call. He couldn't wait any longer. He swung into the room and dropped to one knee defensively. Something sharp bit into his knee, and a blast of arctic-temperature air blew across the top of his head.

Brooks's gaze flicked through the room. Maryse was nowhere to be seen, but the window was open.

You're kidding me.

He looked down. Shards of glass dotted the carpet.

"What in God's name— Oh." *The picture. My uniform. Crap.*

Damning himself for wanting to put out a single memento in the first place, Brooks pushed to his feet and strode toward the window. As he leaned out, he caught sight of her. Sixteen feet off the ground. Inching along the narrow ledge toward his balcony. And just out of grabbing distance.

"Stay there," she said without turning his way.

"I was just going to say the same thing," he replied. "What the hell are you doing?"

"You're a cop."

"And that made you climb out a window?"

"You lied. And even if you *hadn't* lied, my daughter's life is at stake and I'm pretty sure working with a cop is going to get her killed."

"I *am* a cop. But I didn't lie."

"A lie of omission is still a lie."

"You could've just walked out the front door."

"Right."

She moved a little farther down the ledge, and Brooks cringed.

"The front door is *still* an option," he said.

"I'll take my chances with the fire escape and the trees down there, thanks," she told him.

Brooks eyed the foliage in question. It was a cluster of

dense, short evergreens and looked like a safe place to land. Except underneath it—invisible from above—was a small rock garden, framed by a wrought-iron fence.

Brooks cringed again. "Trust me. You don't want to fall into what's down there."

"Trust you?" she called back. "Nice one."

"Listen to me, Maryse. I'm not a cop *here*, okay? I'm only a cop at home in Nevada."

"Right," she said again.

He lifted a knee to the windowsill and gritted his teeth. "I'm not overly fond of heights, but I swear to God, I'm going to come out there. Then we'll probably *both* fall. But I'll make sure to land on the bottom. I'll probably take one of those spikes under the tree straight into an organ I need. I'll be dead. Because you couldn't use the front door. But, hey, you'll be on your way."

She finally tipped her head his way. "That's—"

He cut her off. "The truth. Just like the fact that I don't have a gun, or a badge, or any kind of cross-border authority. I'm on *vacation*."

"But you don't feel obligated to turn and tell the Canadian authorities what's going on?"

"Maybe a little," Brooks admitted. "But I feel *more* obligated to help you. I have considerable firsthand experience solving crimes. And resources I can use. Subtly. Or you can just consider me a bodyguard. But *please*…come back inside."

A gust of wind kicked up, making her coat flap. She wobbled. Then gasped.

Dammit.

Brooks lifted himself into the frame and pushed through. Without looking down, he stretched out his hand.

Come on.

And thankfully, a heartbeat later, her fingers landed in

his palm. He tugged her gently back to the window. Then through it. He slid if shut forcefully behind them and—in an instinctive need to reassure himself that she was safe— he pulled her into his arms.

She fit perfectly against his chest, her head at just the right level to tuck against his chin. He held her that way for a long moment. Fiercely protective and strangely intimate.

Then he pulled away and adjusted her to arm's length so he could look her in the face. "Please don't do that again."

Her eyes were wide. "I won't."

Brooks sagged. "Thank you."

"Are you really not going to call the local police?" she asked.

"I'm really not going to," he confirmed. "If I get tempted, I promise to warn you ahead of time."

Her expression lightened hopefully, then drooped again. "My daughter…"

Brooks nodded. "Let's start with what you know. The hotel, right?"

"Yes."

He slid to his closet, pulled out a hooded gray sweat-shirt—one he liked far better than the parka, anyway—then yanked it over his head. "Did you ask a lot of questions while you were there?"

"No," she said. "I was just trying to get into the room."

"What room?"

"I found a key card in Camille's—that's my daughter's name—room. It was the only thing out of place, so I knew I had to go there."

"Okay." Brooks gestured toward the hall, and Maryse exited in front of him. "Do you think they'd remember you at the desk?"

"I'm not sure. The guy did offer to help me," she replied. "Is it bad if he does?"

He shook his head. "It doesn't really matter. Just need to know what to expect. If you're comfortable with it, I might go in on my own and ask a few things. You can just lie low."

"Lie low where?"

"My rental car." He lifted his keys from the living room table, then led her to the door. "Why don't you tell me a bit about your daughter?"

Her brows knit together, and her lips pursed nervously. Brooks couldn't help but wonder what secrets she was guarding. Something illegal? More dangerous than he'd already witnessed? He forced himself not to ask. When— if—she wanted to share them, she would. But there was no sense in making her any more uncomfortable. She was already enough of a flight risk.

"What do you want to know?" she asked guardedly.

Brooks locked the door, then started toward the stairs. "Anything. What's her favorite color?"

A tiny smile tipped up the corners of Maryse's mouth. "Oh. That kind of stuff? I can talk all day. She likes pink, but pretends that she doesn't, because she's worried someone will think she isn't tough."

"Is she?"

"Tough? Yes." The smile got a bit bigger. "Very. And tries to be even tougher than she is."

"Good."

Over the next few minutes—both on the walk to the underground parking garage and on the short drive over to the Maison Blanc—Maryse painted a thorough picture of her daughter. Brooks had no problems envisioning her— smart and intuitive, with a solid helping of sass. Unlike her mother, she was a blonde cherub. They shared the same blue eyes, though, and also a love of junk food and painting. She didn't mention the little girl's father, and Brooks found himself wondering if the man had something to do with her kidnapping. Sure, Maryse claimed not to know who had Camille, but did that mean she didn't know anything about what prompted the abduction in the first place? Brooks resisted an urge to ask. He suspected she wouldn't tell him anyway. Clearly, she felt that *not* sharing what she knew posed less of a risk to her daughter than actually disclosing it. Because throughout their whole conversation, one thing was abundantly clear—Maryse loved her daughter more than anything.

The obvious caring and commitment was something Brooks found admirable. *More* than admirable, if he was being honest. It was attractive as all hell. And it affirmed his decision to offer his help.

As he pulled his car into the side lot at the hotel, Brooks reached over to give Maryse's hand a reassuring squeeze. "My goal is to be in and out of there in ten minutes."

Her eyes met his, and she held tightly to his hand. "You think you can find something out that quickly?"

"I can definitely find out whether or not there *is* something to know," he assured her. "I'll report back to you as soon as I figure it out, okay?"

She gave him a sharp nod, then released his hand. As he moved to get out of the car, though, she reached for him again.

"Wait," she said, then pulled out her phone, tapped lightly on the screen and flashed a picture at him. "This is her. Just in case."

Brooks stared down at the photo, memorizing the details of the little girl's face. She *was* cherubic, just as Maryse described, with more than a hint of mischief present in her sparkling baby blues.

"She doesn't speak," Maryse added.

Brooks nodded. "She's the reason you sign."

"Yes. She's deaf. But even if you sign with her...she

might not trust you. So tell her that Bunny-Bun-Bun misses her as much as Mommy does." Now her smile was heart-breaking.

Spontaneously, he lifted his hand to her cheek. He cupped it in his palm.

"You got it," he said softly.

She leaned into his touch. "Brooks?"

"Yeah?"

"Thank you."

He nodded. And then he did something he never did. He made a promise he wanted to keep, but wasn't sure he could.

"I'll get her back for you," he said, then pulled away and slipped from the car.

Maryse watched Brooks disappear into Maison Blanc, a strange mix of emotions tugging at her heart. She still felt the swirling fear, and she still had the hard pit of sickness in her stomach. But there was hope, too. And not the one she'd been forcing herself to have since the second she re-alized Cami was missing. *This* hope was concrete. Rooted in a six-foot-three-inch package of calm certainty. Who'd looked at Cami's picture, then softened and touched her face as he assured her—with authority—that he'd retrieve her daughter. There was something to be said for all the pieces of that brief interaction.

Maryse lifted her phone to examine the photo she'd shown him. It was a typical Camille shot. Arms in the air, a wild grin on her face, seemingly oblivious to the snow falling all around her.

Maryse's heart squeezed. And in spite of the way she urged herself not to do it, she couldn't help but scroll through the next few frames. They were all taken the same day, out in the yard on the property where they lived. One on a sled. Another with a rudimentary snowman—Cami had insisted on doing it herself.

She flicked to the next, knowing it would be the one where her daughter had fallen facedown, then got back up, her hat askew and her expression unimpressed. Smiling already, Maryse lifted the phone. Then stopped. In the background, up behind the sled hill, almost blending in with a patch of trees, she could swear she spied a blurry figure.

Maryse squinted. *What* is *that?*

She dragged her fingers across the phone, enlarging the background. Sure enough, there it was. There *he* was, to be more accurate. A man in jeans and a duffle coat.

With her heart thumping, Maryse enlarged the picture even more, then used the auto-enhance feature to clear up the image as much as she could.

Oh, God.

Even with what remained of the blurriness, she could see the man's face. It was tilted down. Fixed on the one thing at the bottom of the hill. *Camille.* And to make things even worse, she recognized him. The concierge from inside the hotel. The man who'd offered to take her to room eight.

It was a trick, she realized.

He'd been working with the gunman to *get* her to that hallway, and she'd played right into it.

Maryse lifted her gaze to the entryway.

Brooks.

She had to warn him.

With limbs like lead, she opened the door and climbed from the vehicle. She hurried over the concrete to the doors. This time when she made her way through them, the rush of warm air didn't provide any relief. Instead, it sent a fresh wave of nausea through her. She paused to push her hand to her stomach in an attempt to stifle it, then looked toward the concierge desk. Brooks was there, his distinctly wide shoulders bent over the counter as he spoke with the person on the other side.

I need to get his attention.

Her eyes traveled around the wide lobby in search of some way to do it. She couldn't find one. The area was quiet enough that any loud noise would draw attention. But it was also quiet enough that it would probably draw *everyone's* notice. Including that of the concierge who'd been spying on her in her own backyard.

Maryse shivered. *Don't think about it.*

She watched as Brooks's head swung toward the hall that led to room eight, and she willed him not to go there. The gunman who'd grabbed *her* might be dead, but she doubted he was the only one involved. She took a small step closer to the desk. Then froze as Brooks moved aside even more, and the uniformed man behind the counter came into view. His gaze landed on Maryse, then slid straight over her and went back to the computer in front of him.

Maryse's body sagged. It wasn't him.

She watched for a moment as he tapped something on the keyboard, then nodded at Brooks, lifted a finger to indicate he'd be right back, then stepped into the office behind the desk.

Thinking quickly—and not wanting to take the chance that the *other* concierge was somewhere nearby, just waiting to show up again—Maryse strode toward Brooks. When she reached him, she pressed her hand to his back and held it there. She didn't know if anyone was listening or watching, and she didn't want to take a chance on that, either.

"Hi, sweetie," she said breathlessly. "I'm having a problem with the car outside. Can you give me a hand?"

If the close contact or overly familiar greeting startled him, he didn't show it. Just the opposite, in fact. In a smooth move, he dropped his head down and settled his mouth against her cheekbone, then slid it up to her ear. A caress that was close enough to a kiss that it made her shiver. She couldn't help but inch a tiny bit closer.

"You all right?" Brooks said, barely loud enough for her to hear. "Nod if you are."

Maryse nodded. Then shook her head. Then nodded again.

He draped an arm over her shoulders and nuzzled her neck. "Which is it?"

"I'm fine," she whispered. "But this hotel isn't."

"You don't want to stay here?"

"I don't think it's—" She cut herself off as the concierge returned to the desk.

She wished she could lean back and finish in sign language. Things were so much easier when she could speak without being heard.

The man smiled at her, then at Brooks. "Looks like your wife made it, after all! Sorry about the interruption."

"No worries at all," Brooks assured him.

"I'm used to a much slower gig," the concierge added. "The day manager went home, and I have to admit…filling in is harder than I thought it would be."

"The day manager?" Maryse repeated, relieved that she wouldn't run into him.

But the concierge's next words gave her pause. "Yep. She's a force. Makes me glad I work the night shift."

She?

Maryse lifted her gaze to Brooks's face, wondering if he noticed the discrepancy between what she'd told him earlier about a man at the desk and the fact that it was *supposed* to be a woman.

"It's funny, actually," the guy behind the desk added almost absently. "She claimed to have to go home to be with her kid. But in the year she's worked here, she's never mentioned that she's a mom before."

"Funny," Brooks echoed, and it was obvious—at least to Maryse—that he knew something was up.

"Guess there's always something new to learn about people." The concierge smiled again, then turned his attention to the computer screen. "All right. The ground-level suite you were asking about—eight—is actually undergoing an upgrade. Whole thing got wrecked in a flood and renovations are scheduled to go well into next month. We *do* have a room available on the second floor, though. Same layout, functional balcony… If you and your wife would like to book there instead, I can give you a last-minute deal."

Maryse jumped in quickly. "Yes, please."

Brooks's hand tightened on her shoulder, and she nodded—more for his benefit than for that man booking the room.

"Even if it's not the room we were hoping for, it'll be nice to stay in the city for the evening." She forced a light laugh. "Sometimes life in a small country town makes you feel like someone's always watching."

"True enough," Brooks murmured, squeezing her shoulder again, then letting her go to pull out his wallet.

Maryse started to argue—to reach for the small handbag she had tucked into her jacket—then stopped as she realized it would look a little odd for a wife to argue with her husband about who would be paying for a room. It was safer, as well. If someone else at the hotel was looking for her, it would be better to be booked in under Brooks's name. She vowed to herself that she would pay him back, but kept silent as he made an excuse for their lack of luggage, accepted the key cards—identical to the one she'd discovered in Cami's room—then led her to the elevators. Brooks stayed quiet, too. Through the ride up, through the short walk to their room, and until the door was firmly locked behind them.

Then he faced her and—in a tone just shy of bossy—said, "Tell me."

Chapter 5

Brooks waited as Maryse dragged out her phone, then clicked it on and held it up for him to see.

"That's the man who helped me at the desk earlier today," she said. "Not the one filling in right now."

"And not a woman, if the beard is any indication," Brooks replied.

She shook her head, then pulled the phone away, tapped on the screen, then showed him again. "It was taken at my house. Two days ago."

Brooks took it from her hand, studying the shot. It gave him a chill to see just how close the man had come to Maryse and her daughter without being detected. How long had he watched them?

"And you'd never seen him before?" he asked.

"No. Never." Her answer was firm.

"Okay. Give me a second to run through what we know." He tapped his thigh thoughtfully. "The man in that picture… Was he definitely a hotel employee?"

"Yes. Well. He was wearing a uniform, and he was on the phone behind his desk."

"Did anyone else see him?"

She closed her eyes as if trying to recall, then opened them and nodded at him. "There were a few other hotel employees around. A baggage guy and a woman talking to some guests."

"And presumably, they would have noticed if some stranger dressed in a fake uniform was behind the front counter."

"I think so."

"So. He *is* an employee. Just not a concierge. And the woman who was supposed to be at the counter went home to a kid that the night guy didn't know she had."

He paused, and Maryse filled in the rest of his thoughts. "It *could* be her kid. But what if it's not?"

"What are the chances that she's been working with him for a whole *year*, but never mentioned that she had a child?" He shook his head. "No mom I've ever met could go that long without bringing up some funny story, or without bringing up some bit of trouble her kid is causing."

He met her eyes, and he saw a glimmer of guarded hope there as she replied. "Sometimes, I'm sure I manage to work Cami into every conversation I have."

He had an overwhelming need to make that glimmer expand. "We need to find out for sure."

"How?"

He tapped his thigh again. "Her personnel file, maybe. Even if it doesn't list her dependents, it will have her contact info. Easy enough to fabricate a reason to give her a call."

"But we need the file first. I doubt they're going to hand it over."

Brooks frowned. She was right. He was too accustomed to simply flashing his badge to get his way. He paced the room for a moment.

"Need to think like a criminal," he muttered.

"You mean steal it?" Maryse asked.

"Yes. Exactly. There has to be an employee contact list in that office behind the concierge desk."

He stilled his movements, sure—even though he hardly knew her at all—that she wasn't going to like what he was about to suggest. He met her worried gaze, then opened his mouth. And he was right. She shook her head before he even got the idea partway out.

"No," she said quickly. "Trying to sneak into the office is too risky."

"It's riskier *not* to try," Brooks replied. "If this woman has your daughter, we have to find out."

"If the current concierge catches you, he might kick us out or call the police. If the guy who was *pretending* to be the concierge does, it'll be even worse." A frown creased her forehead, and her blue eyes clouded for a moment before she closed them and sank down onto the corner of the bed. "If that's even possible."

Brooks stepped to where she sat, then crouched down in front of her. One of his knees brushed her thigh, and a jolt of longing just about made him lose his balance. He gripped the edge of the bed to keep himself up, and fought another urge to pull her close and try to soothe away her aches. He knew what she needed most was to get her daughter back, safe and sound.

"Maryse."

Her lids lifted, and that sad, blue gaze hit him as hard as her whispered reply. "Sorry."

"Nothing to be sorry for," he assured her.

She looked down at her hands. "I always plan things ahead."

"Sounds like a lot of pressure to put on yourself."

"No. It's how I cope with things. And I'm just…not used to not knowing what to do."

He slid his fingers overtop of hers and clasped them tightly. "You don't have to know what to do right this second, okay? *I've* got this part. I've been a cop for more than twelve years. Over a third of my life. I'm *very* good at assessing safety, and I promise you… I won't do anything that will put Camille at risk."

She swallowed, then raised her eyes up again. "I won't ever be able to repay you for this. I mean, the cost of the hotel…yes. But even the way you've helped me in the last couple of hours… I don't think there's enough money in the world."

"I told you I'm old-fashioned. That means getting the job done is reward enough."

A responding smile lit up her face for a moment, and he couldn't help but wish it was a more frequent expression. He wondered if it *was* more frequent in her day-to-day life. He hoped so.

"Thank you, Brooks. Again."

Spontaneously, he pushed up to his knees and leaned forward to place a kiss on her cheek. Nothing more than a quick, tender reassurance—that was his aim. At the same moment, though, Maryse tipped her face to the side, and instead of landing on her face, Brooks's mouth brushed hers. For a startled second, he didn't move. He just hung there, pressed against the soft skin of her lips.

Then her hand came up and found the back of his neck, clinging to it with a surprising amount of need. He couldn't help but want to meet it. In fact, he couldn't remember the last time he'd wanted to do something so badly—especially in regards to a woman. The lingering effects of his last relationship's demise were still far too close to the surface.

Or at least they had been until now.

Brooks deepened the contact into a proper kiss, exploring the contours of her mouth with his own. She was sweet and yielding, warm and inviting. But as her fingers came up a little more to find the edge of his hairline, a brush of cool metal reminded him of the ring he'd spotted on her finger.

She hadn't mentioned a man in her life, husband or otherwise. She hadn't said a word about the missing child's father, either. So chances were good that there *wasn't* a significant other in the picture.

But what do you know about her, really? The answer was easy. *Nothing.*

There were a hundred things he *should* ask, both as a law-enforcement official, and as a man who wanted to take a gentle kiss and turn it into something else entirely. At that moment, though, there was only one question he needed to resolve.

Brooks pulled away. He slid his palm to her hand, then ran his thumb over the ring on her finger and met her eyes.

"Wearing one of these usually carries a specific meaning," he said, working to keep any hint of accusation out of his voice.

Two spots of color formed in her porcelain cheeks. "You think I'm— No."

"No?"

"I'm not married."

He studied her face for less than a second before deciding she was telling the truth. "Good."

He pushed up, then cupped her cheek and kissed her again. Not demanding. Not aggressive. Just a hint—no, *a promise*—of something he wanted to explore in more detail when the time was right.

When her daughter is safe...

He gave her bottom lip a little tug, then dragged himself back to the pressing circumstances of the present.

He stood up. "When I'm done, I'll come back and knock twice. Then I'll pause and knock four more times before I come in, so you'll know it's me. While I'm gone, don't answer the door for any reason. If I have to get ahold of you, I'll find a way to call through to the room. I'll let it ring twice, then hang up. I'll call back, and you pick up. But not until the fourth ring. Got it?"

She nodded. "Two knocks or rings, then four more."

"Perfect. I'll be gone fifteen minutes," he told her. "No more."

"And if you're gone longer?"

"I won't be. If I think my plan isn't going to work, I'll come back right away. If I'm stuck, I'll call." He gave her hand a final squeeze, then slipped to the door, opened it and put the do-not-disturb sign onto the door handle. "Just in case."

His reassurance didn't stop her face from pinching with worry. "Be careful."

She signed the plea as well as spoke it, and Brooks signed back what he hoped was the equivalent of "Always am."

Then he closed the door quickly, and as he made his way up the hall, then toward the stairs, he had to work to keep his mind on the task at hand. It was unusual for him to cross the line between professional and personal.

No, he corrected mentally. *Not just unusual. Unheard of.*

Yet everything about the blue-eyed woman made him want to take the line between the two, toss it aside, then stomp on it.

Why?

Maybe because the job had been his life for the last five years. Maybe because this was the first time he'd stopped to breathe since things went south with his ex.

Brooks shook his head. He didn't have time to question himself any more than he had time to question Maryse. The little girl was the most important thing.

He took a breath, put on a smile and pushed through the stairwell door and into the lobby. He strode confidently toward the front desk, calling out cheerfully before he even reached it.

"Hey! I've got a bit of a concern, and I'd like it if you could take care of it personally."

In under a minute, he talked the concierge into running a phony errand. And the moment the other man disappeared up the hall, Brooks slipped in behind the counter. A quick scan of the office led him to a filing cabinet with the top drawer labeled with the word *Personnel*. Thankful for whoever favored the paper route over the digital, he reached for the handle. It didn't move.

Locked.

Brooks turned his attention back to the room. He immediately spotted a container full of paper clips. Shoving aside a tickle of law-breaking guilt, he snapped up one of the clips. He forced the pliable metal open, then spun back to the filing cabinet and stuck it into the keyhole. It only took a few seconds to jiggle the lock free. Inside, Brooks found a set of tidily organized folders. He tossed a cautious glance out the door, assured himself he was good to go, then began to flip through. His search quickly yielded him the correct set of paperwork.

"White, Dee," it read. "Daytime Concierge."

He pulled it free and tucked it under his shirt, then exited the office, sliding to the customer side of the counter just as the substitute concierge rounded the corner with an armful of fresh blankets. Brooks smiled a genuinely pleased smile, offered the man a tip and his gratitude, then snagged the linen and started back toward the room, a whistle on his lips.

His self-satisfaction was short-lived. As he turned up the hall, a flash out the window end caught his eye. His cop instinct reared its head, and he slowed. A short, squat figure stood at the edge of the nearest ground-level balcony.

Whoever it was had a hood pulled up and over their face, making it impossible to tell anything beyond the fact that it was a man.

As Brooks watched, the figure moved along the grass carefully, head down. After a few steps, the person stopped. He lifted his head and stared straight ahead for several long seconds. Brooks followed the stare with a pointed gaze of his own, and when he spied the goal at the end, his throat constricted with worry.

The fire escape.

Sure enough, the man swung his face back and forth, then reached up to release the metal ladder.

There was no doubt in Brooks's mind that the man was headed for the balcony of his own room.

The room where Maryse sat waiting.

Unguarded.

Unarmed.

Unsuspecting.

Without another thought, Brooks dropped a curse under his breath, cast aside the folded blankets and ran toward the stairs at full speed.

Maryse sat on the edge of the bed, her fingers tapping the plush bedspread. Her heart and her mind had knotted up equally, and she didn't know where to focus her thoughts.

Cami.

Brooks.

The former dominated, as always. Right now, Maryse's worry was a thick lump in her stomach and it wasn't going away anytime soon. Not until she had her daughter back in her arms.

But the latter wasn't going away, either. He and his kind hazel eyes definitely kept sneaking up on her. Just like his kiss had done.

She lifted her fingers to her lips, touching the spot where his mouth had landed. His kiss had been gentle. Unexpected. And admittedly wonderful.

Even though Maryse thought maybe it had started out as an accident, a few quick seconds in had changed that. And it had warmed her from the inside out. A slow, fiery burn.

Which is completely inappropriate, she told herself sternly.

But was there a set of rules that dictated against kissing while in a situation like this? She somehow doubted it. And even if there were…she still had an unreasonable urge to do it again.

She glanced over at the clock on the nightstand. Eight minutes had passed. It felt like forty.

She pushed up from the bed and paced the room, trying to settle down.

Maryse wasn't good at holding still. And she wasn't good at letting someone else do the work, either. A big part of her hands-on nature was brought on by her six years as a single mom. If she didn't get something done…it didn't get done. But she knew she'd been a little like that before Cami ever came into her life. It was probably why her brother relied so heavily on her, even when they became adults. And definitely the reason he'd entrusted his daughter to her.

Maryse's heart squeezed. *Oh, Jean-Paul. What did you do? What could possibly catch up with you this far down the road?*

In the year leading up to his death, she'd been sure he was turning things around. He'd been more upbeat. He hadn't asked for a cent. He'd even secured a job at some company called People With Paper, and he'd talked about finally moving on with his life.

Over the last half a decade, Maryse had wondered if the

last bit had something to do with Cami. If he'd been excited about the prospect of a whole new world.

Maybe he just couldn't escape the old one.

The thought—as always—broke her heart. At one time—before her daughter came into the picture—her brother had been the one who mattered most. It weighed on her.

"And there's another reason not to hold still," she said aloud to the empty room.

Too much stillness led to too much dwelling on the past. Even on the best of days, she had a hard time dealing with thoughts of her brother. And not only was today not the best of days, it was the *worst* day.

Except for Brooks and the kiss.

She had to admit that in spite of her fear, he *was* the tiniest silver lining—a bright speck in an otherwise dismal day. Inappropriate or not, she was grateful for his presence.

The sound of a key card sliding noisily into the door cut through her scattered thoughts then, and with a slight tingle in her limbs, she stopped her pacing and fixed her gaze on the door handle.

Then she remembered.

No preceding knocks.

It's not him.

For the briefest moment, she considered that it might be a hotel employee or someone trying for the wrong room. Just as quickly, she dismissed the idea.

The do-not-disturb sign.

Whoever was on the other side of the door had to have seen it. And the fumbling of the lock had stopped, and the handle was already turning.

She scanned the room, her eyes searching for the nearest loose, heavyish object. She needed something fast. Something she could wield easily.

The phone.

It would be no match for a gun, but it would have to do. It might, at least, provide enough of a distraction that she'd have time to slip out and go in search of Brooks.

She snatched it up, tearing it from the wall, then positioned herself to the side of the door frame. And just in time, too. As she lifted the phone over her head, the door flew open and a bulky figure—definitely *not* dressed in a hotel uniform—darkened the space there. Maryse swung the makeshift weapon with as much force as she could muster.

But the man entering the room was quicker than she anticipated. His wide fingers closed on her wrist and squeezed.

Maryse's hand released, and the phone fell from her grip. It clattered to the ground, useless any longer.

No.

She closed her eyes and dropped open her mouth, prepared to let out a scream. Her attacker was still quicker. A meaty palm landed on her mouth, muffling the sound. Then he was dragging her into the room, ignoring the way she gnashed her teeth against his skin, acting like he couldn't feel the booted foot she slammed into his shin. And he was speaking to her, too. He was saying something in a low, insistent voice that was probably supposed to be soothing.

"Maryse."

He knows my name.

"Maryse!"

She threw back an elbow.

"Dammit, ouch. Maryse, it's *me*. It's Brooks."

And it finally registered. It *was* him.

Her body sagged so hard that she was sure he was now holding her *up* rather than holding her *back*. He released her mouth, but kept the arm around her waist in place for several more seconds.

"You didn't do the knock," Maryse said, her voice breathless.

"I'm sorry. It went out of my head. We have a bigger problem. And I think it's about to—" A sharp crack sounded from the other side of the room and cut him off.

Maryse's eyes flew toward the noise. A heavy curtain covered the source, but she knew on the other side was a set of sliding glass doors. Someone was breaking in.

"C'mon," Brooks urged.

He slid his hand to hers, then turned toward the door. But before they could make it two steps, the click of a cocking gun sounded from behind them.

"Drop her hand," ordered a gruff voice. "Or I'll fire."

Immediately, Brooks's warm fingers left hers.

"Good," added the voice. "Now move back and step apart. Slowly."

And Maryse didn't dare do anything but comply.

Chapter 6

Brooks took a breath and weighed his options, lightning fast. He knew without asking that something about the gunman was off. Over the course of his career, he'd come across his fair share of desperate people, and the man's voice gave away that he was riding that particular line.

Not worth the risk to try and jump him, Brooks decided. *Not yet, anyway.*

He gave Maryse a quick touch in the small of her back, hoping it was enough to reassure her that he would come up with a plan, even if he didn't have one right that second. Then he stepped aside, putting the requested space between them.

"Also good," said the gunman. "Now I need both of you to follow my instructions carefully. Understand?"

Brooks glanced toward Maryse to make sure she was acknowledging the gruff speaker's request. She was nodding shakily, but as she lifted her gaze to the man, she let out a strangled gasp.

Brooks followed her stare, and it only took him a moment to figure out why she'd made the noise.

The fake concierge.

Even though Brooks had only seen the cell phone photo, he recognized him, too. He'd cataloged the man's features as a course of habit.

Thick brow.

Weak jaw, covered with a goatee.

Wide nose and a thin slash of a mouth.

Definitely the same man.

Now, though, he looked far worse off than he had in the picture. His eyes were bloodshot and wild, and a sheen of sweat covered his brow. Under his sweatshirt, his hotel uniform was rumpled, and there was even a small tear visible in its collar. The hand that held the gun shook as he spoke.

"I want *you* to move over there, beside the closet," he commanded, giving his upper lip a nervous lick. "Put your palms above your head and press them flat against the wall. Legs apart, eyes forward."

Brooks curbed his natural instinct, which was to balk, and pushed himself to obey instead. He did keep his gaze on Maryse and the gunman, though, leery of breaking complete contact.

The phony concierge waited until Brooks was in position, then nodded at the pretty brunette. "You can sit down."

Brooks willed her to be strong, and he was glad that she seemed to be holding it together. She took a breath and stepped to the high-backed chair, then perched on the edge, her eyes fixed nervously on the weapon. Its muzzle was pointed firmly at her chest, even though the man wielding it kept flipping his attention back and forth between her and Brooks.

Need to get him to point that over here, he decided.

Keeping his voice level—and conciliatory—he directed a question to the gunman. "Is there a problem we can help you work through?"

The man immediately swung the gun toward Brooks. "What?"

"It seems like you might need some help."

"Help?"

"That's not what you're here for?"

The man licked his lips again, then lifted his free hand to scratch at his chin. "No?"

Distracted. Good.

Brooks offered a small smile. "You sound a little unsure."

The gun wavered, then steadied. "No. I don't need help. I need my brother."

"Okay. Is he somewhere here in the hotel? Or in the city?"

"He's dead."

Damn, Brooks thought, while out loud he said, "I'm sorry to hear that, Mr.…."

The man paused, opened his mouth, then shook his head. "No names."

Damn again.

Brooks still kept his tone agreeable. "Okay. How about if you tell me how your brother died instead."

The phony concierge jabbed the gun back toward Maryse. "She showed up, and they killed him."

"Ah. Was he the man in the street? The one who got shot?"

"Yes." The man nodded, then shifted from foot to foot. "This was his idea. For the money."

"Well. I truly am very sorry for your loss. But I'm not quite following." Brooks dropped one arm to his side, careful to keep the change in stance casual. "For the money? What money?"

This time when the other man scratched at his chin, he used the gun. "We just wanted to make an exchange."

Maryse burst in then, like she couldn't help it. "An exchange? For Camille?"

"We had her," the man confirmed.

"Had?" Maryse repeated.

"We *have* her," the man amended quickly, his eyes darting from Brooks to Maryse, then back again.

"Who's 'we'?" Brooks brought his other arm down, too, then angled himself into the room; he sensed that things were about to take a bad turn and he wanted to be between Maryse and whatever was about to happen.

The gunman shook his head. "It doesn't matter anymore anyway."

Then his face screwed up, his features crunching together. He drew in a choked breath, and for a strange second, Brooks thought he might cry. Instead, he lifted the gun again and took aim. Straight at Maryse.

Brooks didn't think. He didn't hesitate. He just dived hard across the room, his arms closing on the other man's waist. Together, they flew backward and landed on the bed. The folder he'd hidden under his shirt came free in the tussle, and the papers inside scattered across the room.

Brooks ignored them. He needed to concentrate on the threat—the gun. He threw one elbow into the other man's chest, while at the same time reaching for the other man's wrist. A few seconds of flailing and he had it. He squeezed. When that didn't work, he dragged the man's wrist over the bed and slammed it into the nightstand. Once. Twice. On the third time, the gun finally clattered to the ground.

"Grab the weapon!" Brooks shouted.

Maryse blurred past him. Vaguely, he saw her reach for the gun.

Then the man beneath him bucked and kicked, commanding his attention again. For a moment, he retained the upper hand. He used his forearm and his lower body strength to press the man to the bed. But Brooks's strength and skill were overtaken by brute determination and surprise. The phony concierge lifted his head, slammed it into Brooks's own, and the world clouded over in a haze.

* * *

By the time Maryse managed to retrieve the gun from under the bed, then right herself again, it was all but over. And not in a good way. Brooks's eyes rolled back in his head, and he toppled sideways. Then the man below him pushed the big cop over completely and jumped to his feet, wobbling a little.

Maryse fumbled with the gun. She'd never fired one before, and she cursed herself for never learning the basics. It should've been the first thing she'd done in the name of protecting Cami.

Too late now.

And she couldn't get to the trigger fast enough.

The wild-eyed man was stalking toward her, his arms outstretched. With his mangled hand—courtesy of Brooks and the nightstand—and the already-purple welt bulging out on his forehead, he was a terrifying sight.

"Might as well give up now," the thug snarled as he stepped closer. "I'm going to catch you anyway."

He lunged forward, and Maryse ducked out of reach, then tore across the small room. She reached the opposite wall quickly, and there, she finally got a better hold of the gun. But her fingers were slippery with sweat and they refused to simply cock the hammer. She stopped trying and held it out anyway, hoping the red-eyed man would take that as enough of a threat.

"Stop," she ordered, glad that her voice came out with some force.

The man paused. "If you shoot me, you'll never get your kid back."

Maryse sucked in a breath. "Where is she?"

"Safe. And hidden."

"Tell me! Please."

"Give me the gun first."

She was almost sure of what would happen if she did. But that didn't stop her from considering it.

Anything to save Camille.

But the gleam in the man's eyes at her pause was enough to make her shake her head. "If I give you the gun, you'll just kill me. That's what you were going to do a second ago."

"Maybe I'm having a change of heart."

"Where's my daughter? If you tell me, I'll walk away. I'll never say a word to anyone about this."

"Too late for that. He already knows."

Her heart thundered, and her mind reeled with worry. *Too late?* Who was "he"? Wasn't this man the one who held her daughter captive? And how was she going to find out?

The man shook his head and, as he spoke, she realized she'd voiced at least one of the questions aloud. "He's the kind of person who—when he finds you—will make you wish you'd given *me* the gun."

At the dark threat, Maryse gasped, then inched back in an unconscious attempt to get away.

The thug smiled. "There's nowhere to go."

Her eyes flicked over the room, searching. But he was right. Her escape options were limited. There was the broken sliding glass door, which was too far away. There was the main exit, which the fake concierge now blocked. And there was the bathroom, which would only provide a temporary solution.

And there's Brooks.

She couldn't leave him. Not when he'd risked his own life on her and Cami's behalf. She lifted her chin, preparing to issue another warning.

As if he could read her mind, the thug stopped advancing toward her and turned to Brooks instead. He moved closer to the unconscious man, a dangerous glint in his eyes.

"Let's see how brave you are when I'm strangling your boyfriend," he said. "Think you can fire that thing with enough accuracy to hit me but not him?"

As he turned away, Maryse reacted instinctively. She sprang forward, her own safety and her need to get away forgotten. She swung out her arm as she moved, the gun suddenly a blunt force weapon. She smacked it into the side of his head. She only managed to hit his ear.

He spun back, then sideways to face her, fury dominating his features. He lifted a hand to his injured ear, and when he pulled it down, a streak of red covered his palm.

Bleeding. But conscious. Not good enough.

She drew the gun back again. This time, though, he knew she was coming, and he was better prepared to block her blow. He threw up a hand, and Maryse's forearm slammed into it hard enough to jar her whole body. Even her teeth slammed together.

She took a step back. Then tried again. But he was moving, too. He dropped his shoulder and charged.

Maryse did her best to sidestep, but her knee cracked against the desk chair. She let out a cry, then stumbled. The gun flew from her grip, skidded across the floor, then disappeared under the bed.

Maryse didn't waste any time. She dropped to the carpet and crawled forward, her hand outstretched. Her assailant followed, taking full advantage of the fact that she was already down. He jumped onto her back. He clamped a hand on her wrist. Then he pulled.

Thankfully, the carpet was better than the average commercial-grade. It still stung Maryse's skin as her chin hit, but the impact was minimal. She tried to push herself up and, in reward, got a knee in the small of her back. She hit the ground again, this time harder.

Her attacker was winning, and Maryse knew it.

In a last-ditch effort to get free and get to the weapon, she threw back an elbow. It hit its mark, but not hard enough to do more than make the man who held her down grunt. Both of his hands slid to her forearms, then forced her to roll to her back. As he straddled her hips and pinned her down, tears pricked at her eyes, and as his fingers closed on her neck, an unspoken apology to her missing daughter formed in her mind. But before her lids could close in defeat, there was a dull thud.

Maryse's eyes flew wide-open again. Above her, the man's jaw slackened. He teetered. Then a hand appeared at his collar and yanked him away, freeing her.

And Brooks knelt down at her side, concern filling his hazel eyes.

Brooks ignored the dull ache in his head in favor of making sure Maryse was okay.

"Still with me, sweetheart?" he asked, the endearment dropping from his mouth naturally.

She nodded weakly. "Where's…?"

"Breathing noisily over there somewhere." He reached down and cupped her cheek. "You okay for a minute if I go take care of him?"

She blinked, then swallowed, her expression suddenly nervous. "Take care of him?"

In spite of the situation, Brooks laughed. "Not like that. *Secure* him, in case he wakes up."

Her cheeks went pink. "Oh. Yes. I'll be fine."

Still smiling, Brooks brushed his thumb over her cheekbone, then stood up. As he turned toward the unconscious man, his amusement faded.

His hands on her throat.

The sight that had greeted him as he'd dragged himself from his own bout with unwanted oblivion was enough to turn his stomach. In fact, it was impossible to tell whether the churning in his gut was from the violence or from the blow to his head.

Or maybe from the fact that you almost let him get her?

As he grabbed the bedside lamp—the one he'd used as a weapon—from the ground, then wound the cord around the hotel employee's wrists, he had to acknowledge the self-directed question. "Maryse?"

"Yes?"

"If you want to call the local PD, now—"

"No."

"A man just broke into our hotel room. He tried to kill you."

"And he's my only connection to my daughter."

Brooks paused in what he was doing and made himself say the next, hard sentence that had formed in his mind. "It won't matter what the connection is if I can't keep you safe."

She met his stare with an even look of her own. "I don't want to be 'kept safe.' I don't need to be."

"Maryse." He realized a second too late that he'd said her name with entirely more stern force than he needed to.

She looked down at her hands. "I can't sit around waiting for someone else to help her. That's *my* job, and I'm not going to ask permission to do it."

Brooks fought a frustrated sigh. He could see the stubborn set of her shoulders, and he had a sudden vision of the cops showing up and Maryse taking off. Which would not only complicate the investigation. It would cast suspicion where none was due. And it would take *him* out of the equation completely.

"Okay," he said, "but if you change your mind…tell me. Don't hesitate."

She lifted her head, relief and hope mingling in her gaze. "Thank you."

"Yep."

Fighting his lingering guilt, he turned his attention back to the more pressing task at hand. He bent down to yank the phony concierge farther away from Maryse, then tugged at the cord around the man's wrists. When he was satisfied that the plastic-covered wire was pulled tight enough, he stood up again, scanning the room for something to use for the man's feet. He wasn't taking any chances.

His eyes landed on the open closet. Inside hung two bathrobes, and each had a loose belt.

Perfect.

He only made it a half a step, though, before a loud knock on the door interrupted him. He tossed a worried look Maryse's way. She'd pulled herself up to the edge of the bed and sat on the corner, her expression as concerned as he knew his own must be. Another sharp rap made her jump.

A voice followed the second knock. "Sir? Ma'am?"

Brooks slipped to the door and peered through the spy-hole. The concierge stood in the hall, his face tense as he shifted from side to side.

Brooks turned back to Maryse and, in a low voice, said, "It's our friend from the front desk. He looks annoyed."

"Should we answer it?" she whispered back.

"If we don't want him to break it down," Brooks replied, eyeing the bound man lying in the middle of the floor.

"Sir?" The concierge's voice was more insistent now.

Then Maryse's face cleared, and she sprang to her feet. "I've got an idea. Pull *him* up beside the bed. Toss the blanket over him and take off your shirt."

"What?"

"Hurry."

She didn't explain further. As Brooks dropped the blanket over the unmoving man, Maryse slipped off her boots, then her already-askew jacket. She lifted off the soft, red sweater underneath, then snapped up the sheet from the bed and wrapped it around her chest. Finally, she pushed down her bra straps and tucked them under the linen.

Her bare shoulders were the color of warm cream and dotted with a surprising number of freckles. If Brooks had stopped to think about it, which he hadn't—yet—he would've imagined the rest of her skin to be as mark-free as her porcelain-hued face.

But I like this better, he decided, studying the pattern that dipped down past the sheet.

"Shirt?" she prompted, and Brooks realized he was standing very still, just watching as she undressed.

He lifted his hands to the buttons, but clearly didn't do it fast enough, because she stepped toward him and reached out to help. Even though she undid them swiftly, it was impossible *not* to notice how her fingers moved across his chest. How the tips of them warmed his skin as they brushed against it. He even had to stifle a groan as she finished with the buttons, then pushed the shirt back.

As she stepped back to give his newly bared chest a quick once-over, Brooks stared down at her, wondering if she was aware of the effect she was having on him. Or if she felt the same lick of interest. When she lifted her face, and he spotted the lacy blush spreading across her cheeks, he was sure that she must.

"Ready?" she asked, her voice a little breathless.

"Guess I must be," he agreed. "Even if I don't know what it is I'm ready for."

"This." She dropped her pants to the floor, stepped out of them and moved toward the door.

And he finally clued in to her plan.

Chapter 7

Maryse closed her hand on the doorknob, grateful to have an excuse to pull away from Brooks and the temptation of his wide, strong chest. She hadn't expected to have such a strong reaction to his tanned skin, and the pleasant prickles of heat had almost overwhelmed her.

Well, she conceded, *at least it adds an element of realism.*

And her breathless greeting as she cracked open the door definitely screamed of something sexy. "Hi there."

The concierge—the real one—stepped back and eyed her a little warily. "Mrs. Small?"

She inched the door open a little bit more. "Yes?"

"We had a report of some noise?"

"Noise?" Maryse intentionally let the sheet drop, then laughed and pulled it up again before she was fully exposed. "Oh! Oops."

The concierge averted his eyes. "I, uh, tried to call the room a few times, but—"

"We'll pay for it." Brooks's voice came from just above her ear, and his hand landed in the small of her back as he made the announcement.

"Pay for what?" the concierge wanted to know.

Brooks's palm slid from her back to her hip, and he pressed her to his side. He held out the broken phone.

"For this," he said. "And anything else we inadvertently broke during our—"

Maryse jabbed an elbow into his stomach, cutting him off, and she smiled as sweetly as she could manage. "We'll pay. We got a little carried away, but we'll keep it down from now on."

The concierge hesitated. "You sure you're okay, Mrs. Small?"

"Yes."

She might've added something else, but her brain suddenly ceased to work properly because Brooks's lips had landed on her throat. They worked from a spot just below her ear down to her shoulder in a trail of light kisses.

The concierge cleared his throat. "So. Right. I'll just… Right."

"Uh-huh." Brooks's voice rumbled against the sensitive skin of her neck. "Thanks for checking on us."

"You're wel—"

Without warning, he reached around Maryse to slam the door shut. And he didn't let her go as it closed. Instead, he brought up his other hand and turned her to face him, then pulled her close and tipped his head down so that their lips were less than an inch apart.

"That was a good plan," he murmured.

"You think so?" she breathed.

"Can I just ask you for one favor?"

"What?"

"Next time you're going to get mostly naked in front of me…give me a bit of warning. Especially if it's happening directly after a fight and a head injury."

"Okay."

"Thank you."

He dragged his mouth over hers—just barely more than a whisper of a touch—then released her. As she picked up

her pants and watched him button his shirt, desire mingled
with a need for more than that simple, gentle touch.

Maryse knew the timing was off.

Way off, she amended as she thought of Cami.

Her heart squeezed, and her gaze followed Brooks. He'd
bent down beside the blanket-covered man on the other side
of the room and was searching the ground for something.

But she had to admit that in spite of the timing, her want
wasn't quite banked. If anything, Brooks's protective nature
and determination just heightened it. And besides that, he'd
said *next time*. That had an appealing ring to it. Something
to look forward to, when the future seemed painfully un-
certain. In fact, if she really thought about it…*he* was the
only semisure thing in her life at the moment. Which was
strange, considering how little she knew about him.

He's an off-duty cop.

He's willing to help.

And he's got the softest lips in the world.

"Right. What more do I need?"

She didn't realize she'd spoken aloud until he answered.

"What more do you need in regards to what?" he repeated. "Did I miss something?"

Blushing, she shook her head. "Nothing. Never mind."

"If you say so." He pushed himself up from the floor.
"Our unconscious friend is staying that way for a while,
but I've got his phone here and I think we should…um.
Maryse?"

"I'm listening," she said.

One corner of his mouth tipped up. "I'm sure you are.
But you might want to get dressed?"

Her blush deepened as she glanced down at the sheet
she still held wrapped around her body. Wishing there was
a more graceful way of throwing on clothes as fast as she
could, Maryse scrambled to get re-dressed.

"Okay," she said when she'd finally pulled on her second boot, "you've got his phone, and…?"

"I think you should take a look through it. See if anything is familiar." He held out the phone, and she took it.

"I can do that."

"The gun?"

"Under the bed, I think."

He bent down again, and Maryse swiped her finger over the phone, relieved to see that it wasn't password protected. She scrolled through the text messages, but nothing stood out, and there was nothing about Camille. She switched over to the address book. She didn't recognize any of the names except Maison Blanc.

"Any luck?" Brooks asked.

Maryse shook her head. "No. I wish I did recognize something but…nothing."

"What's the last number called?"

As she clicked on the call log to check, her finger slipped to the redial button instead. And before she could correct her mistake, a woman's voice—crackling with irritation and loud enough to be heard without lifting the phone to her ear—carried through the line.

"Greg?"

Maryse held her breath, her finger hovering over the hang-up button. But when she lifted her eyes to Brooks's face, he shook his head and mouthed for her to wait.

"Greg!" the woman repeated, even louder this time, then launched into an angry, muttered monologue. "You've got to be kidding me. He pocket dialed me *again*? We're supposed to be leaving, and instead I'm stuck here with a kid who doesn't talk. And I swear to God there's some car circling the block. You'd think the money would be motivation enough. Hell. Incompetence is gonna kill me."

Then the line went dead and Maryse exhaled, trying to

curb her side-by-side jumps of hope and fear. "The kid who doesn't talk. She has to have been talking about Camille. We have to get to her, Brooks. We have to find her. Call her back and... Oh, God. She said they were supposed to be *leaving*. What's the best thing to do?"

"I don't know what the *best* thing to do is, but the *first* thing...we need to figure out who the woman is."

"The call went to someone named Dee."

"Dee?" Brooks reached out and took the phone from her shaking fingers, then tapped across the screen—far more precisely than she had done—and a frown creased his brow.

"Does that name mean something?"

"I think it does."

He pocketed the phone, then strode across the room where he pushed through the papers that had come loose during his fight with the fake concierge. After a swift search, he lifted one sheet from the messy pile and scanned it.

"'Dee White,'" he read aloud, then looked up at her. "She's the *real* daytime concierge. The woman who was supposed to be at the counter when the man with the gun was there instead."

Maryse eyed the still-unconscious man on the bed. "So they were working together."

"Looks like it. And neither of them has any connection to you or your daughter?"

"Not that I know of." It was the truth, even if it wasn't as complete an answer as she could've offered. "Does that paper say where they're from?"

"Just that Ms. White lives on rue Riel."

Hope surged through her again, and this time she didn't try to tamp it down. "Brooks...that's only ten minutes from here."

"You want to go there?"

She swallowed her fear and looked him in the eye. "I don't want to. I *have* to."

As he followed the simple driving directions Maryse had outlined before they exited the hotel, Brooks strummed his thumbs against the steering wheel. What they were about to do went against his training *and* his better judgment.

He'd left behind a suspect. A felon. Secured and unarmed, yes. But unguarded, too. There was nothing to stop the man from waking up, somehow breaking free, then walking out of the hotel room. It wasn't just a bad decision; it was a crime. A step well above the occasional jaywalk that made up the entire history of Brooks's lawbreaking behavior.

On top of that, he was carrying a possibly—likely—illegal weapon and willfully taking a civilian straight into what was guaranteed to be a very dangerous setting.

You could've said no, he reminded himself.

But when he sneaked a look at Maryse, he had to admit it wasn't quite true. Her need to rescue her daughter herself was palpable, but underneath her outward stoicism he knew she must be terrified. Brooks had learned over the course of his career that people gave away a lot about themselves in times of immense pressure, so there were a few things about Maryse he was pretty sure of.

For one thing, he sensed she needed someone to rely on in the wake of that fear. For another, he got the feeling that she didn't have someone like that in her life already. And he somehow doubted that going through the proper channels would provide it.

So. No. He couldn't have said no. Not so long as he really wanted to help her, and not so long as he let his instincts and conscience have a say in the matter.

And that aside...you have no real *authority in this country.*

That, at least, was true. Sure, he could probably call in some favors and find a way to get a good word put in with the local police, but it wouldn't guarantee him any insight into an ongoing investigation. So this was the best alternative to that, really. And she trusted him, at least a little.

But not enough to tell you her whole story.

That was true, too, and he wished he could find a way around it.

"Brooks?" Her hesitant voice wrapped softly around his name, interrupting his internal argument.

"Yeah, sweetheart?"

"The woman on the phone was talking about money. And the guy who pretended to be the concierge mentioned it, too."

"Pretty standard in a hostage situation like this one. If you want to pay it—"

"I would want to," she said quickly, and with no uncertainty.

"You *would* want to?"

"I'd drain my bank account to get her back. But the person—or people—who took Cami didn't ask me for money."

"No ransom note?"

"Well. There *was* a note." She chewed on her lip for a second before going on. "But it didn't bring up any money. It sounded like they just wanted Cami and that was it."

"Wanted her for what?"

"Personal reasons."

Cursing himself for not asking about the terms of the kidnapping in the first place, Brooks swerved the car to the side of the road, then faced Maryse. "I know we're strangers, and whatever secrets you're keeping are yours and not mine. But if this is a custody issue…"

"What? No."

"Then you really need to give me something else to go on. Something to negotiate with."

She looked down at her hands. "I don't know what to tell you. I didn't think money had anything to do with this."

Brooks fought an urge to demand to know what she'd meant by "personal reasons," and instead he asked, "Is it possible that it's both personal *and* about the money?"

"I guess it could be."

Frustration nipped at him. "Are you sure you don't want to tell me something more?"

She lifted her eyes to meet his gaze, indecision playing across her features. Then she shook her head. "It would take more time than we've got. And I don't think it would help get Cami back."

"Maryse…"

Please, she signed. *Can we just keep going?*

Frustrated, he nodded curtly, then pulled the car back onto the road. She was right that time was of the essence. It always was in a kidnapping case.

He guided the car through the rest of the streets quickly, not speaking again until they reached rue Riel. He found the house with the correct address—a nondescript one-story—then circled the block and parked on the next street over. It would put them just far enough away that they wouldn't draw attention to themselves, but would still be able to make a quick exit if necessary.

He turned to Maryse again, trying to keep his irritation from his voice. "I'm assuming I won't be able to talk you out of coming with me."

Her determined look was back. "No."

"Can you at least do me a favor?"

"What favor?"

"Most of the work I do is in gangs and guns, so hostage negotiation isn't my specialty. But this won't be my first one. I think if Dee sees you right away and recognizes you, she'll panic. And the last thing we need is a panicked, out-of-control kidnapper."

"So what do you want me to do?"

"I want you to expect *not* to rush in there like a SWAT team. We're not going to find an excuse to walk up to the front door and knock, either, because I highly doubt Dee White would just let us in." He paused to make sure she understood, then went on as she nodded. "I want *you* to hang back. Be my lookout while I assess the layout and access points. From there, we come back to the car and we decide on our next move."

"I can do that," she acquiesced quickly.

"Perfect." He reached for the handle, but her voice stopped him before he could push the door open.

"You think I'm crazy for not telling you the whole story, don't you?" she asked.

"Crazy? No. Not the right word."

"Counterproductive, then."

"It's easier for me if I can see all of the puzzle pieces," he admitted.

"I've been on my own with Cami for her entire life," she said. "This is—literally—the first time I've ever trusted someone to help me with anything that has to do with her. Not because I haven't needed or wanted it, but because it would put us both at risk. And I want your help. I really do. But it's hard for me to make a leap this quickly."

He examined her face. The short but impassioned confession had deepened the flush so that it covered her throat, too. It also made him want to ask a hundred other questions. But her eyes held a guarded hope, and a hint of something else, and he wanted to fulfill both desires—to help *and* to respect her need for privacy.

"You're asking me to be patient," he said slowly.

"Yes."

"I'll try, sweetheart. But patience has never been my strongest characteristic, and in my job, it's hard to sit around waiting."

"You're a good cop, aren't you?" she asked.

"I like to think so."

"I didn't mean to say that you're good at your job…" She trailed off, a hint of pink dotting her cheeks, and her hands flashed, *What I meant to say was that you're a good man*.

"I'm not perfect, but I try."

He reached for the door handle again, but this time it was her hand that stopped him. Her fingers landed on his elbow, and warmth immediately crept up his arm.

"Brooks… Cami *isn't* your job," she reminded him softly. "And neither am I."

Frustration slipped away at the emphatic statement. He met her eyes and nodded.

"You're right. You're definitely not a job."

He gave her jawbone a light stroke, then slid from the car and hurried to the passenger side to open her door. He swung it wide, and she started to step out. As she moved, though, her boot caught on the rubber seal at the bottom of the door frame, and she fumbled a bit in an attempt to get it free. Automatically, Brooks reached down to help. One hand gripped her boot, and the other landed on the curve of her calf. Try as he might, he couldn't shake the sudden memory of how that same calf had poked out temptingly from the bedsheet at the hotel room.

Without meaning to, he slid his fingers over it. Maryse let out a little gasp, and he wasn't sure if it was from the heated contact or from the fact that her foot suddenly came free. When he lifted his eyes, though, he was sure it was at least partially the former. He saw desire—the same pull of attraction he felt—reflected in her gaze.

His hands lingered for another heartbeat before he forced himself to pull away, and he stood and held out his palm for her to take. For a long second, Maryse stared at him without moving.

"I'm okay," she finally told him.

"You said you wanted my help," he pointed out.

"I do."

"So take it."

She continued to hold still, and Brooks almost pulled his offer of assistance away. Then her hand snaked out and landed in his, the guarded look dropping into a smile.

"Thank you."

And as he assisted her from the car, Brooks was sure there was something symbolic in the small, simple gesture of trust.

Chapter 8

The look in Brooks's eyes was intense. And full of way too much meaning for five hours of knowing each other. It was also smoldering enough to take Maryse's breath away so badly that her chest kind of ached as he led her up the sidewalk. His warm fingers wrapped around her cool ones, and his presence cut through the chill in the air and warmed her from the inside out. He continued to hold her hand until they reached the house three doors away from their destination, where he dropped it in favor of pulling her into an embrace.

"Sorry to steal your trick, but…" He trailed off, then dipped his head down and spoke into her ear. "To anyone looking, we're just a couple of lovers on a winter stroll. So without being obvious, I want you to look past my shoulder to the corner. There's a big tree over there. No leaves, but an enormous trunk. Tell me when you spot it."

Maryse lifted her arms to Brooks's shoulders, then stood up on her tiptoes and pressed her cheek to his neck. With her eyes half-open, she focused on finding the described tree.

"The oak tree?" she asked.

"That's the one."

"Okay. I see it."

"Good." One of his hands found the small of her back

and rubbed it in a small, pleasant circle. "Dee White's house is around the corner, just a few lots past the one with the tree. So when we get there, we're going to pause again. I'm going to leave you in that spot, and I'm going to run back as if I forgot something in the car. Then I'm going to slip in between the houses on this side and approach from behind to get a look in the house, okay? If I see an opportunity to retrieve Camille, I'm going to take it."

"And if you don't see one?"

"Then I'll find an excuse to get inside. Traveling vacuum cleaner salesman."

Maryse couldn't make herself smile. "Okay."

He gave her a squeeze, then adjusted so that she was on his left, tucked under his arm and out of view of anyone who might be watching from Dee's side of the street. They walked at a leisurely pace, Brooks bending to kiss her head every few steps. The intervals of affection were just enough of a distraction to keep Maryse's nerves at bay as they approached the big tree. But when they actually reached it, her worry spiked again.

"What if none of this works?" she asked.

Brooks guided her to the oak, then pushed her back to the cool trunk and put his arms on either side of her. "It will."

"How can you be so sure?"

"I just am. If I can't break in and take her, I promise you, I can put on a convincing show."

"Convincing enough to make a kidnapper give up?"

He stepped closer, pushing his body to hers and pressing their foreheads together. "Trust me. In another life, I'd have been an award-winning actor."

Maryse's breath caught in her throat as his lips grazed hers.

"You're that good at pretending?" she murmured against his mouth.

"Very good." One of his hands crept up, then slid between the buttons of her coat and skimmed across her waist, and he added, "Plus…the closer it is to the truth, the easier it is to do."

"And this is close enough to the truth to be convincing?"

"Damned straight."

The lip graze became a full-blown kiss, sucking the air out of Maryse's lungs. The hand Brooks had inside her coat traveled up her side, then around her back, then caressed the bottoms of her shoulder blades before it came back to her waist again. And through the exploration of her torso, the kiss got deeper. His tongue darted out to trace the lines of her mouth, then found its way inside, where it met with her own.

Maryse reacted to the attention with an eagerness that surprised her. She stroked the short edges of Brooks's hair and kissed him back as best as she knew how. Like she was trying to make up for the last six years of abstinence in a solitary moment. She could hear her own little gasps of enthusiasm. She didn't care. He'd said he wanted the world to see a pair of lovers, and there was no better way to do it than this. And for the too-short time that the deliberate display of affection lasted, the world around her disappeared. The cold didn't exist. Her fear took a step into the background. Even thoughts of Camille barely dampened the intensity, especially when her brain quietly reminded her that she was doing this *for* her daughter. The fact that she was enjoying it was just a tiny bonus.

And it was Brooks, not her, who at last pulled away.

"Think that'll be convincing enough?" he said, his voice ragged and his eyes hooded.

"I think so," Maryse breathed.

"I want you to do something else for me, okay?"

"Yes." Her face reddened at the quick, forceful agreement, and Brooks smiled down at her.

"Reach up under the back of my sweater to the waistband of my jeans. I've got our friend Greg's gun tucked back there."

"You should hold on to it. It'll do you more good than it will me."

"I need you to take it. If I think you're out here unarmed, it'll distract me."

"And what about you being *in there* unarmed?"

He shook his head. "I've got plenty of training and experience with hand-to-hand fighting. Can you say the same?"

"No, but—"

"Please."

Maryse bit back an urge to tell him that she really didn't know how to use the weapon. She was sure if she emphasized her incompetence with gun use, he'd insist she wait in the car. So she nodded instead and slid her hands to his waist, noting his sharp inhalation as she moved them along his belt until she reached the warmed metal near his back pocket.

"Got it," she said.

"Bring it around slowly," he replied. "And try not to shoot me."

"Not funny."

But she did as she was told, holding her breath as she dragged the weapon so that it was between them. Brooks's hands closed overtop of hers, and he guided them together to the pocket on the inside of her jacket. The gun felt heavy and unnatural against her hip.

"If all else fails," he said. "You can just whack someone in the head with it."

"If I can even get it out fast enough. That didn't work so well with Greg."

"But you're experienced now. So you can do it if you have to. And, sweetheart…if your daughter's in there, we're going to get her back." He dropped another kiss on her mouth—this time lightly—then turned back up the sidewalk.

With her heart in her throat, Maryse watched him slip past a row of shrubs beside the house, then head toward the car. The farther away he got, the more her stomach twisted up in knots. As he reached the vehicle, he turned abruptly and disappeared completely into one of the yards. No wave, no acknowledgment of her presence. And even though she understood why, she couldn't help but wish he'd at least glanced over his shoulder.

Then there was nothing but stillness. Even the cold winter breeze had died down.

She shifted her attention to Dee White's house, scanning the perimeter for any sign of Brooks. She saw none. In fact, the house was silent, too.

And all the quiet gave her too much time to think. Too much time to chew at the fact that Brooks had said *if* Camille was in the house. Too much time to wonder why money had come up, but no ransom demand had been made, and to worry about why this couple seemed to know about her brother, but hadn't mentioned him outside of the note they'd left behind.

It didn't make any sense, no matter how she came at it.

It doesn't matter, she told herself. *So long as Camille is safe. So long as Brooks can get her out.*

Her eyes searched the property once again.

"Please hurry," she murmured, her whisper dragging against the chilly air.

Finally, she caught a flash of gray—just the same color as Brooks's sweater—beside the fence, and she exhaled, sure it was him. For a second, relief eased her worry. But a heartbeat later, it came back with a vengeance. A second flash followed the first, and there was no mistaking it for Brooks. It was something metallic. Something dangerous.

Another gun?

The thought was enough to spur her to action. She fled the relative safety offered by the wide oak and ran toward the house, her feet flying over the snow-covered grass. She reached the house's front yard in moments. She strode up the path to the front door. And there, she paused, unsure what to do next. Try to come up stealthily and hope to use the element of surprise? Call out to Brooks and possibly alert not only whoever was following him, but also whoever was inside?

If you haven't done that already.

Another flicker from the side of the house took away the illusion of choice.

What she had to do was hurry.

Drawing the gun from her pocket as she moved, Maryse pushed herself to the exterior wall of the house and moved in the direction of the metallic gleam.

Brooks took a cautious step toward the back porch.

Something isn't right.

The house was too quiet.

During the accidental phone call, Dee White had been anything but calm and collected. Even her brief, angry monologue had been enough to tell him that she wasn't the kind of person who would sit around sipping tea in silence. She was likely the kind of criminal who would be rash and unpredictable, and she'd be wearing a hole in the floor in frustration as she waited for Greg to get back to her.

So what does that mean for right now?

Had she left, as she'd said she was going to do? Or had

she had Camille held elsewhere from the beginning? Either thing was a possibility.

And either will leave us back at square one, too.

Brooks took another concerned step forward, then froze as the distinct sound of boots crunching on snow carried to his ears. Quick and steady, and definitely headed his way.

Automatically, he dropped into a defensive stance, arms wide, hands open, knees loose and ready to spring. He inched back, careful not to let himself get into a position where he could be cornered against the house.

The footfalls slowed.

Brooks tensed.

The footfalls stopped.

He leaned back, waiting for an attack.

Instead, an icy breeze kicked up, sending a waft of honey-scented air his way. It only took him a moment to place the newly familiar smell.

"Maryse," he hissed, his voice low.

The snow crunched again, quickly this time, and she appeared at the edge of the house. He noted the look on her face—fierce but scared—then spied the weapon in her hands. When she saw him, the gun dropped to her side.

"Brooks?" His name was almost a gasp.

"Just me."

"You're okay?"

"I'm fine," he assured her. "What happened?"

"I saw someone following you. Or I thought I did."

Brooks scanned the yard. It was as empty as it'd been for the last few minutes.

"Looks clear," he said.

She let out a laugh that sounded forced. "I overreacted, I guess."

A tickle of guilt bagged at Brooks's conscience. He'd assumed she would be safe and out of harm's way, and that using her as a lookout would be unnecessary.

"It's my fault for not telling you what to do if you *did* see someone," he said. "But I don't think anyone's here. Outside or inside."

Her eyes pinched with worry. "No one?"

"I'm sorry, sweetheart. I took a look through all the windows I could find, and I didn't see anything. No lights, no movement. I was just about to try to find a way in to confirm."

Her eyes flicked toward the back door. "I think that's going to be pretty easy."

"What do you mean?"

"It's open."

Brooks followed her gaze. Sure enough, the door sat ajar by just a few inches. Hadn't it been closed just a few seconds earlier? The not-quite-right feeling hit him in the gut again.

"Give me the gun, Maryse," he commanded in a low voice.

She held it out, butt-end first. He took it, positioned himself in front of her, then swept the yard again, arcing the gun across the whole area and searching for anything out of the ordinary. He took a step forward.

Need a better view.

"Wait here a second," he said.

He moved a few feet farther out, his feet touching the edge of the snow. He could see the entire flat space, and most of the neighboring yards, too.

Still nothing. So why can't I relax?

He started to turn back, but before he could spin around completely, a small figure—not much larger than a child— came flying out from the side of the house. It collided directly with Maryse, knocking her to the ground.

Cursing the fact that he'd dropped his guard, Brooks fumbled for a second with the gun, trying to get a clear shot. He realized immediately it was unnecessary. The figure was a tiny woman. Barefoot and—judging by the scant amount of clothing she wore—unarmed. If it hadn't been for the element of surprise, he doubted she would've been able to overpower Maryse at all.

Quickly, Brooks shoved the weapon into his waistband, then strode over and grabbed the woman by the back of her sleeveless T-shirt. He yanked her off with as little roughness as he could manage, then dragged her to the wall, kicking and shouting muffled curses.

When he lifted her up, he saw why she couldn't do much more. A strip of duct tape covered her mouth, and she had a huge almost-black bruise on her temple. Her eyes were wild and bloodshot.

She continued to thrash and flail, finally jerking her head back so hard that it smacked the wall behind her.

Brooks cringed and relaxed his arm, expecting her to go limp. But the woman wasn't done. She lifted one of her bare feet and slammed it to his knee. Once again, she had surprise on her side.

Brooks stumbled backward, nearly falling over. He caught himself on the wall, then cursed as the woman bolted. He moved to chase her down, but Maryse beat him to it. Her long, slim legs carried her quickly over the snow, and she caught up before the other woman made it even halfway across the yard. She slammed into her, knocking her to the snow. The two women rolled over the cold ground, and in the ten seconds it took Brooks to reach them, Maryse already had the smaller woman pinned to the ground.

"You can take over anytime," she said, sounding winded.

Brooks bent down, grabbed the still-flailing woman's

arm, pinned her wrists together, then nodded. "Okay. You're good to let go."

Maryse eased off, and Brooks yanked the would-be escapee to her feet. She kicked out one more time, but he held her firmly, and she finally sagged in defeat.

Brooks tipped his head in Maryse's direction. "You all right?"

She was already pushing to her feet, and she nodded. "I'm fine."

"You sure?"

"Yes."

Wishing he could give *her* the attention rather than her ragged attacker, he turned back to the underdressed woman. "You done?"

Her bloodshot eyes were still furious, and Brooks knew no matter how complacent her body seemed, she was still seeking a way to fight back.

"Fine," he muttered. "Don't know why I thought this might be done the easy way."

He threw a belated look toward the neighbors' houses to check if anyone was watching, then pulled her over the snow and back toward the house. Careful to keep his hold on her, he brought her into the relative shelter of the rear wall, then lifted a hand and pulled off the duct tape.

"Got something to explain?" he asked.

The woman spit, then yelled, "You son of a—"

Brooks slapped the tape back in place. "That's about enough of that."

She mumbled something, her nostrils flaring.

"All right." He worked to sound patient. "How about we try this again? More reasonably."

He reached up to free her mouth again. For a few seconds, she just flicked a glare between him and Maryse, who'd followed closely behind. Then she drew in a breath, exhaled it…and started yelling all over again.

"I don't know who the hell you think you are, or what the hell you think you're doing, but if you think *I'm* going to—"

The tape went back up, and Brooks shook his head. He waited until she seemed calm before speaking again.

"I'm willing to talk," he said. "Really. But it's hard to do if you're screaming and swearing at me. If you want to have a conversation—nicely—nod once. Otherwise, the tape stays on until the cops get here."

It was a bluff, of course, but she didn't need to know that.

"Well?" he prodded.

She glared long enough for Brooks to count to twelve, then finally nodded. He freed her mouth again, and this time when she took a breath and spoke, it was in a cold, brittle tone.

"This is *my* house. I have more than a right to know what you're doing here," she said.

Maryse inhaled sharply enough to echo through the air, and she stepped closer, clinging to Brooks's arm as she asked, "This is your house?"

"Whose did you think it was?"

"Does that mean you're Dee White?"

"What about it?"

"Are you her?"

"Yeah. So?"

"Where's my daughter? Where's Camille?"

Dee White's eyes narrowed. "You're Maryse LePrieur. How did you find me?"

"Please. You just have to tell me where she is."

"You're too late."

Brooks tensed at the answer, and he heard the catch in Maryse's voice when she asked her next question.

"What do you mean?"

Dee White shook her head. "She's gone. He took her."

Brooks opened his mouth to ask for more information, but—quite abruptly—the woman began to cry. Big, racking sobs that made him pause and rethink his approach.

"All right," he said gruffly. "Let's move this party inside and see if we get some answers."

Chapter 9

Maryse's body was alight with a need to shake answers out of Dee White. Literally take her by the shoulders and do it.

She'd never in her life considered herself to be an aggressive person, and it had never occurred to her to try to extract information using force. Of course, she'd also never been away from her daughter for more than a few hours, either. And she'd never had Camille's life—or her own— lined up in the crosshairs.

But God help me, she thought as she moved through the crowded kitchen, *if that woman doesn't stop crying and start talking...*

In the five minutes since they'd entered the home, the overblown waterworks hadn't subsided. And Maryse wasn't buying it. She didn't believe for a second that the fury Dee White exuded had turned to concern or remorse, or whatever it was that had the tears rolling. It was an act. Another barrier between her and Cami. And she wanted to call it out. She'd ordered Brooks—in sign language—to let her do it. He'd refused. He hadn't even acknowledged the gestures.

He'd suggested—verbally and in a too-gentle voice— that she might be close to the edge. Then he all but insisted that she put a bit of physical distance between herself and Dee. Just for a few moments. And he'd suggested the tea. What he'd really meant was that she wasn't detached enough to be reasonable. And it was the exact reason she was standing near the stove, waiting for a kettle to boil, when she would rather have been by Brooks's side, demanding to know the truth.

Her eyes sought the clock on the wall. Another full minute had gone by, making the total wasted number six.

Brewing tea for the woman who had Camille. Who took her.

Maryse's stomach knotted up.

Where was Cami now?

How had she looked when Dee saw her?

Had she asked for Maryse?

The tumble of questions made tears prick at her eyes, and her body bristled with tension that she couldn't diffuse. Brooks might be in there, trying to find the answer to the first one, but would he ask the second and third? Would he be thinking of her child's welfare the same way she was?

She shook her head.

He was a good man. But he didn't have a personal attachment to Camille.

The kettle's whistle put a temporary hold on her negative thinking. She lifted the pot, poured the water over the waiting tea bag, then sloshed it directly into the mug. She refused to let it steep. Or to offer the woman milk or sugar. This wasn't some pleasant afternoon party where they needed to play nice. Dee White could just take her tea as it was served.

She stalked from the kitchen back to the living room, half expecting to find Brooks seated beside Dee on the couch, his arm wrapped around the other woman, comforting her.

The mental image made Maryse stop so short that the hot liquid spilled over the side of the cup, scalding her hand.

She bit back a yelp and settled for a wince. And it wasn't just about the pain. It was about the scenario itself.

I'm jealous.

The realization stung.

It was an over-the-top reaction, especially when it wasn't even something that she knew was happening. But that didn't stop the tickle of green-tinged emotion from being real.

Maryse stood just outside the living room door, pondering what it meant. She appreciated Brooks and his help. She liked him. And there was no denying the intense attraction or the way she felt when they kissed. But jealousy? It was a stretch.

She tightened her grip on the mug and forced her feet to move forward. And she was ridiculously relieved to find Dee on the couch with her feet curled under her body, but Brooks standing beside the table with his arms at his sides. Not even in touching distance.

Maryse let out a breath, then stepped toward the table. As she brushed by the big off-duty cop, he pressed a hand to her hip very briefly.

"Better?" he said.

"Hoping to be," she replied pointedly, setting down the mug in front of Dee.

The other woman lifted her eyes. They were still red. Still angry. Maryse glanced Brooks's way, thinking he had to see it, too. But his expression was sympathetic, his shoulders relaxed. Did he actually believe Dee White's act?

Maryse's chest tightened with worry.

"Do you want me to give a recap, so you can drink that tea and relax?" Brooks said, his voice full of compassion.

"Please," said the woman on the couch.

He nodded at Dee. "Ms. White was just telling me about the ordeal she went through."

What about Camille! Maryse wanted to scream.

Brooks bent down, lifted the mug up, then turned the handle toward Dee. "Go ahead."

The woman took a tiny sip, then sighed like he'd done her the biggest favor in the world. In response, he smiled a kind, full-mouthed smile that made Maryse squeeze both of her hands into fists. But she kept her lips pressed tightly together and held in her anger, even when Dee smiled back.

"Thank you."

"No problem."

Maryse thought her head might explode. But then Brooks shifted on his feet and touched the weapon at his waistband, and she remembered what he'd said about being an award-winning actor in another life, and she knew, suddenly, what he was doing.

They were still on the same page.

Thank God.

Brooks turned his easy smile her way, and she saw the slightest hint of tension in his eyes as he spoke. "Ms. White, her boyfriend and his brother have been on the run for a while now, trying to keep ahead of some bad debt."

"Bad debt?" Maryse repeated, careful to keep her voice neutral.

Brooks nodded. "Not your average credit-card kinda debt, though. The knee-capping, finger-breaking kind that needs a whole new identity."

"And?"

"And these guys—very bad men, from what I understand—felt that Ms. White and her friends owed them something more than money."

"Camille." Her name came out a whisper.

Maryse didn't know how her daughter connected to the men in question, but she was sure all the same that it was true, even before Brooks nodded a second time.

"These men came to Ms. White and offered to forgive the debt in exchange for retrieving your daughter."

"But…why?"

The woman on the couch spoke up then. "They said the little girl belonged to them."

It was all Maryse could take. "*Belonged to them?* She's *my* daughter. She doesn't belong to *anyone* because she's a person. And I have no idea who 'they' are!"

"We didn't actually give her back," Dee said.

"Give her *back*?"

The other woman shot her a defensive look, then pointed to her forehead. "That's why I got this. They hit me. I ran and hid in the shed, and they left."

"Because they really just wanted Camille. And you weren't going to hand her over like you promised."

"It was Greg's brother's idea."

"Who?"

"The man who took you from the hotel," Brooks explained.

Dee nodded. "He said if the kid was worth that much to someone else, she'd be worth even more to her mother."

Maryse connected the dots, finally seeing how the money aspect factored in. "You thought *I* would pay you."

"Wouldn't you?"

For the first time, icy fury overrode her fear. She would've taken a step toward Dee, but Brooks's hand closed on her elbow and pulled her back.

She couldn't muster up the strength to push him off and instead sagged against him and said, "But he didn't even ask me for money."

"Dee doesn't know why he didn't ask. But we need to listen to the rest of what she has to say, sweetheart," he said.

"Unless she knows where Cami is—"

"She might not know where she is, but she does know who has her. And that's worth something."

Maryse blew out a breath. He was right. It was worth more than something. It was worth everything. At least so long as it was the *only* thing. But that didn't mean she had to like it.

She made herself speak as calmly as she could manage. "Who has her, Dee?"

"They're a gang. Run by a man named Caleb Nank."

The name meant nothing to Maryse, but Brooks's hand tightened on her elbow. Did it mean something to him? She thought it must. And his next words confirmed it.

"Maryse," he said. "Can you excuse me and Ms. White for a moment?"

"What?" She couldn't keep the surprise from her reply.

"Just for a minute. Maybe two."

Her first instinct was to argue. She wanted to hear whatever it was that Brooks was going to say. Needed to know what he was going to ask, and learn the answers, too. But when she turned to glance his way, the urge fell away with no effort on her part.

His expression was neutral, but that pinch was back around his eyes, and his jaw was just a little bit tenser. He looked like a tightly wound spring, trying its damnedest not to uncoil. Whatever it was that bothered him about the name Caleb Nank, it was something big.

And then he signed, *Please trust me.*

So instead of fighting him on it, Maryse nodded and stepped out of the living room and into the hall, careful to put herself far enough away that she couldn't hear what they were saying. She knew she needed to defer to Brooks's expertise.

But it's not just expertise, is it? It's the whole blind-faith thing.

His silent request had hammered it home.

She'd told him that this was the first time she'd ever trusted anyone else with anything to do with Camille. And she'd been honest about that. But what about herself? When was the last time she'd given over that kind of trust on her own behalf?

She leaned against the wall, considering it. Her friendships were superficial by necessity, limited to the other moms at her daughter's school. In her relationship with her brother, *she'd* been the reliable one, the one who could be counted on and trusted, not the other way around. And as far as romance was concerned...

Seven years.

That gave her good pause.

It had been *seven years* since she last kissed a man. The year before Camille, she'd had a steady boyfriend, but things had fizzled out so slowly that she'd barely noticed. She hadn't even felt a need to call him and tell him that she was leaving town.

Her eyes traveled up the hall toward the living room. Strangely, she felt like if she suddenly needed to run again, she'd want Brooks to know.

Maryse shook her head. It was on the same level of ridiculousness as being jealous of Dee White. But it was true nonetheless.

Somehow, he'd got under her skin. Slipped in behind her wall. And if he could do that in a few hours, what would it be like in a day? Or two?

Her eyes sought the living room door again. But what they found instead was another door, slightly ajar. Maybe it was a need to fill the moments until she was allowed back in the room, or maybe it was plain old curiosity. Either way, she felt a strange compulsion to look inside.

She moved forward, opened the door and stared. The room was full of sophisticated printing equipment.

Broken fingers and new identities. That was what Brooks had said.

Maryse took a step inside. A half a dozen passport pieces—Canadian, American and at least two she couldn't identify—were spread across a large desk. There were pictures and slices of trimmed paper and empty laminated cases.

Not very subtle.

She eyed the nearest set of passport pieces. And froze. The tiny face staring up at her was one she knew as well as she knew her own.

What did it mean?

She took a final step into the room and reached for the photo before she even got to the desk. And as she lifted it up, an object underneath it made her head still, then start up again thunderously.

In one hand, she held a tiny photo of her own daughter. In the other, she held a bracelet she knew well—the silver, heart-shaped beads on an elasticized string were usually around Camille's tiny wrist. Proof that she'd been there. And proof of something else, too.

Brooks was having a hard time maintaining his cool. Everything about Dee White screamed of deception, manipulation and narcissism. As far as suspects went, he knew her type well. At some point in her life, she'd lost control. Now she was making up for it, desperate to feel like she was the one leading the chase. For every fifth or sixth thing she said, only one would be true. Normally, Brooks would be happy enough to feed into it and use it to his advantage. He might even sympathize a bit and try to understand what had made her turn out this way.

Not now.

With Maryse's kid's life on the line, he didn't have the time required for picking through her lies in search of tidbits of truth. Playing along was wearing on him.

And Caleb Nank...

The man wasn't some low-level criminal. He was the chief operator of a company that acted as a front for some very dirty dealings. The man was just smart enough to keep evading the law, somehow managing to orchestrate every one of his shady deals without making himself culpable. Or even visible, for that matter. On paper, the man was a saint. In real life, he was a ghost.

And you were supposed to take him down. No. Scratch that. Are still *supposed to be taking him down now.*

He'd spent years trying to build a case against Nank. Brooks gritted his teeth, forced off the reminder and nodded at whatever falsehood was currently dripping from Dee's mouth. Thinking of Nank had thrown off his game, and it was a scramble to fall back into the congenial role he'd taken on to get the woman on the couch to talk.

So he didn't try.

"Nank runs out of Nevada."

Dee blinked at his abrupt statement. "You know him?"

"*I* run out of Nevada."

"You— Oh. I get it."

He nodded, not caring whether or not she understood which side of the law he was on, and dropped his own tidbit of truth. "Nank is the reason I'm stuck in this town. So, yeah. I know him."

She flipped her scraggly ponytail over her shoulder and glanced toward the door. Her eyes turned shrewd.

"And you don't want *her* to know."

"Her knowing won't help us get her daughter back."

"You're a hundred percent sure the girl is hers?"

"Yes."

Dee shook her head. "You might want to consider that you're wrong. Nank and his men have pretty compelling evidence that says otherwise."

"Unless it's a DNA test, I'm not buying it."

The woman sent him a cool-eyed stare. "And if it *is* a DNA test?"

Brooks refused to bite. "I'd still be hard to convince."

"You said you know Nank, so you probably also know what he normally deals in."

"His guys have been busted for fraud, for prostitution, for possession... He's got a finger in a lot of pies."

"But not kidnapping," Dee said pointedly.

"Maybe he's initiating a career move."

"Why would his men say the kid was Nank's if she wasn't?"

It was a valid question. What *did* the crime boss want with a deaf child? Clearly, she wasn't implying that Nank was the kid's biological father. Or was she? His hand tightened into his fist.

No.

There was no way Maryse would've been involved with a man like that.

Brooks schooled his expression into an impassive one and said, "I'd never pretend to understand what motivates Caleb Nank."

"If you don't believe me, why don't you bring your girlfriend back in and ask *her* why someone like Caleb would take the kid?"

Brooks didn't answer. The details of why Camille had been taken had been on his mind from the get-go—motivation for the crime was probably even key to finding her—but he'd made the decision to trust Maryse's judgment. She wouldn't risk her daughter's life for the sake of a few details.

He opened his mouth to say as much, then stopped when Maryse herself appeared in the door. Her face was even paler than usual, and she had two small, dark-colored notebooks and a stack of papers in one hand and a slim laptop computer in the other. She held them out, her face ashen.

"What were you doing with these?" She directed the question to Dee, and Brooks could hear every ounce of tension in her voice. "Were you trying to pass her off as your own?"

"It was just another option," Dee responded.

"Where were you taking her?"

Brooks eyed the notebooks a second time and realized what they really were. *Passports.*

Maryse turned his way, fear and worry evident in her eyes. "One for her. One for Greg. And all these pieces of paper are left over from making one for Camille. And the laptop was left on a travel website."

With sickness churning in his gut, Brooks took the passports and opened them. They looked as good as real, and he had a feeling they'd stand up under closer scrutiny, too. He turned to Dee.

What the hell had *they been planning?*

He didn't get a chance to ask. The tiny woman was suddenly on the move. She sprang up from the couch, reached under the coffee table and drew out a gun. By the time Brooks could get his own weapon free from his side, she had hers pointed at Maryse.

He raised the barrel and automatically tried to move in between the two women, but Dee cocked her gun, freezing him to the spot.

"Stay right there," she ordered. "Put down the gun slowly or I'll shoot her."

Brooks did as he was told, cursing inwardly. He should've

anticipated the woman's forethought and he shouldn't have underestimated her palpable need for control.

"You don't want to do this," he said, dropping into police-negotiation mode as he set his weapon on the coffee table. "Whatever it is you need, we can get. No one has to get hurt."

Dee shook her head. "Little too late for bargaining. Nank has the girl. I've got the gun. And you two have nothing."

"What about Greg?" Brooks replied.

The woman shook her head a second time. "Idle threat. You didn't kill him. And I don't think you will. So it'll just be a matter of time before he shows up to help me. Give me the passports."

As Brooks handed them over, Maryse inhaled sharply. He wished he could offer her some reassurance. Instead, he had to concentrate all his efforts on getting them out of the situation.

"There has to be something else you want," he said, careful *not* to sound desperate.

"You have a car?"

He nodded. "You need a ride somewhere?"

"No, actually. I just need your keys." She held out her hand.

He reached into his pocket, grabbed the metal ring, then pulled it out and tossed it toward her. In the split second she raised her free hand to catch the keys, Brooks leaped into action. He threw his body forward, arms out. His calf cracked the table, and Dee jumped back at the last second, but he still managed to catch her forearm with the side of his hand. The gun wobbled, then fell. They both went after it, scrambling across the floor. The petite woman was closer, and she reached the weapon first.

"Get down!" Brooks shouted at Maryse as Dee lifted the gun from the ground.

A blur, gasp and thump let him know she'd complied.

Which was a damned good thing because the second she hit the ground, a shot rang through the air. It only took a second—and a few chunks of flying drywall—to figure out where the bullet had landed. Straight into the wall where Maryse had been standing just a moment earlier.

With his ears ringing and a growl building in his throat, Brooks grabbed the edge of the coffee table and propelled himself toward Dee. She was just readying the weapon again when he reached her. He snapped out a hand in an attempt to grab it. She stumbled back and out of reach. He lunged again. His hand closed on the barrel of the gun, and he lifted it up. With just a moment to spare, he noted that Dee's finger was on the trigger. He dropped his grip as she squeezed, narrowly missing the searing heat as the weapon fired a second time.

The ceiling above them cracked then shuddered, and somewhere in the distance, sirens sprang to life. They were far off, but there was no doubt about where they were headed. Someone with quick fingers had clearly dialed 9-1-1, and the nearest patrol car was on its way.

Time was about to run out.

Dee White appeared to realize it, too. She stepped backward, hands out, gun up.

"I'll take a ninety-second head start," she announced, then eyed Maryse up and down. "And just for fun, why don't you use the time to explain to *him* how Camille's not actually your daughter?"

"She *is* my daughter."

"My grandmother had a saying. *Don't split hairs.* She's not your *biological* daughter. Don't bother lying." The tiny woman's eyes flicked to the window as the sirens got a little louder. "Ninety seconds."

Then she bolted from the living room. Moments later, a door slammed from somewhere in the house, and with the exception of the approaching sirens, silence reigned. Brooks moved through the room, using his sleeve to wipe anything he thought he'd touched. He snapped up the pieces of phony passport with Camille's info, then grabbed the keys Dee had discarded. Finally, he turned his attention to Maryse. She stood stiffly, her gaze on the laptop in her hands.

Doubt tickled at Brooks's conscience, but he refused to acknowledge it. His instincts were rarely off. He didn't see how they could have failed him in regards to this situation.

Tension hung in the air, and he knew the only way to clear it was to get the truth from her. But not right then.

"I think our minute and a half is up," he said instead.

She didn't move, and when she spoke, her voice was barely loud enough to be heard. "Brooks… I told you it was complicated."

"I believed you. I still believe you."

"I understand if you don't."

Brooks took a step forward and reached out. "I do, sweetheart. But now we've got to go."

Finally, she lifted her eyes. Then one of her hands. And she let him pull her through the house and out the back, just as the flash of red and blue rounded the corner near the front of the house.

Chapter 10

As Maryse followed closely alongside Brooks, guilt ate her conscience. She knew that the source of the discomfort hanging over them was her own trite statement.

It's complicated? Seriously? she scoffed silently. *You went with that tired line again? You couldn't come up with something better?*

But something had compelled her to tell Brooks the truth. The way he put his life on the line for her, maybe? Or the way he was looking at her right that second, his eyes full of both muted curiosity *and* a willingness to understand?

"You okay?" Brooks asked.

She opened her mouth, then closed it and nodded instead, clutching the laptop to her chest like a lifeline. It was better not to risk saying something that could just make things worse for her. And they'd reached the end of the fence that met up with the rear neighbor's yard, anyway.

"All right." Brooks's voice was low, his words rushed as he nodded toward the corner of the property. "We're going to go through those bushes over there, then head to the edge of the house. We'll take a walk around the block on the other side and see if we can get to the car without being noticed."

Maryse managed to find her own voice. "What will the cops do?"

"They'll examine the perimeter. Secure it. Then move inside. When they figure out it was real gunshots, they'll probably shut down the street and start looking for anything that stands out. Which is why we need to move."

"Right."

They picked their way through the shrubs at the end of the yard and stepped into the open lawn. For the few seconds it took to cross from the back to the front, they were exposed, and Maryse prayed that the neighbors were at work. Or at least too scared to look out their windows.

And her prayers were answered.

They made it to the street without notice. They slipped to the sidewalk and even made it to the car with no problems. There, Maryse let herself enjoy a moment of relief. But as soon as Brooks turned the key in the ignition, the fear came back full force. It only grew worse as they pulled off the curb and the flashing lights disappeared from sight.

"Hey." Brooks's voice cut through her fear, and she realized she'd closed her eyes.

She opened them and swallowed against the thickness blocking her vocal cords, then repeated his softly spoken word. "Hey."

His gaze moved from the road to her. It landed on her wrist, where she'd slipped on Cami's bracelet. The elastic was stretched, the beads spread wide. Brooks's expression grew curious.

"It's hers," Maryse explained. "I found it with the passports. It's not worth anything. But I didn't want to leave it there."

"I get it." His eyes moved back to the windshield.

"Brooks…" Maryse trailed off as a lump formed in her throat.

She shook her head. She didn't *want* to relive the past. Or talk about her brother and his criminal ties or his death. But it had nothing to do with Brooks. It wasn't that she didn't want to give the details to *him*. It was just that she hadn't ever told the story aloud.

"Whatever it is…" he said. "You don't have to tell me. You don't owe me an explanation."

"I owe you more than an explanation. I owe you my *life*."

"I'll hold you to the last bit." A smile tipped up his mouth for a second. "But seriously. If you don't want to go over the complications, I understand. I'm not going to try any less hard to find Cami."

"I know. And that's one of the reasons I *want* to tell you." She sighed, then smoothed her hands over the laptop sitting on her knees and looked out the window as she went on. "Dee White is right. Camille *isn't* my biological daughter. But I didn't steal her from her parents. Or from anyone else. Her dad… He left her to me."

"Left her to you? In the legal sense of issuing guardianship?"

"I don't think that was an option. In fact, I don't think my brother ever did *anything* in a legal sense, even when it was an option."

"Your brother."

"Yeah." Maryse smiled. "He was a rebellious kid. I loved that about him. I used to wish I had a bit of it in myself."

"Until…?"

"Until the rebellion became the kind of thing that turned into arrests. And bail outs. I kind of thought he was turning it around near the end there, but…" She shrugged. "Then he left Camille to me *literally*. On a doorstep with a note attached."

"While he did what?"

"While he died."

Brooks's eyes turned her way. "I'm sorry, Maryse."

"So am I," she said.

"Did it happen long after he left Camille behind?"

"No. He knew it was going to happen. Which is why he left her in the first place."

"What happened?"

"Wrong place, wrong time. Brought on by whatever he was mixed up in."

"That's kind of vague," Brooks pointed out.

Maryse forced herself to explain. "It was a fire. Arson. He died, and so did three other people. And everyone said it was my brother who set it. The papers, the cops…"

"Ah."

"He didn't."

"You sound sure."

"His note said so."

Brooks was silent for a long moment. "So your brother the troublemaker became your brother the lawbreaker. He got mixed up in an arson that he didn't commit, left a baby on your doorstep and here we are."

She could tell he was musing over the details rather than making light of the situation, so she nodded. "Yes. More or less."

"And Camille is your niece."

"Biologically. My niece… God. That sounds so weird to say. I've been raising her since she was a newborn."

"I need to ask—"

"About her mother."

"Yeah."

"I don't know who she was," Maryse admitted.

"Was?"

"My brother didn't say anything about her. But I've always assumed that if she was alive, he wouldn't have given Cami to me." She paused, thinking about it for a second before she corrected herself. "Maybe *assumed* isn't the right word. I *knew* there was no way Camille's biological mother could be alive. Family was the only thing that mattered to him. Literally the only thing that he had any kind of commitment to. So if there was any chance…"

"I understand."

Maryse waited as Brooks tapped his fingers on the steering wheel, his brow furrowed in concentration. After a minute, he flicked on the turn signal, then navigated the car onto the shoulder of the road.

He faced her, his eyes a mask of concern. "Where did all of this happen, sweetheart?"

"Las Vegas."

"Nevada."

"Yes. He was living there at the time. It's where he left Camille."

"And that's where Caleb Nank is from."

Maryse's chest tightened. "Who is he, Brooks?"

Brooks sighed, then ran a hand over his head. "He's a bad guy. Truly. He came out of nowhere a few years ago, and he's clever and creative and in control and elusive. The man deals in favors as much as he deals in cash."

"Like Dee and Greg."

"Exactly. Everyone who works under him owes him something in one way or another. A real puppet master."

"Exactly the kind of man who'd attract a guy like my brother," Maryse responded softly. "And the note—the one the kidnapper left—said he was taking what *Jean-Paul* owed them."

"So the kidnapping wasn't to do with you."

"No. Is that a good thing?"

"It's good that they see Camille as a valuable commodity. It's good that they were willing to wait this long to take her, and I'd even go so far as to say that in this case, it's good that they haven't asked for ransom."

"It is?"

Brooks met her eyes and shook his head slowly. "It means they'll keep her alive."

The breath she drew in was sharp enough that her lips vibrated, and the sound of it bounced through the car. Of course it had crossed her mind that Camille's life might be in danger. It went without saying. But having that particular truth acknowledged out loud—even if it was in the name of dismissing it—sent a chill through her.

"What else?" she made herself say.

"I probably shouldn't be telling you anything about him because the investigation is ongoing, but I don't want to lie to you about the seriousness of Nank and his business. I've been personally chasing the man for over half a decade. Slippery as all hell. Never lets anything get tied directly back to him. And the truth is, I've never had the pleasure of meeting him personally."

"You're chasing a man you've never met?"

"It's less crazy than it sounds. His reputation and the actions that've been timed to him on a tertiary level make it worth the wild-goose hunt."

"So what do we do now?"

"If we want to get Cami back, we've only got two choices. We can find her and physically remove her, or we can try to find something he wants *more*…" He trailed off, his face full of something he didn't want to suggest.

But Maryse knew what it was anyway.

"And make a trade," she filled in, her heart somehow twisting and sinking at the same time.

The first option was undoubtedly rife with danger. The second was awful. At the moment, neither seemed viable.

"Maryse?"

It took a second to realize Brooks had been talking. She forced her attention back to what he was saying. *Something about planes?* She wasn't sure.

She shook her head. "I'm sorry. I got lost for a second."

"It's okay, sweetheart."

"I'm scared."

"I know," Brooks said. "But we've got a few things on our side. Nank doesn't know I'm helping you. He doesn't know we're coming. And I'm guessing he's the kind of man who doesn't deal well with surprises."

He reached across the console and closed his hand on hers. Maryse squeezed back, grateful for the contact, and thankful also that he didn't just dismiss or minimize her concern.

"If you need to get lost for a second now and then," he added, "do it. I promise I'll be here when you get back."

The look in his hazel eyes told her he meant it. The warm security she found there made her cheeks flush, and the heat of their clasped hands became a burn that drove away both the cold and her worry, at least enough that she could breathe.

"I know I keep saying it…but thank you."

"Happy to help," he replied, and he squeezed her fingers again. "You want to talk about our next move? Or you need another minute?"

Maryse shook her head. "Next move. Please."

"You sure?"

"Yes."

"Okay. I was just telling you that Nank must've sent someone to make sure that Dee and Greg and Greg's brother did what they were supposed to do. When they failed, his men took control. And an educated guess would say they're likely on their way directly to Vegas."

"And we should go there."

"Whether we choose option one or option two, it's the best way to do either," Brooks said. "Have you got a passport?"

Maryse nodded. With the passport her brother had provided six years earlier, she'd managed to secure supplementary ID. With that, she'd been able to get a renewal for the old passport with no problems. It had surprised her, really, that she'd been able to go through legal channels to obtain the illegal document.

"I'm guessing you're not carrying it with you?" he asked.

"No."

"Okay. We'll swing by my place, then yours. We'll book the next flight out of Montreal, and we'll be on our way."

Brooks sounded confident and determined. And Maryse was glad. But suddenly nervous, too. And the added bout of nerves had nothing to do with her daughter's kidnapping and everything to do with the fact that she was about to embark on a journey with the singularly most attractive man she'd ever met.

Holding Maryse's hand tightly—a position that was fast becoming a habit—Brooks moved from the car to his apartment building at a pace that was just below a run. Even though the stop provided a much-needed breather, Brooks wanted to make the trip back to his apartment as quick as possible. No one had identified him yet, but that didn't mean they wouldn't.

And the moment someone does...

It would fall apart. Caleb Nank's dogs would be on him. His boss and the PD dogs would be on him. And he'd be officially asked to step aside. He could imagine how Maryse would react. Her desire for secrecy broken, her need to be involved directly in finding her daughter subverted. Worse than that, the authorities would have a field day with Camille's parentage. There was no paper trail linking the two of them together. Even with the blood connection, Maryse had taken the child across the border and they'd undoubtedly been living in Canada illegally. There would be nothing Brooks could do to help her if all of that came out.

As they reached his door, he had no choice but to shake off the concern. He'd deal with the potential scenario when—*if*—it came up, and not before. He squeezed her hand before freeing his fingers to unlock the door.

"Shouldn't take me more than five minutes to get ready," he said. "You want to have a look on that laptop for flights that'll take us from Montreal to Las Vegas?"

"Sure." The quaver in her voice made her sound anything but.

Brooks closed the door. "Aside from the obvious...is everything all right?"

"I was just wondering if this can possibly be a coincidence," she replied. "I mean, what are the chances that *you*—the cop investigating Caleb Nank—would be in this exact spot on the exact day that I'm here, looking for my daughter, who's been taken by the same guy's men?"

"Slim to none," he admitted.

"What do you think it means?"

He reached out and cupped her cheeks in his hands. "Honestly, sweetheart, I'm not sure. I could work through the details. Look for other places our paths have crossed, or try to find some reason that someone might've deliberately driven us together. But if I do that, I'll have to take time away from looking for Cami. And that's something I don't want to do."

She stared up at him, little flecks of navy playing across her otherwise light blue irises. Brooks noted the mix of emotions there. Distress and fear. Appreciation and trust. Under any other circumstance, he'd toss aside everything he was doing just to get lost in that gaze and prove that she could give him the latter two and forget about the former two. He wished he could find an excuse to do it now. Instead, he had no choice but to push aside his feelings. He gave her a light kiss, then took the laptop from her and carried it to the coffee table, glad to see that it was fully charged and didn't need a password to get in. With the exception of his phone, he'd deliberately left his own electronics back in Nevada, so the stolen computer would come in handy now.

"I'll set you up with my frequent-flier account. All of my info is in there, so you can just add yours," he told her as he clicked through and logged in to the website. "You're probably the best judge of how quickly we can get from here to your place and back to the airport. So pick a flight that works."

Maryse seated herself on the couch. "One way?"

Brooks hesitated, then shook his head and said what he knew she needed to hear. "No. We're going to do this. Give us a forty-eight-hour window. And don't forget to include a ticket for Camille on the way back."

"Okay."

She turned her attention to the computer, and he moved to the bedroom. He was still eager to get going as soon as possible, but he felt a need to pause and consider what Maryse had said about coincidence. It had been in the back of his mind, too, since the moment Dee White dropped Nank's name. It had seemed odd from the beginning that of all the places in the world to choose from for a forced leave of absence, his boss would pick this one.

Laval, Quebec. A nice city... Brooks thought. *If you can get past the ice.*

He'd kind of assumed that was what had fueled the choice. It was no secret that he was a man who loved the blazing sun. And what good would the thinly veiled punishment have done if the captain had shipped him off to Honolulu for two months? He supposed he could've simply not taken his boss's "suggestion" that Laval, Quebec, be his destination. But at the time, it seemed like ticking the man off even further was a bad idea. Brooks let out a sound, midway between a frustrated growl and an exasperated sigh.

The easiest solution was to call his boss and simply ask. Except if the man *had* gone so far out of his way to orchestrate this setup, drawing attention to it could bring down the operation, whatever it might be.

And so could hightailing it back to Nevada.

This time, the noise that escaped his mouth was all growl. "Little bit of insight would be nice right about now, boss."

He moved his fingers over the pocket that held his phone, thinking over the idea of using it in spite of his worries. After a second, he dismissed it. His gaze sought the bedroom door. He wasn't ashamed to admit that his decision to keep working on this independently was almost solely because of the woman sitting in his living room. He couldn't yet pinpoint what it was that filled him with such a strong need to assist her—possibly at the risk of his own career—but he wasn't going to deny its existence. Her understated bravery…her willingness to accept the help of a virtual stranger…both added to her allure.

And the fact that she's beautiful doesn't hurt, either.

Yeah, there was that, he acknowledged. Except there was way *more* than that, too. Even in the scant few hours they'd spent together, he sensed a connection that could run deeper, given the chance. Before he could stop himself, he wondered how she'd like the desert heat. Would she mind living there, or was she attached to the cold winters?

"You're clearly going insane," he muttered, forcing his eyes away from the door.

The brief glance he caught of his reflection in the mirror

over his dresser confirmed it. His eyes were a little shiny, his face stuck in some kind of stickily sweet smile.

Seriously, Small. Get your crap together.

He mentally grabbed ahold of the command and made himself move toward the small pile of clothes that already sat atop his suitcase. He eyed it skeptically. Forty-eight hours, he'd told Maryse. How much stuff could he really need? Jeans and a couple of T-shirts. A single pair of dress pants and a collared shirt. A few smaller essentials, and he'd be good to go. His passport was handy, and he always kept a stack of emergency cash aside, just in case. In the end, he was pulling things out of his bag rather than sticking them in. When he had everything arranged tidily on one side, he clued in to what he was doing. Making some space for Maryse's things.

Because if we're going down there as a couple, we should look like one from the start, and sharing a bag makes sense.

The thought made him pause again in his final moment of rearranging. He hadn't realized until that second that continuing the already-used ruse was a part of his plan. It made sense, though. They'd gone to the hotel posing as a couple. They'd approached Dee White's house as a couple. Their chemistry made it workable.

More than workable.

He stood and zipped up the suitcase. As he lifted it from the bed and started toward the door, his reflection caught his eye again. The smile was back in full force, and there was no way he could wipe it from his face. Not completely, anyway.

Because however bad the circumstances were, he had to admit that he was looking forward to pretending to be Maryse's significant other.

Chapter 11

Maryse clicked her seat belt, then tugged it to make sure it was secure. For some reason, the tightness seemed important right that second. A little bit of added safety. Not that Brooks didn't provide a large measure of it. His physical presence—big, strong and undeniable—was more than enough to make her feel protected.

So why do I feel like I need something else?

As they pulled onto the road, she eyed Brooks as surreptitiously as the small space would allow. Then swallowed as she clued in to what was bothering her. It was *him*. His big, strong, undeniable presence *itself* was making her nerves twitter uncontrollably. He made her feel safer, yes. But vulnerable, too. It got worse when he tipped his head her way and offered a smile. It was definitely an added flutter factor. And when he swiveled his gaze back to the front windshield…she wanted to see it again. She *wanted* to feel the syncopated rhythm of her heart.

"I've never had company," she blurted.

She was rewarded with another glance, this one surprised. "What?"

"At my house," she said. "I've never had company."

"Ever?"

"No. The closest I've ever come is having one of the

moms from Cami's school step inside for dropping off her kid. I've never even offered anyone a cup of tea."

"Hmm. I thought all moms were IV coffee users."

"Funny." She sighed. "But I'm serious, Brooks. Even though we settled here years ago, I've never *felt* settled."

"You were afraid of letting anyone in."

"Literally and figuratively."

"But Camille has friends."

"She's made a few at school. But the program she's in is small, and with her deafness…" Maryse shrugged. "She's not exposed to big groups, and she kind of keeps to herself."

Brooks was silent for a minute before replying. "You know that I'm not going to judge you based on how dusty your knickknacks are, right, sweetheart?"

"I know."

"So what are you worried about?"

"Everything."

"Something less vague might be helpful."

Maryse squeezed her hands into fists. She'd already told him more than she'd told anyone. There wasn't another soul on the planet who knew about her brother and who he was to Camille.

Except Caleb Nank and whoever took her on his behalf.

Her stomach knotted. That truth alone was enough to motivate her to speak.

"I'm worried that if I *do* let someone in, it'll become an expectation. They'll come over *un*expectedly. They'll expect tea."

"Whoa."

"Whoa, what?"

"That's a lot of uses of *expect* and its various forms."

"Whoops. Sorry."

Brooks's hand dropped down to nudge her knee teasingly. "Should be."

She sighed and leaned back against the headrest. "All I've ever wanted to do was keep Camille safe and happy. When my brother left her behind and told me to run, I did. For a full year, I moved around, assuming at every step that someone was watching. But it's hard to do with a kid— especially one who needs regular medical attention. And I was never very adventurous."

"So you crossed the border and found a place so cold that no one in their right mind would follow?"

"I crossed the border because I thought maybe whoever was after us wouldn't be *able* to. And because I finally clued in that maybe my brother left us the passports for a reason." She corrected with a smile. "And it *does* get hot here in the summer, just FYI."

"Right."

"Seriously. We have a pond on our property. In July, we use it for swimming, and in January, we use it for ice-skating."

"I'm guessing you *actually* ice-skate October through April, then chip away at the permafrost for a single, icy plunge at high noon on *one* mid-July day."

In spite of herself, Maryse laughed, and some of the tension in her body eased. "Sometimes we go sledding."

"Sledding?"

"You know. Sliding down a snow-covered hill?"

He chuckled. "Yeah, I know what sledding is, sweetheart. I just prefer sitting in my pool on a piece of inflatable plastic to sitting in the snow on a piece of wood. Less chance of splinters or broken legs, and the only thing that's cold is my beer."

"Well. So long as you have a hobby you love."

"You don't have one?"

"Besides sledding and ice-skating and my annual polar bear swim?"

"Mmm-hmm."

Maryse took a moment to think about it. And she was stumped. She had as few hobbies as she did friends.

"Nothing?" Brooks pushed.

She shook her head. "I guess not. Everything I do is with Camille. Or for her."

"Ah."

Her cheeks warmed. "It's not as lame as it sounds."

"It doesn't sound lame."

"No?"

"No," he said, his face serious. "I'm impressed by your commitment to her."

"That sounds like something someone would say if they wanted to offer admiration for something lame that they would never want to do themselves."

"So you *do* have a hobby."

"What do you mean?"

"Psychoanalysis."

A lopsided grin tipped up his mouth, and Maryse's pulse jumped. Then it tripled as he dropped a wink her way.

"You might want to find a new one, though," he added. "You're not good at this one."

"I'm not?" The question came out a little breathy.

"Uh-uh. You clearly can't tell the genuine admiration from the grudging kind."

"Maybe it's just hard to imagine that *you* think sacrificing any semblance of a personal life for the sake of my kid—"

"Stop right there."

Maryse blinked at the abrupt change in his tone. "Why? I mean—"

He cut her off a second time. "If we weren't in such a hurry, I'd pull over the car dramatically and tell you *exactly* how wrong you are about what I think of everything you've done for that little girl. Even though you don't know Nank, or anything about him, you must've known it was dangerous. So I don't just *admire* you. It's incredible to me, Maryse, that you put aside your life to raise her."

The heat in her cheeks came back, this time searing. "I've broken a few laws in the process, I'm sure."

"More than a few, *I'm* sure," he replied.

"And you're a cop."

"I am."

"So I'm not all that admirable from a cop's point of view."

He went quiet, and for several long minutes, the silence hung between them heavily. They were out of the main part of the city now, and heading toward the small community where Maryse lived. She kept her gaze ahead, her eyes on the increasingly bare landscape. She was afraid that if she looked directly at Brooks, the tears that waited just under the surface would find their way out.

It wasn't that she was intentionally selling herself short. She knew she'd made hard decisions, then stayed committed. But that didn't mean what she'd done was above criticism. And if anyone could find the flaws in her chosen path, it was a police officer like Brooks. He'd said he wasn't perfect. A statement she could relate to easily.

She stared out the windshield, thinking about what she could've done differently. It was a question—a series of questions, really—that had kept her awake for a lot of nights. Especially in the beginning. Could she have gone to the authorities back then? Tried to clear her brother's name?

Anything at all?

Brooks's voice—firm but soft—interrupted the old, internal worries.

"I'm a cop," he said, "but that doesn't mean I only see

things in black and white. And it doesn't mean you should've made a different choice."

Another twinge of doubt bit at her. "But maybe if I'd made different choices, this wouldn't have happened."

"Or maybe Nank would've got his way a long time ago." Brooks's hands were tight on the wheel. "You made the *right* choices, sweetheart. Camille is lucky to have you as her mom."

"Thank you."

It was funny that hearing him say it was so soothing. Her dedication had been unwavering for six years, and though she questioned the steps that got her where she was, she hadn't had a moment of regret. In fact, aside from the fear of being caught—which had become more and more muted over time—Maryse had never thought she was missing anything. She said as much aloud, and Brooks's grip loosened. It was almost as though he'd been genuinely concerned that she might *not* feel that way.

Strange.

"I've always thought parenting required a special kind of selflessness," he said to her, shaking his head a little as he spoke. "Not everyone has it, and not everyone is willing to try and gain it, either."

And something in his tone made her sure he was no longer talking about her and Camille.

If Brooks could've somehow reached his foot around to kick his own butt, he would've. He hadn't meant to leave a potential opening like that.

But you did, didn't you?

Maryse's next question, spoken in a carefully neutral voice, told him she'd picked up on the fact that he'd been referring to more than the current situation.

"You don't think you could do it?" she asked.

Brooks heard the secondary implication in spite of her casual tone. *Or maybe you just don't want to?*

It bothered him that she might think that. So much so that it overrode his general need to keep his past to himself.

"Me?" he said. "No."

"No?" She sounded disappointed.

"I don't *think* I could do it. I *know* I could. I wanted to, in fact."

"You did?"

"Try not to sound too surprised."

She colored. "If you wanted to, how come you didn't?"

Brooks smiled. "Unlike you…I didn't have a baby left on my doorstep. And the conventional way requires a woman."

"Right."

He didn't have to look over at her to know that the pink in her cheeks had likely turned crimson.

His smile widened for a second, then fell as he told her the truth. "If I'm being honest…I *had* the woman. Or thought I did."

"What happened?"

Surprising himself, he didn't hesitate. "My girlfriend—fiancée, actually, for all of about three weeks—and I were looking for a house. We'd been shopping since I gave Gia the ring, and we just couldn't seem to find something we both liked. She was pushing for a condo. But I'd been renting an apartment for years, and I was over the single guy life and ready to move on to something more. She kept complaining about her parents' house and how perfectly domestic it was and telling me how she didn't want that."

"Hard to find a compromise," Maryse said.

"Very," Brooks agreed. "There's not much middle ground between a one-bedroom condo and a four-bedroom house with a white picket fence. And believe me, we tried. Row homes and bigger, ground-level suites. I finally found one I thought could be perfect. A bungalow with three bedrooms. Big yard. Pool. Good neighborhood and close to schools. I was pretty damned excited to show it to her."

"But she didn't like it?"

"She hated it. Found fault in every bit of it. We were standing in the middle of the living room having this quiet argument while the Realtor stood awkwardly to one side. I got frustrated, and I told Gia that I didn't want to move again in a few years. She had no clue what I meant. When I brought up kids and needing space for them, she was shocked. Told me she *never* wanted kids. And that shocked *me*. The fight ended, and so did our relationship." He paused and chuckled, finding true amusement in the memory for the first time. "Feel a bit sorry for that sales agent now. Although I *did* buy the house, so I guess I shouldn't feel too bad."

"You bought it?"

"I said it was perfect, didn't I?"

"But…weren't you worried about it being a bad reminder?"

"No. Well. Maybe for a few days. Then I decided it was ridiculous to pass up on a good deal that suited what my future needs. And the truth is…" He trailed off, wondering what it was that compelled him to disclose everything.

He cast a sidelong look at Maryse. She was leaning forward a little, her body language telling him she was interested in what he had to say. There was no judgment in her eyes, no indication that she had any bad feelings about his story.

"The truth is what?" she prodded, sounding curious rather than prying.

Brooks plunged on. "After those few days, I didn't feel like I was missing anything. Gia and I were a couple, and then we weren't. I sifted through my life and I realized how little we had in common. How rarely our priorities lined up. It seemed strange that we'd managed a harmonious, four-year relationship at all. We weren't meant to be together. I was actually *glad* it was over."

Maryse didn't answer, and for a moment, he thought the admission wasn't sitting right with her. The old guilt—not over ending the relationship, but over the fact that he was happy about its demise—crept in. But when Maryse did speak, it was clear that she understood.

"And you feel bad about that," she stated. "Because you're not *supposed* to be glad when an engagement gets broken."

"Exactly. Gia dealt with it properly. Called her friends and rallied them into a frenzied hatred. Had her dad come by and tell me where to go. She was basically a montage of breakup clichés."

"Did she flush the ring down the toilet?"

He couldn't help but laugh. "Returned it and used the money to buy herself a solo vacation."

From the corner of his eye, he caught her smile as it tipped her mouth into a tempting curve. "Perfect."

"Pretty much. And she came back from Mexico *much* happier, actually."

"The power of tequila and cabana boys."

"Yep."

"Did her good mood last?"

Brooks felt his jaw want to tighten, and he forced it to stay loose. "Not really. Mostly *my* fault. I wasn't miserable enough for her. She wanted the screaming and the crying and all the other emotional crap."

"But you couldn't fake it."

"No."

"What did you do?"

"Hid in the house she hated. Went to work and came

home and not much else. After a few months, Gia decided
that was good enough. My hermit status had to be an in-
dicator of my unhappiness. She spread that around town,
everyone assumed I was as heartbroken as she was, and a
year later Gia moved away and life carried on."

"Did you stop wanting that life?"

"The kids and the white picket fence? Not at all. Just
never found the right woman."

The statement carried an undeniable weight. And suddenly, Brooks was picturing *her* in the life she was asking about. Maryse, seated at his handcrafted wood table.
Maryse, lounging on a chair beside his pool. And Camille,
too. Her little blond head bobbing as she pranced around
the cactus-dotted garden. The three of them laughing together as Brooks struggled to keep up with their rapid-fire
sign language.

Seriously? he chastised himself. *You're imagining all of
that? Now? Already?*

"Brooks?"

He felt a trickle of heat crawl up his neck, and if he didn't
know better, he would've thought he was about to blush.
Had she read something into his silence? If so…how much?

He cleared his throat and adjusted his collar. "Yeah?"

"The turn is just up there."

He blinked and refocused his attention on the landscape.
In spite of the relatively short distance traveled, the scenery
had changed dramatically. The city had given way to country, and a big green sign ahead announced that they were
nearing LaHache, the town where Maryse and Camille
lived. He flicked on the turn signal and followed the curve
of the road. In moments, the highway was invisible. In its
place was a long strip of frozen farmland—pretty but cold.

"So this is home?" Brooks asked.

"Is it weird to say home-*ish*?" Maryse replied.

"Weird, yes. Surprising, no."

"No?"

"Mmm-mmm. Like you said, you never felt settled. I'm guessing LaHache was just a safe option for you. Far from the threat, and—" He cut himself off as something about his own words made his mind buzz.

"What?"

"I'm not sure," Brooks admitted. "Something about what I just said makes me want to sit at my desk at the PD, make a bunch of charts, then draw a bunch of lines connecting things together."

"If you had time." She sounded apologetic now.

"Kidnapping cases are always time sensitive, sweetheart. This is only different because I don't have a collection of other detectives and police resources at my fingertips. And before you say anything, that's not your fault, either, and I'm not even close to asking you to let me get some reinforcements in. I respect your decision."

"Brooks…"

"Yeah, sweetheart?"

"How do you *do* that?"

"Do what?"

She waved a hand around in the air. "Say a bunch of things that immediately make me feel better. And stay so calm and reasonable while you're doing it."

His mouth tipped up into a grin—partly because he was glad to make her feel better and partly because the last part was a first. "I don't think I've *ever* been accused of being calm before."

"Seriously?"

"Part of the reason my boss sent me up here was my short temper."

"He sent you up here?"

"Forced vacation."

"So...vacation-*ish*?" Maryse asked.

"Yep. Vacationish," he agreed, slowing down to match the posted speed limit at the edge of town. "You want to give me directions from here?"

"Straight through, all the way to the end of this road. There's a stop sign and a T and you'll want to go left. Hang a left again at the second run-down barn, then follow that road to the duck-shaped mailbox. That's us."

He lifted an eyebrow. "Duck-shaped mailbox?"

"Cami didn't want the regular one. She has a thing for ducks, so I indulged." She shrugged, her lips turning up, then down quickly.

"You have real ones in the pond?"

"No."

"You can get some."

"Live ducks?"

"Yeah. People even hatch them from eggs." He winked at her as he turned at the promised T in the road. "You're not very good at living the country life if you don't raise animals."

"Is that a specialty of yours out there in the desert?"

"As a matter of fact... I've got a cat. Rufus. My neighbor's kid is probably spoiling him rotten as we speak."

She smiled again, and this time it didn't fall away. "Cats are probably tied with ducks in Cami's mind."

"Ah. The great battle between waterfowl and house pets. Not a good combo in the same pond, though," Brooks said, then nodded out the windshield. "Is that the second barn up there?"

"That's the one."

He stepped on the gas pedal a little. "What would you choose?"

"Choose?"

"A desert cat or a Canadian duck?"

Once again, he felt the shift. It was a seemingly casual question. A teasing one. Yet somehow the pause after he asked it turned it into something loaded.

"I guess that would depend," Maryse said slowly.

"On what?"

"What Camille had to say about it."

And as he pulled up to the duck-shaped mailbox, he knew for certain that rescuing Maryse's daughter was only slightly more important than one other thing—making sure that once he did, her little girl liked him. A lot.

Chapter 12

Maryse led Brooks up the driveway, feeling an enormous pressure for him to appreciate her living space. She was admittedly an untidy housekeeper. Her life with Camille was chaotic and full, and she didn't waste moments worrying about whether or not she'd put away the laundry as soon as it came out of the dryer. And Brooks's assurance that he wasn't there to judge didn't put her mind at ease.

She opened the front door slowly, flicking on the light as she stepped inside, then stood still as the big man scanned the small entryway. His whole body seemed to fill the space, making it even tinier than it already was, and Maryse might've noticed that more if she hadn't been so busy being self-conscious about the disarray. Camille's jacket and snow pants hung from a hook over a wide plastic mat, and several pairs of boots—rain, winter and dressy—sat in a pile on a bench. Why hadn't she wiped up the melted snow? Or at least opened the bench and shoved the footwear into it?

Self-consciously, she slipped out of her boots and coat. He did the same, hanging his sweater beside her jacket like it belonged there and lining his boots up beside hers, too.

Maryse cleared her throat. "So."

"So," Brooks repeated.

"This is it."

"It's a great place to put your shoes," he joked.

"Oh. Right. Come in." Maryse hoped her embarrassed flush wasn't too obvious as she led him from the foyer to the adjoining living room. "Sorry it's so cold in here. I guess I left the heat down this morning. I usually light a fire first thing, but…"

"You had more important things on your mind," he filled in.

"Yes."

His wide shoulders took up the entire doorway for a moment. Then he moved into the room, his gaze sweeping the space. Maryse bit her lip, worrying more than necessary about what he thought. About what he saw when he looked at the mismatched set of furniture—one brown love seat, one forest green ottoman and a beige chair—which sat quiet and empty. Did he notice the patchwork quilt that she'd fallen asleep under the night before? It hung between the coffee table and the love seat. Did he see the stack of socks without mates that took up one corner of the room and the pile of firewood that filled another? Was it too crowded? Too full in unfinished home-life business?

She was very aware that there was evidence everywhere of Cami. Children's books and macaroni art. A half-finished fleet of paper airplanes and a doll sitting in a plastic high chair. The biggest source of pride in her life.

But not very sexy.

The thought caught Maryse by surprise. Being sexy was about as low on her list of priorities as something could get. But as she eyed Brooks, following his continued perusal of her cozy home, she wished she'd put it somewhere a little higher up. Like maybe somewhere in the top three. Because for the first time since taking Camille into her life, she wanted someone to see her as a woman as well as a mother.

No. Not just someone, she corrected mentally. *Brooks.*

Yes, it was definitely a specific-to-him desire. The way

he moved through the room made Maryse tingle with a need to be noticed. She watched as his hands found the back of the love seat then ran over its worn fabric, and she had to admit—at least to herself—that she was a little envious of the attention the material was getting. When he turned a smile her way, though, envy slipped to the back of her mind. His eyes were full of appreciation and enough warmth to cut through the chill in the air.

"It's nice," he said, the two words somehow conveying much more.

"You think so?"

"Suits you, I think."

She couldn't help but ask, "Why?"

He swept his hand across the room. "It's not new and shiny, and it doesn't need to be, because it's got solid class. It's clean, but not sterile, so it's comfortable. Lots of personal touches."

"Is that how you see *me*? As classy and comfortable?"

"When you say it like that, it sounds like an insult."

"Was it a compliment?"

He took a small step toward her. "Definitely."

"So you *like* classy and comfortable."

He took another step, putting him within touching distance. Within *feeling* distance. The heat in his gaze was matched by the heat emanating from his body, warming Maryse, inside and out.

"I like those things, yes," he said, his voice low and full of promise.

Maryse's heart was beating faster and faster. "And you haven't been able to find a woman like that?"

"*Hadn't* been able to."

"Oh."

At her squeaky reply, Brooks's mouth tipped up in a slow, sexy smile. "What about you?"

"Me? No. I've never been able to find a classy, comfortable woman to settle down with."

"Do you *want* to settle down?"

"More than I want most things."

"Just you and Camille?"

"That's all it's ever been."

"Never been tempted to date? Get married? Give Cami a brother or sister?"

"I never really thought about it."

"But if you had…what would you be looking for?"

Now the heat in her body traveled up to settle in her cheeks as she answered with the first things that came to mind. "Someone smart. Hardworking. Someone not afraid of a challenge and not afraid of having fun. Who would love Cami the way I do—as if she were his own."

"That's it?" he teased.

"It's more comprehensive than classy and comfortable."

"Hmm. Comprehensive. Then I guess I'd better add to my list. I also like a strong, capable woman who recognizes that asking for help when she needs it isn't a sign of weakness."

"That's it?" Maryse echoed breathily.

"No."

"What else?"

"I appreciate a woman whose name starts with the letter *M*. And who has a heart big enough to drop her life to raise a child, and who can take a tiny house in the middle of nowhere and make it her home."

"Home…ish."

"Ish," he confirmed.

"So nothing too specific, then."

"Very general."

He reached out to touch her cheekbone with the back of his hand. Automatically, she tipped her head up to lean

into the caress. As she did, his hand turned and his palm
cradled her jawline, drawing her mouth close to his. And
even though she was already anticipating the newly familiar feel of his lips, the contact sent a shock wave of desire
ricocheting through her body. It moved from her mouth to
her throat, to her chest to her abdomen, to her thighs to her
calves, then back up again. And the want was as specific as
it was startling. *This man* lit her on fire. Turned her blood
to molten lava. Made her want to slip away from the world
and explore everything he had to offer.

And she couldn't hold back a little moan as his hands
slid to her back, one set of fingers finding a sensitive spot
just above her waistband and the other pressing between her
shoulder blades. He dragged his palms back and forth, pulling her closer. Maryse was more than happy to sink into the
attention. Eager to deepen the kiss. She brought her arms
up to his shoulders and tucked her curves as closely to his
hard lines as she could. Then she tasted the edges of his lips
with her tongue. Tentatively at first, then with more fervor.
Very quickly it was hard to tell where her mouth started
and his began, and when the backs of Maryse's knees hit
the edge of the love seat, she honestly couldn't have said if
she was the one who propelled them toward it, or if it was
he who initiated the move. Either way, the result was the
same. She leaned back—just a little—and they tumbled
together into the soft, familiar fabric.

As she landed beneath him, her denim-clad knees
parted, and Brooks fell between them with just enough
force to make her gasp. Before Maryse could recover, he
let out a low growl, clasped her waist and flipped them
over so that she was on top. Immediately, he lifted his head
and his mouth sought hers again. He nipped at her lips,
then trailed kisses along her cheek to her earlobe, which he
pulled between his teeth and tugged. His mouth was diz-

zyingly thorough. Deliciously warm. And his hands were equally attentive and just as shiver-inducing. They traversed up her thighs. His fingers spread over her hips. He kneaded and squeezed and stroked his way up to the bottom of her sweater. For a blissful second, his rough palm was on the sensitive skin just below her rib cage. Then it slid out again, working its way up her sweater. At the lower edge of her covered bra, he paused.

"Brooks," Maryse murmured against his mouth.

She wriggled a little to get him to keep going, and both of his hands moved. The first one cupped her breast, his thumb tracing an unhurried circle over the curve. The second landed on her hip, rocking forward into him. And in spite of the layers between them, there was no mistaking his reciprocal desire.

Oh, God.

The fabric blocking her from what she craved was going to make her crazy. She had to do something about it. Urgently. Her fingers flew to the almost-nonexistent space between them, fumbling for the button on his jeans. She didn't get far in her search. Brooks grabbed her again and swung her so that her back was pushed to the love-seat cushions again.

He held himself poised above her, his wide pupils darkening the hazel of his irises to an almond brown under his sandy lashes. His gaze was full of heated desire, and the strong ridges of his wide chest were visible, even through his sweater. They begged to be bared. Maryse wanted nothing more than to lift off his shirt and let it happen. She even brought her hands to its hem and slid her fingers underneath it. But Brooks spoke then, stopping her from giving in to her wanton need.

"Sweetheart…" he said, the endearment sounding raw

and ragged. "You have no idea how very little I want to ask this, but…how much time do we have?"

The plane.

Guilt trickled in. Not quite a bucket of icy water, but at least a cool breeze. Just enough to ease the intensity of her ache.

"Not long," she told him. "A little more than five hours."

"Not long *enough*." His tone was imbued with regret, but he pushed up to a sitting position, then pulled Maryse up, too. "Two hours to the airport from here if we don't have any problems. And you know they want us there three hours early."

She wanted to argue that they could hurry. That they could make good use of the few minutes they had to spare. But ultimately…what she wanted wasn't a quick fix. And judging from the serious look on Brooks's face, it wasn't what he was after, either.

Which is a good thing, she told herself. *And this flight is what gets you to Camille.*

The reminder was enough to bank the intensity of Maryse's urgency.

"You're right," she said, moving to stand. "I'll get my passport and pack my bag."

Brooks grabbed her arm gently. She met his eyes, which were full of undisguised concern.

"It's not that I want to stop," he stated. "But I don't think I would forgive myself if I was the reason we missed our flight and slowed down our search for Camille."

Maryse's chest filled with a different kind of a heat. Her appreciation of Brooks's help had nothing on her appreciation of his genuine care. He didn't know Cami. He barely knew *her*—though he'd made it clear that he could read her just fine—but his face told her he meant what he'd just said. The fact that he used the words *we* and *our* so casually, so naturally… For a second, Maryse's throat closed and she actually thought she might cry at the feeling of overwhelming gratitude.

She fought it and bent down to give him a swift kiss. "Back in a minute."

Then she hurried away. And it was just in time. Because the tears came anyway.

Brooks watched Maryse's curves disappear up the narrow hall, and he seriously debated going after her. Most of him wanted to.

Okay, more than most, he admitted silently.

He was damned sure, though, that it could—*would*— only end one way. A way that he wanted to savor. To give meaning to. Not something he wanted to rush through or minimize.

And nothing I ever want to become a possible source of regret.

So he battled the urge to chase her down the hall and instead distracted himself by moving around the room, examining the glimpses into Camille's and Maryse's life together. What he saw made him smile. Unfinished projects and mementos galore. He got the feeling that most of the chaos was Cami-induced. The little bits of grown-up-themed space—few and far between—were organized. A collection of books, arranged tallest to shortest. An entertainment system, each wire carefully untangled and fed through a color-coded organizer that attached to the wall. A small desk that housed a sticky-note-covered computer and stack of tidy papers that gave him the impression that whatever she did for a living, she must work from home in that exact spot. Probably while Cami played in the background.

Brooks smiled. What had Maryse been like, pre-kid? Had she been neat and tidy? Fastidious, even? He suspected at the very least she'd been an everything-in-its-place kinda girl. But he liked that she'd adapted, and that she didn't try to tuck away the mess.

Whistling a little under his breath, he stepped past a clay sculpture that looked like a toss-up between a snake and a horse. A row of photographs above the fireplace caught his eye. Curious, he moved closer and examined them. Most were of Camille involved in varying activities. He chuckled at the one of the little girl dressed in a swimsuit and hurtling toward a good-sized body of water, presumably the pond. Her blond hair was pulled back in braids, which were streaming out behind her, and she had a wildly ecstatic grin on her face.

Behind that photo was an older one of both Maryse and her daughter. The two were dressed in matching red-and-black dresses, and the background was a professional backdrop sheet. The picture itself, though, was unposed. Maryse's head was thrown back in laughter, and a smaller, chubbier Camille had a hand on her mother's cheek and an adoring look in her eyes. The love between them was obvious. It made Brooks envious. The story he'd told her about Gia was completely true. A family had always been on his agenda, and he'd taken for granted that he'd start one sooner rather than later. Kids and Popsicles and bedtime stories. Something happy to come home to after the hard things he witnessed at work.

Suppressing a regretful sigh, he turned his attention to the next picture. What he saw made him frown. It was another older shot, this time of Maryse as a teenager. She stood beside another teen—a young man with his arm slung across her shoulders. But it wasn't jealousy that gave Brooks pause. It was something else.

Recognition.

He knew the other kid in the photo from somewhere.

Slowly, he reached out and picked it up so he could examine it more closely. For a second, the only thing that really stood out was the guy's blue eyes. The same shade as Maryse's. As Camille's. Brooks made the connection quickly.

Her brother.

That wasn't where the familiarity came from, though. Mentally, he added some years to the teen's face, trying to bring the image up to present day.

A few lines in the forehead, a touch of premature gray...

Brooks just about dropped the picture as he clued in.

"Crap!"

The frame slipped between his fingers, and he fumbled to keep it in his grasp. He secured it and lifted it up again. Yeah, there was no doubt about who the guy was. Sure that he was right, he set it back on the mantel. Then he thought better of putting it back. He grabbed it again and turned to stride up the hall after Maryse.

Chapter 13

Brooks pushed open the bedroom door, then stopped in the doorway, his brain ceasing to work as he caught sight of Maryse. She stood inside the tiny room, beside the bed in a state of near complete undress. Her long, well-muscled legs were bare, every creamy inch in view. A pair of black satin panties left nothing to the imagination. Brooks forced his eyes up from the smooth, tempting curve of her hip. Dragging his gaze up was worse. She was topless. The swell of her breasts was on full display. And though she held her bra in her hands, she seemed as frozen as he was, her only movement a slow, stunned blink. It was impossible to look away. Even more impossible *not* to drink her in. She was hands down the most beautiful thing he'd ever seen.

Renewed desire coursed through Brooks, and as the heat filled him, his body came back to life. Suddenly he wasn't frozen. Instead, he had to work to keep still. It required serious effort to fight the urge to stride across the room so he could take her in his arms and lay her down on the bed.

Time constraint be damned.

He balled his fist in an attempt to keep from reaching for her.

Finally, she drew in a breath—one that made her quiver visibly—and lifted the skimpy fabric in her hands to her chest.

"Just thought I'd change," she said in barely more than a whisper.

Brooks ran his eyes over her again. "It's warm in Vegas. But not *that* warm."

With a pretty blush creeping across her chest, she slid the bra into place. As she fastened the clasp without looking, he decided that the effect was no less alluring. Yeah, he wanted to pull it all off, but the contrast of the black satin against her porcelain skin had an undeniable appeal just as it was.

She stared back at him for a second, then shot an awkward look over his shoulder. "My stuff…"

"Sorry."

He stepped to the side, and she moved forward. There still wasn't room for her to get by. Brooks knew he should probably leave the room. Except he couldn't. Even when her bare arm brushed his elbow, and she stopped and cleared her throat, he felt the need to stay.

She met his eyes and gestured to a spot behind him. "Could you…?"

He turned sideways and spied a stack of clothes on the dresser. "Oh. Yeah."

He grabbed them and handed them over, then watched as Maryse slid into the pale yellow T-shirt and jeans. He was torn between appreciating the way the clothes hugged her body and wishing he could still see her in entirety.

"The room's a little small," she said apologetically. "It was a den before I got ahold of it. I gave the real bedroom to Camille."

"It's cozy."

"Comfortable?"

"Yeah, that."

"Sure. If you're a munchkin," she joked, then reached

up and undid the still-tight bun she'd somehow managed to keep fastened.

Brooks realized it was the first time he'd seen the cascade of brunette waves truly free. It tumbled over her shoulder in a way that made him wonder what it would look like spread across his sheets. His gaze drifted to *her* bed, seeking the plush white pillow tucked just under the blanket. The mere thought of the sharp contrast made his mouth dry.

"I think I'm ready," she said, drawing his attention back to where it should be.

She'd pulled her hair up again, this time into a less severe ponytail. She tossed it over her shoulder, then bent down and zipped up the suitcase that sat in the middle of the bed.

"Sorry if I was taking too long," she added as she straightened up. "It's been so long since I went anywhere that I wasn't sure what to pack, and I stuck a few of Camille's things in before I started getting my own."

He waved off her apology. "You're fine."

She smiled. "If I was fine, you wouldn't be here, rushing me."

The photograph slipped back to the surface of his mind. "I didn't come here to make you hurry up. I came to ask you about your brother."

"My brother? Okay. What would you like to know?"

"What was his name, sweetheart?"

"Jean-Paul Kline."

"Did he ever go by another one?"

"Like, an official alias? I don't know. But I'm sure he didn't always give out his full credentials when he was running scams."

Brooks reached around her to grab the suitcase. "C'mon. We can talk and move."

Together, they made their way from the bedroom to the front hall, then out to the car. Brooks waited until they'd turned down the driveway before he pursued his questions again.

"There was a picture on your mantel," he said. "Two teenagers standing in front of a big brick building."

"Right. That's me and Jean-Paul. It was the day he graduated high school. He was eighteen and I was sixteen. That was right before things started to get really rough for him. Why are you asking about it?"

"Does the name Elias Franco mean anything to you?"

She shook her head. "Should it?"

"It was the name of one of my confidential informants. And not just *any* CI… This is the guy who first brought Nank to my attention."

"Okay."

Her lips were pursed thoughtfully, and he knew she was considering his words carefully, thinking them through and connecting them to their current situation.

"You think Elias and my brother were the same man," she said after a second.

"I know they were," Brooks replied. "About eight years ago, this guy—the same one in your photo—came to me at the precinct. I can't even remember how I wound up at the desk with him. I was still pretty fresh to the detective gig, so maybe someone thought what he had to say wasn't important and just passed him along."

Brooks paused, remembering how Franco had looked. Nervous enough that he could've easily been mistaken as high. But something about him reeked of genuine fear, and when he said he'd deliberately come from Las Vegas into Rain Falls to avoid being seen, Brooks had given him the benefit of the doubt.

"But you did listen?" Maryse prodded.

"Sure did," Brooks agreed. "And he told me he'd been trying to get out of the game for a while, but kept getting sucked back in, a little deeper each time. A few months earlier, he'd been recruited to do a job for a company called People With Paper."

"Yes. That's where he was working when he was killed."

"Right. As a security guard. But it turned out the job was under a man named Caleb Nank—like I said, it was the first I'd heard of the guy—and the security position was far darker than he thought. He said the company was a front for a whole bunch of illegal activity. One thing led to another, and the next thing he knew, he was too far in to get out. But he wanted to walk away, and he was willing to tell us what he knew in exchange for a guarantee of protection."

"And you accepted his offer?"

Brooks nodded. "Yep. Not right away, though. Vetted his story first. Got permission from my captain and the one over at the Vegas detachment to pursue the case. At the time, Nank was a complete unknown. Still looked like a legitimate businessman from the outside. Elias—Jean-Paul, I mean—was quickly able to prove that it really was just a front."

"But you couldn't link anything to Nank directly. Like you said before."

"That's right. We busted his guys for small stuff. Possession with intent. Solicitation. Not one of them would turn on Nank, though. Never saw the guy in person, and all his lackeys said the same thing. They'd rather face time in jail. We spent months trying to build a case. Trying to find a crack. Came up dry every time."

"And my brother?"

"He said that what Nank's guys really meant was that they'd do anything to avoid facing their boss. They all owed him something. And the only way they would help us out was if they were like *him* and found something that was more important than fulfilling the debt. He never told me what it was that he owed Nank himself, but I could hazard a pretty good guess on what it was that he thought was more important."

"Camille," Maryse filled in.

"The dates line up," Brooks said. "He worked for me for a little over thirteen months, so it makes sense that he might've come in right around the time he found out he was going to be a father. And from what you told me about family being the only thing he valued, I'd say that could definitely be his motivation for wanting to turn his life around."

"Brooks…" She spoke without looking at him, her voice even. "Do you think Nank found out that he'd become an informant and had him killed?"

There was no point in lying. "It's a strong possibility, sweetheart."

"Did you know?"

"That he died? No. Sometimes, CIs change their minds and disappear. And since we never actually charged him with any crimes, we had no reason to chase him down."

"What about the fire that killed him?"

Brooks's heart ached at the small, sad-sounding question, but he still answered honestly. "I heard about the fire itself. But it wasn't in my jurisdiction and it was never connected to Nank, who was my main focus. The reports all stated that the arsonist perished in the fire and I never looked into the details. Never saw a picture or thought it might have something to do with my case."

"It's probably what Nank wanted."

"Undoubtedly."

Maryse went silent, staring out the windshield as he navigated the car through the countryside. The flat white scenery flashed by quickly, matching the somber mood. Brooks wished he had comforting words to offer, but nothing he said would change the past. He cast a glance toward her. Her expression was unreadable. Was she relieved to hear that her brother had been on the right side? Or angry that his police involvement was likely what got him killed? It was impossible to say what she was thinking.

But a moment later, she spoke, and her tone was anything but neutral.

"I hate him." Maryse spit out the words with a vehemence that surprised her. "I don't know Caleb Nank. You could put two men in a room and I couldn't tell you which one he was. But he ruined my brother's life, then killed him and blamed his death on Jean-Paul himself. He *destroyed* that piece of my family. Maybe I love Camille more fiercely because of that, I don't know. But now he's trying to take her for some perceived debt, and I can't wrap my head around the cruelty. I hate him, Brooks."

The big policeman didn't balk at her impassioned speech. "I've been chasing the man for eight years, sweetheart. Dead ends every time. And I normally try to keep my personal feelings out of my cases, but with this one... good cops have been killed trying to pin him down. And now all this. I'm not ashamed to say that I hate him, too. Probably why my boss finally put some distance between me and the case."

Maryse took a steadying breath. It felt good to release the emotion; it felt even better to have Brooks share it.

"Tell me what made him send you out here," she said.

"You sure you want to hear about it right now?"

"I could use the distraction."

He shot her a glance and a nod, and Maryse was glad to listen as he launched into an explanation. "Rain Falls was thinking about passing off the case. Back to the main station at Vegas, where it belonged. We're all part of LVMPD, but technically they're closer to everything that happened.

My boss apparently informed everyone but me that it was his plan to hand the reins back over to them. And he was right to worry about my reaction. We'd *just* got someone on the inside again, so when I caught wind of what was happening, I was more than angry. Blew up in front of half the station and stormed out. What I didn't realize was that the captain's favorite rookie—who was also working for *me*—was listening. And what neither the captain *nor* I realized was that the same rookie was directly involved with our new CI."

Maryse could see the guilt-ridden pinch of his mouth. "You couldn't have known."

"I *should* have known. Kept better tabs on the kid." Brooks shook his head. "When Parler—the rookie—realized the girl wasn't going to be *ours* anymore, he freaked. Scared he couldn't keep her safe. He ran straight to her. I'm guessing he wanted to pull her out completely."

"You're guessing?"

"We never got a chance to ask him. Two days later, Parler and the girl were found dead in the girl's apartment. Shot."

"Nank?"

"No doubt. But the case was run as an open and shut. The gun was left at the scene. Fingerprints on it belonged to a known felon. He'd had ties to Nank in the past, and even though he claimed he'd gone straight and said he'd been framed, the guy *still* wouldn't say a word against his former boss."

"But it's not your fault, Brooks."

His hands flexed on the steering wheel. "The rookie was *my* responsibility. The girl was *my* informant. I should've seen what was going on, but I didn't. I should've kept my temper under control, but I didn't. All the things I should've done…but didn't. And two people died as a result."

Maryse reached out and placed her hand on his tense

forearm and said again, "That's not your *fault*. It's sad, but it's not something you should take the blame for. The rookie should've known better. The girl must've been aware of the risk. And if you lost your temper, it's because you're passionate about doing your job. That's not something you should be punished for."

The big man exhaled. "That's what I've been telling myself for months. Or trying to. Told my boss, too. For all the good it did."

She studied his face for a second. "Did you believe it, when you told him?"

"What?"

"You said you were *trying* to tell yourself that it wasn't your fault. Like you needed to convince yourself. Maybe your boss didn't believe that *you* believed it. Maybe he sent you away to gain some perspective."

"You're saying he might actually have believed that it wasn't my fault." Brooks frowned so hard that Maryse knew he hadn't considered the idea before.

"You don't think it's a possibility?" she asked.

"It's been…" He paused, then turned his hazel eyes her way for such a long second that she was surprised he didn't run them right off the road.

"It's been what?"

He turned away and replied in a rough voice. "It's been killing me. Thinking about what a waste of life it was. About how—even if it was the smallest chance in the world—I could've prevented the loss. So, no. I guess I didn't really believe it wasn't my fault. Logic and emotion don't mix well, do they?"

"Not so much."

"Thank you, sweetheart."

"For what?"

"For making me say it aloud."

He looked so relieved that she almost laughed.

"That's it?" she said. "You admit that you've been blaming yourself for this, and now you can move on?"

"No. But I feel a hell of a lot better." He smiled for a second, then frowned again. "As far as the captain's concerned, though… I just keep coming back to the idea that it's too much of a coincidence that he picked this spot."

"Well. What reason did he give you for choosing Laval?"

"Told me he wanted to send me to the coldest hell he could think of. Then he slapped down the one-way ticket and the rental agreement for the apartment. Made me pretty mad."

Maryse thought about it for a second, puzzling over whether or not the forced vacation could be a cover. And if so, what was it a cover *for*? She could only think of one thing.

"If it wasn't a legitimate punishment," she said slowly, "then your boss must've known Nank's activities had crossed the border and sent you up to follow him."

Brooks nodded. "And it begs the question of why he didn't tell me. Because he could've sent me up here legitimately. Made the arrangements for cross-border jurisdiction. He sure as hell wasn't in a hurry. I've been in Laval for eight weeks already. So I have to wonder what he hoped would happen."

"Maybe he wasn't sure he was right."

"I don't know. It'd be a pretty gutsy financial move if he wasn't sure."

"Did he use police money to bring you here?"

"The opposite. He forcibly dipped into my banked hours to fund this trip. Told me I was lucky he wasn't docking my pay, then made me cash in every vacation hour I had. Called it paid leave. But if he'd used police funds, he'd be accountable."

"Is he even allowed to do that?"

"No. Well, we're required by our union to use our banked hours and vacation by the end of each year, so I guess he could use the excuse that he thought I wouldn't and he was being proactive. Pretty sure he was just doing his usual things and strong-arming his way into getting what he wants."

Something in his tone made her heart skip a nervous beat. "What are you thinking? That he might be corrupt?"

"If you'd asked me a few months ago, I would've said no way. Hell, if you'd asked me a few *hours* ago, I would've said it. He has his own way of doing things. Bends rules left, right and center. Always in the name of bringing down the bad guy, though. But right now, I have to consider the possibility that he's not. It stinks of a cover-up."

Maryse turned over the possibility in her mind. It had been bad enough to know that a gang of career criminals had Camille. It was a whole other thing to wonder if someone in law enforcement was involved, too. A police captain had an awful lot to lose if he was caught, and she didn't want to think about what it would mean for her daughter.

She swallowed nervously. "So much for a distraction."

"Sorry, sweetheart. I wasn't trying to make you worry even more."

"It's like a snowball in my gut. It keeps building and building, and every time I think there's a little bit of hope…" She shrugged. "The hill gets a little steeper and the snowball rolls even faster."

"We can talk about something else, if it'll help."

"Is it fair that I want to say yes to that?"

"More than fair. A brain break is a good thing. It'll give us a chance to rest. And besides that, we still have another hour until we get to the airport, then a few hours on the plane. Plenty of time to make that snowball into an avalanche."

In spite of the heaviness in her heart, Maryse laughed. "Was that supposed to be reassuring?"

"Yep. That's what I'm here for," Brooks told her. "Being a butt-kicking cop is only a secondary role."

"Before we change the subject, can I tell you one thing?"

"You can tell me *any*thing."

"Whatever your boss's reason was for sending you up here…I'm glad he did. There's no way I could do this without you."

Chapter 14

As the conversation shifted to lighter topics—favorite foods, favorite bands and favorite pastimes—Brooks continued to sift subconsciously through the case.

He couldn't accept that his boss was working for Nank. Or that the older man—whom he'd known since he was a kid, and who had been a friend of his own police officer father—would deliberately put Brooks in harm's way. He itched to call the station. Might even have done it, if it weren't for his increasingly personal obligation to Maryse.

He sneaked a glance her way. Her face was relaxed, the only hint of tension in the way her eyes darted out the window now and then. But he knew her head, like his, couldn't be far from the details. For six years, she thought she was safe. Moving through life at her settled-ish pace. Worry always there, but pushed to the back of her mind. The small town probably seemed like a good choice.

Brooks's thoughts paused. Why *had* she picked LaHache? It was quaint, no doubt. Did it have some other significance?

He tried to bring his attention back to the current conversation, but the nagging sensation of needing to connect the dots persisted.

Obviously, Maryse needed somewhere that doesn't appear prominently on any map, but what was it about that place specifically that drew her? Was there a reason? Or was it another coincidence?

He didn't realize he'd muttered his concerns aloud until she answered in a soft voice.

"It's not a coincidence," she said. "We visited LaHache when we were kids. My mom had this crazy idea that she should take us on a winter road trip. Seattle to Quebec. She grew up near Montreal, and that was our end destination. But somehow we managed to miss it. Don't ask how—my mom always just said it was fate. But we kept driving north and eventually we hit the town. We stayed for a week. I never forgot how much fun it was or how much I liked it."

"Did your brother feel the same?"

"Yes. I think so. I mean, Jean-Paul was always kind of flip about emotions. If things got serious, he'd make a joke and change the subject. But he once told me it was the last happy memory he had of us before our mom died."

Brooks considered her statement, weighing what to say next. He was curious about her childhood and her relationship with her brother. He was sympathetic toward the loss of her mother, and he wondered whether her father was alive or if he was gone, too. The loss of his own parents had shaped his early adulthood. He wondered if it had shaped hers, too. But in the end, he settled for a question that might help them with their current problem instead.

"Would Jean-Paul have told anyone else about your road trip?"

"I don't know," she admitted. "But I never thought he'd stick with a girl long enough to— Oh."

Brooks nodded at the clear understanding on her face. "It makes sense that if he cared enough about a woman to stick with her through the pregnancy that he might've trusted her enough to share a few secrets."

"And you're thinking that it somehow got back to Nank?"

"It's at least a possibility."

She frowned. "But Dee White has been in Laval for a year. The other concierge said so."

"I have a theory about that. And—" He cut himself off as a flash in the rearview mirror caught his eye.

They'd just cleared a wide corner, and zipping out from behind the same curve was another car. It wasn't one he recognized, but its speed was entirely unnecessary, and his gut instinct told him the motivation behind the sudden approach was anything but good.

"And what?" Maryse prodded.

"And it's going to have to wait. Have a look behind us."

She swiveled her head and let out a gasp. "Are they following us?"

"I'd bet my right arm on it."

"What are we going to do?"

Brooks mentally reeled through their options. Trying to outrun the other car would be unreasonable. The highway was long, and with the exception of a few curves like the one they'd just passed, it was more or less a straight shot. Even if that hadn't been the case, a high-speed chase along a major highway would undoubtedly draw attention. If anyone was going to get pulled over, he sure as hell didn't want it to be them.

Deciding it would be a better bet to beat their pursuer to the next major turnoff and try to lose them in a more crowded area, he pushed down on the gas pedal, accelerating to a speed that was still within reason.

"Are we any farther ahead?" he asked, his voice as grim as his shift in mood.

Maryse, who still faced the other direction, nodded. "A little bit."

"Good."

A directional sign loomed ahead, bringing hope. When they neared it, though, Brooks saw that it announced that another thirty kilometers lay between them and the nearest town. A quick calculation told him that was almost twenty miles.

Too far.

A car whizzed past in the other direction, and he knew that if he punched the gas much more, someone would alert the police.

"They're getting closer," Maryse said, turning his way.

"Dammit."

He shot a cursory look in the rearview mirror. The driver of the other car clearly didn't care about getting caught. The vehicle was definitely gaining on them again.

"What's he planning?" he muttered.

"They."

"What?"

"It's a couple in the front seat. They're close enough to see." She paused. "I'm pretty sure it's Dee and Greg."

"You've got to be kidding me."

He knew without even looking that she had to be right. Just like he knew he never should have left the man alone in the hotel room.

But...how did they find us? And why the hell are they even bothering to?

There didn't seem to be a point. The girl was gone. Already on her way to Nank, so—

Damn, damn, triple damn.

A possible explanation—no, a *likely* one—jumped to mind. They'd informed the crime boss that he and Maryse were coming, and he'd cut the couple some kind of deal in exchange for chasing them down. And even if they got away, they'd now lost the element of surprise. Which was bad.

Very bad.

"Brooks?" Her soft voice cut through his mounting concern.

He worked to maintain his composure and to contain his worry. "Yeah, sweetheart?"

"This might sound weird…but I think I know what they're trying to do."

"Better tell me quick, then."

"I know this area. I think anyone who's driven the road between LaHache and Laval does. That means that Dee and Greg probably do, too." She spoke rapidly, gesturing out the front windshield. "About five miles up, there's a rest stop. A few years back there were several back-to-back crashes. They were all reported as road-rage incidents, but it turned out the same man committed all offenses."

"He was using the road and the rest stop as a weapon."

"And I think they're going to try to do the same thing."

"And this time the accident might be fatal."

She nodded. "And if that doesn't work, they'll have us cornered anyway. There's no way to get out of the rest stop without turning around completely. And it's out of view of the road, so…"

"A good spot for an execution," he filled in.

"Yes." It wasn't much more than a whisper.

"So we just don't let ourselves be pushed off the road."

"I don't know if we'll be able to avoid it. The road gets really narrow right before the turnoff. It'll be a choice between the rest area and a ditch."

"Then we need to get past it quicker than Dee and Greg can catch up."

Forgoing his need to maintain a low speed and an even lower profile, Brooks pressed his booted foot to the gas pedal. The car groaned a protest, then jerked and shot forward. Another glance in the mirror told him the distance between them and their pursuers had increased only marginally. A look out the windshield also told him they hadn't gained enough ground, either, and there was no sign yet of the infamous rest stop.

"C'mon, c'mon," Brooks urged under his breath.

The speedometer was climbing steadily, but the car shook at the rough treatment. And Maryse had one hand squeezed tightly, gripping the seat under her thigh, and the other lifted to the handle above the door.

Brooks fought a need to slow down in order to reassure her.

Safety over comfort. But as quickly as that reminder came, so did another. *Since when is driving twenty miles above the speed limit* safe?

He shoved aside the thoughts and pushed on, and a few seconds later, he spotted the sign ahead. Relief flooded through him. He didn't know yet what they would do once they passed the spot, but at least they'd have a few moments of reprieve. As he turned to tell Maryse they were almost there, his eyes skimmed over the side mirror. Then stayed there. Dee held the wheel in the car behind them. But Greg was hanging out the passenger window.

What the— Oh, crap.

Brooks barely had time to react. He swerved just as a shot echoed through the air. The bullet missed. But the abrupt motion sent his head flying into the steering wheel. A sharp pain slammed through his jaw. The world spun. The road blurred. Then—for the second time that day— everything went black.

As the car careened across the road into the wrong lane, Maryse screamed Brooks's name, and it exited her mouth at a pitch she didn't even recognize as her own. It was almost a shriek.

But he didn't react. His head just slumped to one side, making her want to cover her face and hide. She wanted him to lift his face and take the wheel and guide them to safety.

But she knew the latter was unlikely and the former would get them killed. So with as much calmness as she could muster, Maryse undid her seat belt, pushed Brooks's head back, forced her shoulder under his heavy arm and grabbed the wheel. But she knew almost immediately it was a mistake. Though she'd given herself some control over the direction of the vehicle, she'd accidentally pressed down on Brooks's leg, sending his foot into the gas pedal. The car immediately accelerated. And lifting her elbow to release the pressure did nothing to slow it again.

Panic building, Maryse shifted her gaze from him to the front windshield. The road sloped down in front of them, and even if their speed decreased considerably more, their current course had them headed straight for a deep ditch. And if by some miracle the car managed to get enough air to carry them over the ditch instead of into it, they'd hit a solid wall of brush and trees.

And things got worse quickly.

Dee and Greg zipped past. Maryse heard a screech, and she knew they must have pulled a wild U-turn far up on the highway ahead. In a moment, the criminal duo would be bearing down on them.

She *needed* to slow the car. Like, two minutes ago.

Leaving one hand on the wheel, Maryse freed the other and tried to dislodge Brooks's foot by shoving his thigh. The effort was in vain. His leg was dead weight. She shook his shoulder, but his body just slid forward even more.

"Brooks!"

He's not going to wake up, no matter how loud you yell. Do something constructive, dammit.

Maryse lifted her gaze to the window again, and tears pricked at her eyes. Just ahead, the other vehicle had recovered from its turn. It now sat blocking the road. They clearly thought it would be enough to stop her. And it might've been, if she had any choice. But right that second, it was just going to result in a T-bone collision.

Maryse cast her gaze heavenward. *A break. You can give me one anytime, universe.*

But she was pretty sure the only break she was going to get was one she created for herself.

And how are you going to do that?

Even if she managed by some miracle to swerve out of Dee and Greg's way, she'd likely crash the car into something else. What she needed was control of both the speed and direction of the car.

Taking a breath, she tried again to free Brooks's foot, this time by reaching down to his calf. It was just as fruitless as her first effort. She couldn't fit her torso between him and the steering column cover. She started to sit up again, but her hand brushed a hard piece of plastic under the seat. She paused and dragged her fingers back to it.

The adjustment handle.

Struck by an idea, she gripped it tightly and pulled. Immediately, Brooks's seat slid back. But it wasn't quite far enough. She grabbed the handle a second time and yanked even harder. Finally, her efforts were rewarded. The seat flew back as far as it could go. The car decelerated abruptly, and for a second, Maryse's hand slipped from the wheel. The car skittered and jerked, the tires bumping hard against the pavement.

Thinking quickly—and knowing there wasn't a way to move Brooks out of the seat—she clambered over the center console and straight into the unconscious man's lap. She took hold of the wheel again, shoved one leg between both of his and found the gas pedal. In moments, she had what she needed. Or at least *part* of what she needed. Because she also had to come up with a plan, and judging from how close she was to where the other car was now—she could see the hot exhaust in the cold air—she had about ten seconds to do it.

Chicken.

The word popped into her mind without explanation, but it only took her a moment to figure out why it had surfaced. And only a moment more to put it into action. She held the wheel straight. She fixed her gaze on Greg, who sat in the passenger seat, his gun-arm out the window. And she slammed on the gas.

She was near enough to see the widening of the man's eyes. He shook his head like he couldn't believe what was happening. He flailed with the gun. He dropped it. Then he mouthed something and grabbed Dee's arm.

Maryse pressed down harder and angled the car just an inch to the left. An adjustment that put her in line to hit the front end of the other vehicle.

Greg's motions became frantic.

Maryse closed her eyes.

This is going to work.

She lifted her lids again with just enough time to be triumphant. The tires on the other car squealed, and the scent of burning rubber filled the air as Greg kicked it into Reverse. They were almost quick enough. But not quite. The passenger side door scraped against the other vehicle's front bumper, and the ear-piercing screech of metal on metal filled the air. Maryse held tight to the steering wheel and refused to let the grazing impact slow her down. She glanced in the rearview mirror. Dee and Greg didn't seem to be recovering well. The frame of their car sagged down on the side, and the bumper hung to the ground in a satisfying way.

Maryse breathed out. "Chicken."

It had been one of Jean-Paul's favorite games. It had scared the hell out of her every time he challenged one of the other local hoodlums. He'd wrecked two cars. He'd broken ribs. He'd even had his license suspended at one point. But he'd never lost.

Thankful that she'd at last been able to channel some of her brother's guts, Maryse continued to keep her foot firmly on the pedal for another few miles. When she was satisfied that she'd put enough distance between her and Dee and Greg, she eased up and dropped down to the speed limit. She started to lean back, then froze as Brooks groaned underneath her.

Brooks.

In the intensity of the last few moments, she'd forgotten about him. It almost made her laugh. It should've been impossible to forget that she had two hundred pounds of very attractive man beneath her rear end. *Really* impossible. And now that she was reminded he was there, she realized she was going to have to pull over and do something about it. His groan was a bit reassuring—at least he was definitely breathing—but it was still *just* a groan, and she needed to check on him.

She glanced at the clock. They had another hour and a half until the suggested check-in time, and probably another hour and a quarter before they actually arrived at the airport. Which meant they could stop in Laval—or one of the two towns before the city—for at least a few minutes.

But...

Maryse shook her head and shoved down an argument against stopping. She was sitting in an unconscious man's lap while driving on the highway. And the unconscious man in question was the only reason she was alive, and the only person who could help her find Camille. She owed him. She needed him. And on top of that…she liked him. A lot. So even if she didn't owe him or need him, she *wanted* him to be okay.

He shifted underneath her, and one of his hands came up to brush her thigh. The contact sent a zap of attraction through her, and she chastised herself for enjoying the touch of an unconscious man. But a moment later, his fingers squeezed, he groaned again, and she realized he was awake, after all.

"Maryse?"

"I'm here."

"In my lap?"

"Yes."

"I thought it was just a really good dream."

She was glad he couldn't see the blush that crept up her face. "It's real."

He sighed. "Then I guess the really bad parts of the dream were real, too."

"Unfortunately."

"Dammit." He shifted slightly, which pushed Maryse forward into the horn. It blared loudly for a second before he shifted again. "Whoops."

"How's your head?"

"Not bad."

"Not bad?" she repeated, wishing she could turn to give him an incredulous look to go with her tone.

"Not bad for being knocked out for the second time in a day," he amended. "I think my chin took most of the impact this time."

"Dizziness? Nausea?"

"No, sweetheart. The worst I am is a little sore and a little cramped."

"I'll pull over as soon as I can."

"No rush."

He adjusted again, this time with obvious care, and Maryse slipped down so that she rested between his thighs. The position was slightly more comfortable. For a minute, anyway. But when Brooks put his palm on her hip, the atmosphere immediately became more intimate.

It got worse when he spoke right beside her ear. "How long was I out?"

Maryse took a near-shallow breath. "Five minutes."

He chuckled. "You work quickly."

She fought another blush. "Someone had to save our butts."

His fingers flexed on her body. "Thank you."

"I think they call that *quid pro quo.*"

"Doesn't mean I appreciate it any less."

"You might appreciate it less when you see your car."

"It's a rental."

"Well, then I wouldn't count on getting your deposit back."

"You gonna tell me what you did to it, or just make guilty little comments?"

Maryse winced. "I played chicken with Dee and Greg."

Brooks laughed again, the buzz in his chest tickling her back pleasantly. "Did you win?"

"I did. I don't think they'll be catching up to us anytime soon."

"Well. That's really all that matters."

"You would've liked him," she blurted.

Somehow—she wasn't sure how—he knew what she meant. "Jean-Paul?"

She nodded. "I mean, I know you said he was your CI, but I think on a personal level, you guys would've gotten along."

"Cop-role versus robber-role aside?" he teased.

"Yes."

She must've sounded a bit earnest, because he was suddenly embracing her tightly from behind, both arms locked around her waist. His lips brushed her cheekbone, and then his chin—which she knew had to be aching—came to rest on her shoulder.

"There's no doubt I would've liked him, sweetheart," he said. "He was *your* brother."

Warmth bloomed in Maryse's chest. It swelled wide across her ribs. Then it settled into a smaller, permanent-feeling pulse in her heart.

Chapter 15

Riding with Maryse between his thighs walked a thin line between being thoroughly enjoyable and utterly frustrating. On the one hand, there was no doubt in Brooks's mind that she fit there just right. Like she was supposed to be there. Or always had been there. Or whatever other sappy statement he could muster up about fate.

But on the other hand...

The fact that she did fit him so well made it hard not to act on the desire that filled his mind. It was even tougher to control his body's automatic reaction. With every little move, it got more difficult to contain it. Each bump in the road jarred his concentration, and he kept thinking of the way she looked in her tiny bedroom in nothing but her little bits of satin when he knew he should be thinking of ways to confront Caleb Nank.

Little bit heaven, little bit hell.

So when she finally said something about seeing a wide enough shoulder ahead, he couldn't help but let out a relieved sigh. Damned if it didn't sound like a barely restrained growl.

As Maryse pulled the car to the side of the road and eased to a full stop, Brooks reached for the handle and flung open the door. Icy air blasted through the small space, temporarily cooling the fiery need that raced through his veins.

The reprieve didn't last long. Maryse swung a leg sideways and twisted her body toward the door. Then stopped. One of her hands was outstretched, the other pressed dangerously high on his thigh.

"Uh-oh," she said.

"What?"

"I'm stuck."

"Seriously?"

"Yes. Hang on."

Brooks sat very still as she wriggled back again. She only succeeded in getting herself sideways, her firm rear end balanced between his legs, her hip resting against the zipper of his jeans. Now she was breathing a little heavily, too, which did nothing to bank Brooks's libido.

"I think my coat is pinned to something under the steering wheel," she told him, reaching up to pull on the zipper, which didn't move. "Dammit. Can you help me? Maybe hold the front part down while I try to get it open?"

Fighting a groan, Brooks brought up his left hand. He grabbed the jacket and pulled down firmly while she worked at the buttons. After what seemed like a full minute of struggle, Maryse at last got all but one undone. The little sigh she let out as she finally popped open the last button was almost an aphrodisiac. The way she wriggled herself out of the coat was as good as a plate of oysters. When she was free of the jacket, though, she stayed in his lap.

"Are you unstuck?" he asked.

"Um. No."

"Not the coat?"

There was a pause, and a crimson flush crept up her throat. "No."

Brooks's eyes followed the line of bright pink to the V of her T-shirt. "What, then?"

"I'm not sure. Could you…?" She tipped her head over her shoulder, indicating what she meant.

"Sure."

He reached around her body, trying not to inhale too much of her honey-laced scent. He ran his fingers along the lower edge of the steering wheel until he found the source of the jam.

"Your belt loop is hooked to something under here."

"Can you get it loose?"

Brooks wiggled the denim to no avail. "Don't think so. Maybe if you swing a bit more toward me."

She inched back, then lifted her knee. The move knocked away his grip of the snagged pants.

"Gonna have to try again."

"Okay."

She started to move her leg again, and he stopped her just before her knee slammed into his already-sore chin. He grabbed her calf, slid his palm to her heel, then ducked and swept her foot past his head. She was straddling him now, and he knew that wasn't a good thing.

"Hold still a sec," he said.

She complied, balancing overtop of him. She went so motionless that he knew she had to be holding her breath. Holding his own to match, he dug behind her, feeling for the offending piece of fabric and whatever random thing it was that held it in place. His thumb finally found the loop and slid through it. He pulled, and the denim sprang free, triggering a chain reaction.

Maryse yelped and flew forward.

Brooks tried to move back and out of the way and failed. His hands came up in a slightly delayed attempt to stop her from smacking into him, and that effort failed, too. Her chest slammed—not unpleasantly—against his own. The impact forced his arms back, and one smacked into something plastic. With a noisy creak, the seat fell back. Finally, a gust of wind sent the driver's side door to an echoing close.

For several seconds after it happened, neither of them moved. They lay there, pressed together, both breathing heavily. Then Maryse's body vibrated against his, racked by silent tears. With a thickness in his throat, Brooks freed his other hand—which had somehow managed to get wedged between them—to stroke her hair.

"Hey," he said softly. "It's going to be okay. We're going to get moving and make it to the airport with plenty of time to spare."

She didn't lift her head, and she continued to shake.

"Sweetheart?"

"I'm—I—I— Oh, God."

Her face finally came up, and he saw that she wasn't crying at all. Her eyes were sparkling, her cheeks were pinched up and her mouth was open in silent laughter.

"Maryse?"

"I'm sorry," she gasped, collapsing down onto his chest again.

"You're *sorry*?"

"It's not funny. I know it's not. Nothing about it is. So I'm sorry. But—" She cut herself off with something that rode the line between a giggle and a hiccup. "Am I hysterical?"

Brooks couldn't help but smile. "Might be."

"Good."

"Good?"

"It gives me an excuse for laughing when I should be crying."

He traced a thumb along her jawline. "It's okay to laugh."

"Camille would be," she told him.

His smile widened. "Oh, yeah? She'd be amused by you being stuck in my lap?"

"Well. She'd be amused by me being stuck in *anyone's* lap. She thinks slapstick humor is the best kind. Laughs like crazy when people fall down, Three Stooges–style."

"Me, too."

"You do?"

"Yep. In fact, I was once chasing down this guy who'd stolen some lady's purse, and he was pretty damned close to getting away, but his foot got stuck in a catch basin. He kept trying to pull himself out and almost did. Right before I got to him, his foot got free. But his shoe stayed behind. He flew out of the damned thing and straight into a tree. Splatted like a cartoon cat."

She propped herself up on her side and stared down at him. "Is any of that true?"

"No."

She burst out laughing, and this time it didn't have the edge to it. "Brooks!"

He grinned. "See?"

"What?"

"It's okay to laugh. Even when you're having the worst moment of your life, there's a little part of you that wants to be happy. And I swear to you that it's really and truly all right to do it. Trust me on this one. I've seen a lot of worst moments."

"I *do* trust you," she said, a hesitation clear in her voice.

"But?" he pushed.

"But even under the *best* circumstance, it seems wrong to be happy without Camille. Whenever something good happens to me, I want to share it with her. So this…"

"This what?"

"You."

"Me?" he teased.

"Stop it. I'm serious."

"Okay. *I* make you want to be happy in this otherwise awful situation. And you want to share me with Cami."

Her blush was back in full force. "Yes."

"I'm okay with that." In fact, he was more than okay with it; he was honored that she thought enough of him to want to introduce him to her daughter.

She shook her head. "It's not that simple. What makes it really wrong is that if Camille hadn't been taken, we wouldn't have met. So being happy about *you* is contingent on admitting that something good came of her kidnapping. And I just don't think I can do that."

"Life is never simple, sweetheart. But you can't overanalyze every detail. You'll make yourself crazy, and you'll miss out on the moments that matter. Moments like *this*." He brought his fingers to the back of her neck and dragged her mouth to his for a slow kiss.

"I don't think I'll be sharing *that* with Cami," she breathed as he pulled away.

"Yeah. Maybe gloss over a few of the details."

"Good plan."

This time, *she* kissed *him*, her soft mouth roving over his with an enthusiasm that made him burn. Her hands slid across his chest, then up to his shoulder, then under the collar of his jacket to caress his T-shirt-covered skin.

"We should go," he murmured against her mouth.

"We have a few minutes."

"Not enough—"

"Time. I know. You said that before."

She kissed him again, even more deeply, and Brooks knew his control was wavering. Heated desire coursed through him, threatening to overtake all else.

He forced himself to break away. "Maryse."

"This is a moment, Brooks."

"I want more than a moment, sweetheart." His voice was hoarse with the admission.

"I do, too," she said. "But what if we don't get another one? What if this is it?"

The question darkened his mind. Even though they'd known each other for less than a day, he was damned sure he didn't want to miss out on a future with her. The idea that this might literally be it for them pained him.

"Don't overanalyze it," she said, echoing his own sentiment. "Just embrace it."

She pushed his sweatshirt off his shoulders. Then she yanked it off completely, tossed it aside and slid her hand down to the bottom of his shirt. She worked her way underneath it, her fingers trailing across his stomach and circling up his chest.

He tried to argue once more, but she brushed her lips over his, silencing him. And as she darted her tongue into his mouth, Brooks knew he wasn't just helpless to say no. He was all hers, plain and simple.

As Maryse traced the inches of Brooks's taut muscles, her hands shook. Not with nerves—she was 100 percent sure that this was what she wanted—but with anticipation. Brooks was right. She'd spent years thinking through every detail of her life. Scrutinizing how each move would affect the next. Even the moments of spontaneity were never *truly* spontaneous. She had everything so carefully planned out that the odd step outside of routine was completely without risk.

And look where that got you.

She shoved aside the thought in favor of sitting up so she could push Brooks's T-shirt up, then lift it over his head. Her breath caught at the sight of him. His chest was wide and thick and had the kind of definition that came from hard work rather than working out.

Perfection.

She ran her hands over the corded muscles without shame, then lifted her gaze to meet his. He was smiling, and his eyes had darkened to the color of maple syrup. The warmth she found there held her, stilling her completely.

"Hey there," he said.

"Hi."

"You're beautiful up there, you know."

"Likewise. Well. Down there. And you know. Handsome."

He chuckled and reached up to touch her cheek. "I've got an idea. How about a little bit more of that quid pro quo."

She frowned. "You want to save my life again?"

He laughed again, then tugged on the bottom of her shirt. "Nope. Yellow looks good on you, but I feel like we should even the playing field."

"Oh." Pushing through a renewed shyness, Maryse used both hands to pull off the top. "Better?"

Brooks's eyes traveled over every inch of exposed skin before he answered. "You have no idea."

"I have *some* idea." She gave him an equally thorough once-over, then bent to kiss him once more.

The tempo increased almost immediately, and while Maryse knew it was because of their limited time, a large portion of her ached to slow it down. To relish it. To sweeten it, and to make it the kind of first time that could be cherished.

But eagerness quickly overshadowed both the desire to go slower *and* the need to hurry. Elbows and knees bumped awkwardly, hitting door handles and each other. Low laughter filled the car almost as much as their rapid breaths. In moments, pants and caution had been cast aside. Skin met skin. Lips met lips. And Maryse was ready for all of it. She almost couldn't restrain herself as his fingers unfastened her bra and slid it down between them. In fact, when his thumbs circled up across her bare breasts, she couldn't quite hold in a little thrust forward. He lifted his hips at the same moment, driving every boxer-clad inch of him between her thighs. Dizzying need filled her. The fabric between them was a wall that had to be torn down.

"Brooks?" His name was a gasp.

He leaned back. "Yeah, sweetheart?"

"Take them off." She didn't bother to disguise the desperation in her voice. "Please."

In seconds, he'd stripped off both his underwear and her own, and they lay together, their frantic movements temporarily suspended.

"Maryse," he said, a raw edge clear in his tone. "I want this. I want you. But I need to make something clear."

"Um. Now?"

"Now."

"Okay."

"I'm not a short-term guy." He cupped her cheek. "So if what you're looking for is—"

She cut him off, unable to fight a bemused smile. "It's not."

"No second thoughts?"

"None."

"Good. Because when we're done with all of this...when we've succeeded...I never want to hurry ever again."

The firm statement made Maryse's heart swell. "Me, neither."

She threaded her fingers through his and pressed them up over his head. Then she lifted up to her knees and—with her gaze locked on Brooks's hazel eyes—eased down slowly. Her body ached as he filled her, and for a moment, she simply sat still, in awe of the sweetly torturous feeling. Then she rocked forward. His eyes dropped shut. And the world of conscious thought slipped away, replaced by instinct. They moved together, faster and faster, locked in a rhythm that was all their own.

The heat built quickly, fueled how well they fit, how perfectly in tune their bodies were. The pace became near frenzied, need outweighing everything else. And soon it reached a crescendo. Brooks clutched at her hips. He drove upward and said her name, his voice throaty and full of want. And that was her undoing. She cried something back—wordless, but far from meaningless—and she shuddered against him, then collapsed to his chest. She tried to speak, but her mouth was as spent as the rest of her body, so she settled for a satisfied murmur and tucked herself into his embrace instead.

As Brooks trailed his fingers up and down her spine, her eyes wanted to close. She realized this was the first time she'd been truly still since she found Cami's bed empty. And with good reason. But now exhaustion crept in. Her mind and body both wanted to drift, and she could feel sleep pulling at her. She wished she could give in. She knew she couldn't.

"Brooks…"

He sighed. "I know, sweetheart. We gotta move or we won't make our flight."

"Sorry."

"You've been in Canada too long. You're apologizing for things you don't need to be sorry for."

"Sor—er. I mean."

"See?"

She laughed and started to reply, but as her gaze slipped out the fogged-up windows, she froze.

Brooks immediately pushed to his elbow. "What's wrong?"

She swallowed. "There's a patrol car headed this way. Lights on, sirens off."

"Crap."

"To put it mildly."

She made herself move, fumbling around in search of something—anything to use to cover herself up. Why were her clothes suddenly so elusive? Even her coat was nowhere to be seen. And the flash of red and blue was bright now, cutting through the recently darkened sky.

Brooks's hand closed on her wrist. "Stop."

"But the car's going to be here any second!"

"I know. Just lie back down."

Pushing aside the need to do anything *but* be calm, Maryse flopped back onto his chest. Brooks reached around her to pull up his sweatshirt. He tucked it around her just as the lights flooded the car and the sound of tires crunching on gravel carried through the air.

"What now?" Maryse whispered.

"Wait."

Moments later, a fist rapped sharply on the driver's side window. Still holding her close, he sat up and made a show of peering out the window. The officer tapped again, and this time, Brooks opened the door a crack.

The policeman—a surprisingly older patrolman with ample gray peeking out from under his hat and a stern, fatherly look on his face—cleared his throat. "Sir. Ma'am."

Brooks blinked at him. "Yeah?"

"Everything all right in here?"

"I'd go with more than 'all right.'" Brooks sounded so offended that Maryse almost laughed.

But her amusement died as the cop directed his attention her way. "You here because you want to be?"

She nodded. "Yes, sir."

"You sure?"

"A hundred percent."

He scrutinized her for a moment longer, then looked back at Brooks. "Kind of a public spot."

"Kind of the *point*," Brooks said, now sounding smug rather than offended.

"You been out here awhile?"

"Not long enough."

"Too long, I think," the cop replied drily. "Time to think about packing up. You headed into Laval?"

"Montreal," Brooks corrected, then added, "Everything all right out *there*?"

"Bit of trouble up the road. Abandoned car. Still probably best if you take off."

"You got it, Officer."

The cop offered them a smile and tipped his hat. "Stay safe."

Then he closed the door firmly and headed back to his car.

Maryse stared after the vehicle as it pulled away.

Stay safe.

The words sent a tickle of concern and guilt through her. Through the course of their encounter—and her enthusiasm for spontaneity—she hadn't thought about safety at all.

Stupid.

Biting her lip, she tossed back the jacket, climbed over to the passenger seat and scrambled to find her clothes.

She spoke breathlessly as she tossed them on, piece by piece. "You think he knew we had something to do with the supposedly abandoned car?"

Brooks pulled his T-shirt over his head slowly. "Nope. Wouldn't have let us go if he did."

"Or he could be waiting up the road."

"Trust me, sweetheart. I've been in his shoes enough times to know he wasn't suspicious."

"Thank God he didn't see the other side of *our* car." She did up her jeans button and stared straight ahead. "Ready?"

"Something wrong?"

For a second, she thought about not answering. Or at least not answering *truthfully*. But she knew it was just a defensive, knee-jerk reaction that could have bad consequences in the long run.

"We weren't…um. Safe." The sentence felt as awkward as it sounded.

"Safe?"

"We didn't…" She trailed off, shrugged and met Brooks's puzzled gaze, then tried again. "We didn't use any protection."

His face cleared. "Oh. On the safety side of things, sweetheart, I'm in the clear."

"Me, too," she said quickly.

"And on the *baby* side of things…"

Maryse's stomach was somewhere around her knees. "Yes."

"We'll deal with that in nine months. If we have to."

"Brooks. This is serious."

"I know. I'm *being* serious."

"But…"

"But what? It's not a reality yet. And if it *does* happen that way, I have no doubt that we'll work it out."

"Okay," she managed to get out.

"Okay," he agreed, sounding far surer than she did.

She stared at him. She couldn't help it. He did sound serious. And not the slightest bit worried. A man she'd known less than a day was really telling her—more or less—that he didn't mind if she wound up pregnant.

"Ready?" he asked again.

She nodded, took a breath, tried for her own sake to lighten things. "Well. At least we have a thing."

"A thing?"

"You know. Pretending to be a couple so no one asks questions."

She expected him to laugh. Instead, he shook his head.

"You're wrong," he said.

"About that being our thing?"

"Oh, we have a thing."

"But that's not it?"

"Nope. Nothing *pretend* about us being a couple."

Then he leaned across the console and gave her a kiss. Firm. Possessive. Desire-inducing in spite of her recent satiation. And without another word—but with a small, pleased smile on his face—he put the car into Drive and pulled out onto the road.

Chapter 16

The quickness of the rest of the trip surprised Maryse, as did the lack of awkwardness and the ease of conversation. In no time, she knew that Brooks was an only child who'd become a cop because his dad and grandfather were both cops, too. She learned that his father had lost his life in the line of duty when Brooks was just twenty, and that his mother had succumbed to cancer a few short years later. His traveling had been limited to the continental US—and now Canada—and he'd once won a hot dog–eating contest. Most significantly, she discovered that it wasn't strange for him to place *her* into his life.

Like when he said, "I've got this insane orange tree in my backyard, and people always tell me it should be dead. But every September—totally off-season—it grows exactly eleven oranges. Best damned things I've tasted, and ten American dollars says you'll think so, too." It didn't seem odd to believe that in five months, they'd be sitting by his pool, eating a homegrown piece of fruit.

He was visibly pleased to hear that she worked a portable job, and he told her data entry was probably more enjoyable in a palm-lined sunroom than in a freezing-cold living room. And it should've been scary. Or at least mildly intimidating. She should've been wondering if she was riding some kind of adrenaline-endorphin-pheromone high. Instead, she was assuming every bit of it would come true.

And the best parts were the ones that included Camille.

When Brooks told her his pool had a slide, and he was glad someone would finally want to use it, her heart swelled. His questions about her daughter's favorite foods and color preferences were endearing. And maybe it should've seemed presumptuous—both on his part and on hers—but it really just seemed exciting. All of it made Maryse long for the ordeal to be over so they could get on with a life that hadn't even been on her radar as of that morning.

By the time they made it into the airport and through customs, she was practically bouncing with anticipation. She couldn't even muster up any subtlety, and as they boarded the plane, the woman at the ticket counter took one look at them and laughed.

"If you two don't come back married," she said, "I'll eat my left shoe."

Maryse blushed as Brooks pulled her a little closer and replied, "I hope you packed something other than that for dinner, then."

"I always know," said the attendant, then handed back their passports. "I've moved you up to business class. I like to do that for the ones I'm sure are going to make it. Good luck!"

"Thanks."

He led her up the gangway with his fingers threaded through hers, and she swore he was whistling under his breath.

When they reached their seats—sixth row—he ushered her in first, then raised an eyebrow. "So?"

"What?"

"You wanna talk wedding dresses, or plan the details of our trip?"

"Very funny. But the wedding wasn't my idea."

"Doesn't every girl dream of a white dress and a bouquet?" he teased.

She wrinkled her nose. "Vegas is more about Elvis impersonators and short skirts, isn't it? And besides that, *I* was never one of those girls."

"Never?"

"Nope."

He studied her face. "I'm not sure I believe you."

Her face heated. "Why would I lie?"

"Because discussing flower arrangements with a man you just met might make him think you're a crazy person?"

She opened her mouth to argue, but the flight attendant stepped between the rows just then to give his safety speech. Maryse watched the demonstration with exaggerated interest, trying not to give in to the sudden doubt that was creeping in.

Because this is *crazy*, she thought, not daring to hazard a glance his way. *And when it's over...*

She swallowed. When it was over, it would make sense for them to go their separate ways. In spite of the infatuation-fueled plans for the future, and no matter what the psychic, shoe-eating woman at the counter said, she and Brooks led very different lives. He was a cop. He put his life on the line every day. Deliberately. She, on the other hand, spent her days *hiding.* Not exactly living in fear, but definitely being careful to stay off the radar. He was guns. She was board games.

Beyond the obvious chemistry, were they even compatible?

As the flight attendant finished his last seat-belt click and the plane started to taxi up the runway, Maryse kept her eyes forward. She hoped that Brooks would drop the marriage discussion. He didn't. Instead, he reached over and took her hand.

"You don't have to pretend with me," he said.

"It's not that I'm pretending," she replied.

"You've never thought about a fairy-tale wedding?"

"When I was a kid I thought about it, I guess." She frowned. "Or maybe just the *being* married part. Not the getting there."

Brooks smiled. "Always the Elvis type, then?"

"Always the realist type," she corrected.

"So a white dress isn't realistic?"

"I don't know."

He squeezed her hand. "You can wear a fire-engine-red miniskirt if you want."

She suddenly felt like she was going to cry. "It's not that I'm jaded."

"I know."

"Do you?"

"Of course I do, sweetheart. You took in a baby, no questions asked. You did it without looking back." He leaned closer and spoke into her ear. "And when that kid went missing, you dropped everything to chase her down. You're so far from jaded that it's not even funny."

She darted a nervous glance at the passenger in the row across from them, then leaned back and freed her hands so she could sign. *I thought we weren't talking about that on the plane.*

It seems like maybe we should, he said back. *At least to make a plan.*

Underneath them, the floor shuddered. The sound of the powerful engines filled the cabin. Then the speed picked up, the noise masking the increased thump of Maryse's heart. The rev continued for another few minutes before the plane leveled out in the air.

She turned back to Brooks. *This scares me.*

Are we back to the wedding? he asked. *Or are we still talking about your daughter?*

"They're connected, aren't they?" she said aloud.

"Ah."

"What?"

Brooks shook his head slightly, and a moment later the flight attendant stopped his cart beside them and smiled down. "Complimentary wine?"

"No, thank you," said Maryse at the same second that Brooks said, "Yes, please."

The flight attendant laughed. "Which'll it be?"

"No," said Brooks right as Maryse said, "Yes."

He set down two plastic glasses. "I'll just leave these both here."

This time, they spoke in unison. "Thank you."

The flight attendant grinned. "You're welcome."

Maryse waited until he'd moved a little farther up the aisle, then lifted the cup. "It's like this."

"It's like cheap champagne?"

She took a tiny sip. "This is the first taste of alcohol I've had since my twenty-first birthday."

He gave her a scrutinizing look. "You were twenty-one when Camille was born."

"I was."

"So you put your life on hold."

She shook her head. "No."

Surprise crossed his features. "No?"

"No. I just adjusted. Quickly. I started a *new* life. And I never looked back. Never regretted it. *That's* how I am."

"Sweetheart… I don't think you're as much of a realist as *you* think you are." He said it with a smile.

"What do you mean?"

"You labeled yourself a planner, but you're actually really good at dealing with the unexpected. You avoid thinking of yourself as spontaneous, but I haven't once seen you back down from a challenge, and you've met everything that's been thrown your way with a creative solution. And the whole time, you've just *known* it's going to work out. You're an idealist, Maryse."

She blinked at him, wondering how he managed to see her so much better than she saw herself. "So maybe my real *is* ideal."

"Maybe."

Her hands flicked, asking a weighted question. *Is that a bad thing?*

No, Brooks replied. *I just wish you'd toss some of that idealism my way.*

What?

Assume that I'm going to work out, too. Even if it scares you.

She breathed in, then took another sip of the wine. She let it fill her mouth, the bubbles dancing across her tongue as her thoughts danced through her head. Every time she let her guard down, she *did* assume things were going to go the right way. It was only when she stopped to think that she started to doubt. And while she was sure some skepticism was necessary—that blind optimism wasn't the answer—there was something to be said for trusting her instincts, too. Wasn't there?

Brooks's hand closed overtop of hers. "You're thinking so hard that you're going to break the cup and waste the free win."

She looked down and saw that she'd bent the plastic almost in half. "Whoops."

"I'll cut you a deal," he said, freeing the wine from her grasp. "You give us the benefit of the doubt, and I'll spend every moment proving it's worth it."

"Every moment until when?"

He lifted his hand to her chin. "Every moment of forever."

Her breath caught at the intense look in his eyes. "Now who's the crazy one dreaming of white dresses?"

He winked, and he dropped his hands to move them through the air. *I'm the Elvis type, actually.*

She couldn't help but smile. *Of course you are.*

"So do we have a deal? You'll stop worrying about us so that we can concentrate on making sure we get the rest of our puzzle pieces put together?" Once again, his hazel gaze was unwavering.

"Yes." Maryse nodded, and the word was like a weight lifting off her shoulders. "So what now?"

"Now...I put my arm around you. Then you put your head on my chest. And you take a nap."

"A nap?"

"Yep. Because once we get to Vegas, it might be a long time before we get to rest again."

"I somehow doubt I'm going to be able to sleep."

"Don't underestimate the comfort level of my chest." To emphasize his words, he lifted his arm, draped it over her and pulled her close. "Try it."

"I don't think I can."

But a yawn escaped her lips anyway. And he felt safe. And warm. And after just a few short minutes, Maryse felt herself slipping away in spite of her protests.

Once he was sure Maryse was asleep, Brooks closed his own eyes. Not to rest, but to give himself some time to think. He wasn't used to approaching a case without the law on his side, and he needed to come up with a solid plan.

But his body ached. His head throbbed. He *wanted* to sleep, too. And if he was being honest, he wasn't sure where to start. On the one hand, he thought it might be best to just swoop in to Nank's headquarters and demand that he give back the kid. In his experience, directness often worked best. Of course, he had no clue whether or not a headquarters even existed, let alone where it might be. In his pursuit of Nank, they'd managed to examine nearly every facet of People With Paper. Never once had they located a secret lair or the man in question. Brooks had told Maryse that the man was elusive, and he'd meant it. Presumably, he spent time in his varying offices and factories. Damned if Brooks had seen any proof of it.

Probably wouldn't take Cami there, anyway.

Which was a whole other problem.

Under normal circumstances, he would've connected with one of his contacts at McCarren International. He would've put a bulletin out, searching for the girl. Whoever had her was only a few hours ahead at most. They would've been intercepted. Arrested. This would've been over.

But then we'd be taking the chance that the authorities would take Cami away.

He knew it wasn't a risk Maryse was willing to take. Which meant it wasn't one he was willing to take, either.

His gaze dropped down to sweep over her face. Had he just seen it for the first time this morning? It seemed impossible. She'd quickly wound her way into his heart. The thought of doing something that would drive her away— like placing a call that would endanger her future with her daughter—dug into him. He swept a strand of hair off her cheek. In sleep, she looked more peaceful than she had in any of the last twelve hours they'd spent together. Still beautiful, but less pristine. Not that she'd been pristine in the front seat of his rental car.

Brooks couldn't help but grin at the memory. *Pristine? Hell, no. She was downright wanton.*

He couldn't say he didn't like it. Or that he didn't want

to see that side of her again. Preferably sooner rather than later.

All the more reason to stop thinking in circles and come up with a workable plan, he reminded himself.

He sighed and pushed a soft kiss onto her forehead. Deciding maybe a bit of movement would help, he eased his arm free, unbuckled, then stood and stretched.

The flight attendant appeared immediately. "Can I help you with anything, sir?"

"Just point me toward the restroom."

"Straight up the aisle, just before the curtain, little room with the toilet."

"Hard to miss."

"Yes, sir."

"Thanks."

Brooks picked his way past the other business-class passengers, turning over the options—and complications—in his mind. Ruling out the direct confrontation meant they needed to go for something more subtle. Which in turn meant they needed to know exactly where Camille was being held.

"Impossible without someone on the inside," he muttered.

And his last two informants—Jean-Paul and the girl who'd got involved with the captain's favorite rookie—were both dead.

He stopped in front of the bathroom door and scowled at the little red Occupied sign, then stepped back to wait. As he did, he bumped the curtain that separated the front of the plane from the back. His eyes flicked to the little opening. Then they locked on a familiar face.

Dee White.

The sight of her stunned him so badly that he couldn't even blink. She was cleaner than the last time they'd run into her, her clothes tidy and conservative. A square bandage covered the bruise on her head. None of it really mattered. What *did* matter was how the hell she'd managed to get on their plane and why the hell she continued to be so persistent.

Forgoing a need for caution—and trusting that she'd have a need to *not* cause a scene on the flight—he pushed through the curtains, strode up the more crowded aisle, then seated himself in the empty seat beside her.

"Hello there, Dee. Funny to see you here," he said through gritted teeth.

She moved like she was going to stand, but he closed a hand to her wrist and held it firmly to the armrest between their seats.

"We need to chat."

"It's not what you think."

"I can't say what I think because of our current location, but I guarantee you it's not pretty." He relaxed his face into a phony smile as another cheerful flight attendant passed by. "One thing I can say, though, is that you're awfully good at following us."

"Listen. Brooks—"

"So you know who I am."

She sucked in a breath. "You told me."

"No, I didn't."

"Then *she* must've said your name in front of me."

"Possibly." He flicked a cool look her way. "But I doubt that's it."

She leaned a little closer, and he could see the sheen of sweat on her upper lip as she spoke. "I'd tell you more. But I can't."

"All I want to know right now is whether or not you're alone."

"I am."

"If you're lying…"

"I'm not lying," she said quickly.

"Where's Greg?" Brooks wanted to know.

"He's not good at blending in."

"I'm sure."

"He would've got made in a second." She licked her lips nervously. "The guy in the blue suit…two rows up… He's an air marshal."

"Uh-huh."

"He is."

He shook his head. "At this point, I don't care if he's the president himself. I just want you to know that when we get off the plane, I'll be waiting."

She opened her mouth again, but Brooks didn't want to hear what she had to say. He just wanted to get away from her. To get back to Maryse, and to give himself time to think a bit more. So he spun away and moved back up to business class with as little fuss as possible. Already, a plan was forming in his mind. Dee knew Nank personally. She could be bought, her loyalty swayed. He knew that for a fact, as evidenced by her actions with Cami. She *wanted* a ransom. She would've taken it from Maryse, who would've given it.

Brooks paused beside their row, staring down at her. He knew she was willing to pay. She'd flat-out said so. But he was leery of asking her. Mostly because he knew she'd jump at anything that could possibly help. It would give her even more hope, and she'd fall that much harder if Dee let them down. Which she might do.

He slid in his seat, and Maryse shifted a little and blinked up at him.

"Everything okay?" she murmured.

"Yep. Just fine, sweetheart. A few more hours. Go back to sleep."

"You sure?"

"Mmm-hmm. Nothing to worry about until we land."

"Okay."

He gave her a squeeze and shoved aside a tickle of guilt in favor of enjoying the way she fit so perfectly beside him. He *would* tell her his idea. But not until he had to.

Chapter 17

A squawking voice dragged Maryse from a deep sleep. For a minute, she was disoriented. Then Brooks's hand tightened on her shoulder, and she remembered.

The plane. Cami.

Her heart dropped, and she sucked in a breath.

"We're on the ground." Brooks's voice was low and somehow reassuring in spite of the fact that he hadn't really said anything significant.

"I missed the landing?"

"Well. It was a smooth one," he teased.

"Must've been."

"We're one step closer to Camille. And I've got something to show you."

"To show me?"

"Yep. I was going to explain, but I thought it was better this way."

"Okay," she said cautiously.

Something about the brightness of his words made her nerves flutter. Not that she didn't trust him. But she was pretty sure he'd make an effort to disguise his own worry in an attempt to assuage hers. She opted for waiting it out and threaded her fingers through his as the captain announced they were ready to deplane.

Brooks didn't add anything, either. He just pulled her to

her feet, then led her quickly into the airport. But the second their feet hit the carpet, he stopped short and turned her to face the rest of the passengers, and she knew her trepidation was valid.

"What are we waiting for?" she asked, dreading the answer.

He gave her hand a squeeze and inclined his head. "That."

Maryse felt the blood drain from her face as she spotted the petite woman exiting just then. "That's Dee White."

"Yes, it is," he murmured back.

The other woman looked up. She met Maryse's gaze and blinked nervously before nodding once at Brooks. Then she stepped forward, bumped her foot on a ridge in the floor and dropped her purse, spilling the contents.

As she bent to pick everything up, Maryse used the opportunity to squeeze Brooks's hand back—hard—and ask, "You *knew* she was on the plane?"

"Yeah. I talked to her while you slept."

"And you didn't wake me up?"

"I didn't want to worry you."

"Well. I'm worried *now*."

"She's going to help us."

"How? Why?"

He bent down and spoke close to her ear. "She knows Nank, sweetheart. She's our only in. All we need her to do is find where they're holding Cami. And as far as why is concerned…she's not much more than a mercenary. For the right price…"

"And why would we trust her?"

"We wouldn't. We won't."

She tipped her head up, watching him watch Dee guardedly. "So…"

"She knows I'm a cop."

"What?"

"I'm pretty damned sure she knows, anyway. So. You're going to offer to pay her, and I'm going to offer to keep her out of jail."

"Can you do that?"

"Possibly. But all that matters is *she* believes it."

"Unless she decides to sue you for not following through."

"Fine. I'll just promise to *try* and keep her out of jail."

Maryse couldn't quite muster up a laugh. Especially not when she realized that Dee had finished fishing her items from the ground and was now headed their way. Though the other woman held her head straight ahead, her eyes darted nervously around the airport.

It made Maryse more nervous herself. So much so that she didn't notice the four uniformed men until they were already brushing past. Brooks slid his hand down her arm and tugged her away.

"Brooks," she hissed. "What's going on?"

"Look. Subtly."

She tipped her head just as one of the men slapped a pair of cuffs onto Dee's wrists.

"What are they doing?" she asked.

"Taking her in."

"I can see that. But for *what*?"

"Who knows? I'm sure there's a list."

"But—" She cut herself off as the police moved by again.

Two cleared the way while the other two held Dee's arms. The petite woman kept her head down as they passed.

"This is bad," Brooks said. "And not just because she can't help us."

"She knows who you are."

"And she can identify *you*."

"And…oh, God. She knows about Cami." Dizziness hit

Maryse hard as she realized how much more precarious their already-precarious situation had become.

"C'mon. We need to get our bags and get moving."

"To where?"

"Anywhere but here."

They made it all the way to the carousel. But just as the bags from their flights started dropping, Brooks's phone chimed, and when he pulled it out and glanced at the screen, Maryse knew it wasn't good news.

"What's wrong?" she asked.

"A text message from my partner."

"What does it say?"

"It says 'look up.'"

"What does that mean?"

Slowly, Brooks lifted his head. Maryse followed his gaze. At first, she saw nothing. But as she continued to stare, she spotted a flurry of activity just past the throng of people waiting for their luggage. Passengers and their families parted to make room for yet another set of uni- formed police, these ones moving with the subtlety of a herd of rhinos.

Brooks drew in a noisy breath and spoke grimly. "That's my captain and his favorite group of men."

"I thought you said they didn't work out of Vegas."

"They don't." His phone pinged another message, and he glanced down, then back up again, scanning one side of the airport.

"What did that one say?" Maryse asked, trying again to see what he saw.

"'Look left.' And there he is. Come on."

He didn't wait for her to answer, or mention the bags they were leaving behind. He just grabbed ahold of her hand again and tugged her along. He swiped sideways, out of view of the oncoming officers, then ducked into the crowd. He pulled and pulled, and for a while, she thought their weaving path was random. But after a few minutes, she realized that the same man had been ahead of them the whole time. Dressed in khakis, a T-shirt and pulled-down ball cap, he moved along at a pace that was just too fast to be called meandering.

They moved through several crowds of people and past multiple baggage carousels. They went through a hall and curved into a newspaper kiosk. Pretty soon, Maryse was lost. Which she guessed was the intent behind the whole thing. She wasn't sure she could've found her way back to their starting point for a million dollars.

But at last, the crowd thinned. For a second, the man in khakis was nowhere to be seen, but as they rounded a corner and Brooks slowed, Maryse spotted him again. He'd moved through a set of wide automatic doors and stood on the other side, his elbow resting on the roof of an off-duty taxi. He inclined his head slightly in their direction as they hurried toward the door themselves, and then he climbed into the driver's seat.

As they followed outside, Maryse inhaled. Factoring in the five-hour flight and the time difference, it had to be about midnight. But the air was warm and dry even though it was fully dark, and the city lights illuminated the horizon. She knew that if they got closer to the strip itself, the time wouldn't matter. It was one of the few things that she remembered clearly from her last trip—that strange feeling that no one in Vegas ever slept.

Everything else about those few days was a blur, drowned out by her new reality. She'd been terrified and alone except for a very tiny, very quiet Camille. She hadn't yet figured out that the near-silence came from the newborn's deafness. She hadn't yet figured out *anything*. The world had seemed too big, and her prospects were dim.

"You all right, sweetheart?"

She glanced up and realized she'd stopped just a few steps from the cab. Brooks was looking down at her with a concerned expression on his face, clearly waiting for her to answer.

"I'm fine," she said.

"You sure?"

"Yes."

"Okay, sweetheart." Brooks let go of her hand, offered her a smile, then kissed her lightly before opening the back door and signing, *Welcome to Vegas*.

Nervous, but trusting him nonetheless, she slid into the backseat. He followed, and in seconds, they were moving out of the terminal and toward the lights.

For several minutes, the inside of the cab was quiet. Brooks could practically feel the questions building up in his partner's mind. Could almost see them adding more gray to the man's salt-and-pepper hair. They'd worked together for four years, and though they were very different men, this was the first time he'd felt the need to keep anything from Masters.

Not your secrets to tell, he reminded himself.

Which was why he needed to approach things carefully. And he had his own questions, too. Like how his partner had known he'd be at the airport, and why their mutual boss was there, too.

The other man broke the silence first, his near-black gaze boring into Brooks. "Hey, Small?"

He braced himself. "Yeah, Masters?"

"Did you call her 'sweetheart'?"

"That's what you're going with?"

"Seems pretty significant considering just this morning you told me there were zero pretty girls up there in Canada."

"I took your advice and found one."

"She *is* pretty."

"Sure is."

"And I'm guessing she's calling the shots."

Brooks relaxed, just a little. "You guess right."

Masters paused, then glanced in the rearview mirror, his eyes on Maryse. "Hi, honey."

"Sweetheart," she corrected, making Brooks grin.

"Maryse, meet my partner, Shepherd Masters," he said. "Masters, this is Maryse."

His partner tipped his hat. "Miss. Must've pulled a hell of a good trick to get this guy to break this many rules."

"Does he usually follow them?"

Masters's shoulders lifted up and down. "He usually follows at least a *few* at a time."

"I didn't ask for his help." Maryse didn't sound defensive—just honest.

"Not surprised at all. He's stubbornly helpful. 'Specially when it comes to things that involve Caleb Nank."

Brooks's mouth twisted. "Subtle segue."

"Not a lot of time to be subtle." Masters threw another glance at Maryse. "It's fine if you don't want to tell me how it ties together, but I sure as hell wouldn't *mind* knowing why I'm taking risks with my career to save your butts."

Maryse's hand slipped across the car to slide into Brooks's palm. "You trust him."

It was a statement rather than a question, but he nodded anyway. "A hundred percent."

"Then I do, too."

"Girlfriend seal of approval," Masters said.

Brooks knew his partner had dropped the label to irritate him. Or possibly just to get a read on his reaction. It didn't bother him at all. In fact, it felt right.

Or maybe not quite strong enough, he admitted.

He stole a glance at Maryse. Just a look was enough to make his chest squeeze. Yeah, she was definitely more than a girlfriend.

Brooks cleared his throat. "Tell me what's happening on your end, Masters."

"You mean how did I devolve from being a perfectly sane cop this morning to being a taxi thief tonight?"

"Exactly."

His friend tossed the ball cap aside and gave his head a scratch, then sighed. "Well. I was thinking about you coming home…"

"Pining for me?" Brooks interjected.

"Can you shut up for a few seconds?"

"Probably not."

His partner shot him a dirty look over his shoulder. "Anyway. It was bugging me a bit. So I went to the captain this afternoon and asked him if you'd be back anytime soon. He got kinda buggy. Not like him at all. Nervous, you know? So I stuck around the station, thinking something was up."

"You spied on the captain?"

"Had to."

"I'm impressed."

"I said shut up, right?"

Brooks squeezed Maryse's fingers. She was smiling a little, which was good, because he was damned sure things were about to get a lot darker. Masters was looking at her again, too.

"You sure you want to stick with this guy? He's a serious thorn," he said.

"I'm sure," she said, her voice tinged with amusement.

Masters sighed. "Fine. Your life."

"Back to the spying," Brooks ordered.

"I did some paperwork. Just kinda watched what was going on. The captain was on the phone, mostly. Really sweating. Called a few of his favorite guys in."

"And usually *you're* one of those guys."

"Usually I am. But today I wasn't. So I was thinking about it a little more. You were already on my radar, and also the only thing I could think of that could make the captain *not* want to tell me what was going on. So I hit up Chatty Patty."

"She's one of our desk sergeants," Brooks told Maryse. "Tends to know just about everything."

"Right," Masters agreed. "And she *did* know what was going on. At least enough to tell me it had something to do with Nank and Canada. So then I'm back to the same common denominator."

"Me."

"Yeah. You. Pain in the—"

"I get it. I interrupted your day off. How did you figure out I was coming in on this flight?"

His partner shook his head. "I didn't. The captain came out and sent me home. So I left for a while. But it was bugging me. And you know how I can't let something go if it doesn't feel right, so..."

"So you stole a cab."

"Borrowed one from my cousin. I waited for the captain to put together his unit, then I tailed them here. Wasn't expecting you, actually. From everything I overheard, they were picking up a girl. Got clearance from both the Vegas people and the TSA to come in and grab her."

"Dee White," Maryse said.

"You know who the girl is?" Masters asked.

"We do," Brooks replied.

Maryse frowned. "But that doesn't make sense, does it?"

"No," he agreed. "It doesn't."

"Why the hell not?" his partner wanted to know.

"Because the captain and his guys didn't get to her. TSA grabbed her as she came off the plane," he explained. "Why would they do that if they'd cleared *Rain Falls* to do it?"

Masters tapped his fingers on the wheel while Brooks turned it over in his head. He couldn't see the TSA agreeing to something, then rescinding it with no notice.

"Whoever grabbed her wasn't TSA," he said. "I don't know how they got past all the security, but they did. The captain is going to be pretty damned ticked off."

"So who took her?" Maryse asked.

"My guess is Nank's men."

Her lips pressed together in a tight line for a second. "That's worse, isn't it, than the police having her?"

He ran a frustrated hand over his hair. "It depends on what they want from her. I was assuming Dee had told Nank we were coming. So were they here to rescue her from us? Keep her from talking the way we wanted her to? Or did they do what my sneaky partner here did and intercept the captain's plans? And why the hell did the captain want her in the first place? Does he know about *you*?"

"Lot more questions than answers," Masters said.

"No kidding." Brooks sighed. "We need to regroup."

"I've got a safe house just outside of Rain Falls," his partner told him. "We can use it. If the shot-caller agrees?"

Maryse nodded her assent quickly.

"Good," said Masters. "Now maybe you can tell me a bit about what's happening on *your* end?"

"You mean how I went from a single cop on forced vacation to a stepdad-hopeful on a rogue mission in under twenty-four hours?"

The car jerked to the side as the other man flung his head to the side in surprise. The look on his partner's face might've made Brooks laugh under other circumstances. But right that second, he was having a hard time finding anything funny. All he wanted to do was get to their destination so he could put his police skills to work and bring home the little girl.

Chapter 18

Brooks stared at the little pieces of paper taped to the living room wall. They hadn't moved, or given him any new insight for a good hour, and he could feel a tension headache building up behind his temples. The minutes were ticking by. Each second wasted time that could be spent retrieving Camille.

"I'm getting back to the part where I just want to storm into one of Nank's places with my guns blazing," he muttered, sinking into the couch.

Maryse shifted over to make a little room for him, rubbing her eyes. She'd been growing steadily quieter since he'd disclosed the majority of her story to Masters. Though Brooks had left out a few of the finer points—like the fact that Cami wasn't her biological daughter and that her brother had once been his CI—it had still taken the full forty-mile trip from the airport to Rain Falls to do it. He suspected that hearing it all laid out had taken a new toll on her. The display of information on the wall was overwhelming, too. And not in a good way. Like Masters had said, there were a lot more questions than answers, and at the moment, he honestly wasn't sure what their next move should be.

"Maybe we should take a break," Masters said.

Brooks shook his head. "You know that's not an option."

"What I know is that we're not making any headway. It's two in the morning, your girlfriend looks like she might collapse, and *you* look like hell."

He pinched the bridge of his nose. "We're missing something."

"Yeah. Food and sleep," his partner replied.

"I don't understand the connection between Dee White and our department. That little piece is the key, I can feel it." Brooks sighed. "At least we can more or less rule out the idea that the captain is in Nank's pocket. They wouldn't have *both* shown up if they were working together."

"*That* was an idea?" Masters sounded surprised.

"Just a thought."

"Did you think *I* might be corrupt, too?"

"If I did, would you be in here with me now?"

"Hell. I don't know *what* you're thinking, man. You show up back home, unannounced, a woman in tow, all googly-gaga…so there's a good chance you could've been abducted by aliens and replaced with a robot."

"Googly-gaga?"

"Exactly."

Brooks chuckled and glanced down at Maryse. Her eyes had closed completely, and the soft rise and fall of her chest indicated she'd fallen asleep.

"Just a sec, okay?" he said. "I'm gonna move her to the bedroom."

"I'll bet you are."

"Shut up."

He stood, scooped her up gently, then carried her from the living room to the hall. She was solid against his chest and felt right tucked into his arms. So right that he was truly regretful of having to let her go. He knew she needed the rest, though. The nap on the plane couldn't have done her that much good. She barely stirred as he pulled back the sheets and set her down. When he slipped her boots off her feet, she just curled up her legs and sighed.

"All right, sweetheart." He pulled the blankets around her shoulders and stared down at her for a second. "Hopefully, by the time you wake up, Masters and I have things sorted out enough that we can go rescue that kid of yours."

He gave the window a quick check—locked and secure—then moved back to the living room, where he found his partner standing in front of all the sticky notes, one hand in his back pocket, the other on their mutual boss's name.

"He sent you to Laval on purpose," Masters stated without turning around.

"That's where the corruption speculation came in. But putting aside that theory…"

"Why the hell would he send you there without telling you why?"

"I dunno. Something off the books, maybe?"

"Maybe. But what?"

His partner moved to tap another set of sticky notes. "Dee White. Is she a CI?"

"The thought crossed my mind," Brooks replied.

"But you don't think it fits?"

"We'd have to put aside the fact that *I'm* the one who's run the whole Nank operation from the start."

"So maybe she was a CI in for something unrelated and this just came up coincidentally."

"Cross border?"

"Okay. Maybe the captain wanted some insurance and forgot to tell you about it."

"Forgot?"

"Conveniently."

"Ha." Brooks studied the notes again. "Let's look at it again. We know Dee's been in Laval for at least a year. The concierge at Maison Blanc told Maryse and me that she'd been employed there—legitimately—for that long. So she couldn't have been working with Nank directly during that time. Pretty useless as an informant. Captain wouldn't be able to offer her any perks, either, since she was cross border."

"Fine. Not a CI," said Masters. "You're a real buzzkill, you know that, right?"

"Wild speculation is *your* thing. I'm just here to knock some sense into you."

"Hilarious."

"I thought so."

"Could Dee White be a witness? Or is that, also, too wild?"

"Not wild. But still unlikely." Brooks grabbed another sticky note and added to the increasing pile. "She came here willingly."

Masters shook his head. "You're right. If she was a willing witness, they wouldn't have been trying to grab her. If she was an *un*willing one, she probably wouldn't have chanced coming at all."

"Why wouldn't she keep running? Why not do what she said she'd been doing already and get out again? Nank's men left her behind once they had Cami. She was in the clear."

"Hey, Small?"

"Yeah?"

"This girl and her daughter…"

"I know. Googly-gaga."

"Hell. You don't even *date*."

Brooks tensed. "Are we really having a heart-to-heart?"

Masters shrugged. "Think it's important to know if my partner's gone off the deep end."

"I'm still on the ledge."

"So reassuring."

"Look. I wasn't planning on going up to Canada and meeting the woman I want to spend my life with, but—"

"Hang on. The *rest of your life*? Did you pull a love-at-first-sight deal?"

Brooks ran a hand over his short hair and said nothing. *Love.* The word hadn't come into his mind. Not yet. Or maybe just not consciously. But it sure as hell explained that solid wall of warmth that filled him when he thought her name. It made sense of the way he kept thinking about a future together. So even if he hadn't labeled his feelings yet, there was no denying that love definitely fit.

Masters let out a low whistle. "Well, damn. *Brooks Small.* Who's all wild and crazy now?"

"Didn't I tell you to shut up?"

"Probably. But since when does that do any good?"

"Never."

"You want me to sing the kissing song?"

"I *want* you to help me solve this case."

"So you can go back to kissing?" Masters laughed, then lifted his hands in mock defeat. "I know. Shut up. Back to the case. Back to Dee White."

"Dee White," Brooks agreed firmly.

"Okay. So. Her. Nank. You. The only person who really knows the connection is the captain. He sent you up to Laval. He wanted to get to Dee when she came back to Las Vegas. And the Nank case is on his watch, technically. You're sure he's not in on any kind of conspiracy, so why not call him and ask him?"

"Because it puts Camille and Maryse at risk."

"You want to give me a bit more to go on?"

"I can't. That'd make you culpable."

"Look. The captain doesn't even know you're in Vegas, right? If he did, he wouldn't have let you just walk away at the airport. He would've sent someone to stop you, too."

Masters had a point. There sure as hell wasn't anything easygoing about their boss. If the captain knew he'd come back before his leave was terminated...he would've unleashed the damned hounds. Which meant that he probably didn't know anything about Maryse's presence, either.

"So maybe it wouldn't hurt to call," Masters said. "Even if you just drop a few hints to see if he bites. I can't think of another—quicker—way to find out what we want to know."

Brooks considered it, his eyes sliding to the hall that led to the room where Maryse slept. Then he shook his head slowly.

"I can't, man. I just can't risk doing something that could hurt her. We have to find something else."

They both went silent, staring at the maddening pile of information. After a good minute and a half, Brooks opened his mouth, not even sure what he was going to say, but his partner's stomach growled loudly, beating him to the punch.

"That's it," said Masters. "I'm taking twenty minutes. I'm getting us some pizza. Possibly a beer, if time allows. Do what you want with that time, but my gut is currently in control, and it will remain that way until I've stuffed it with something remarkably unhealthy."

Brooks couldn't help but grin. "Guess I can't argue with that. Just go easy on the anchovies."

"You got it."

He clapped his partner on the back, then walked him out. As he closed the door, he couldn't fight a need to take a breath, metaphorically *and* literally. He paused in the hall and leaned against the wall. He felt like they were even further away from getting back Maryse's daughter. Physically, they might be closer. Being able to *use* that proximity was proving to be difficult.

For the first time, Brooks really wondered if he was going to be able to follow through on his promise to bring

Camille home. He wasn't prone to false bravado. His case closure rate was over 90 percent. He and Masters were at the top of the precinct. At the top of their *game*.

Except where Nank's concerned.

Maybe that was the source of doubt. When he'd first said he could help, he'd assumed this case was a separate entity. Not something he'd failed at in the past, and definitely not anything that could be so closely tied to his own life.

He exhaled in frustration and pushed up from the wall, prepared to get back to work. He stilled, though, as a sudden clatter from the bedroom carried to his ears. With no pretense of calm, he bolted down the hall. He pushed through the door, then stopped. The bed was empty. The pillow was on the floor, and the boots he'd left beside the nightstand were missing.

"Maryse?"

There was no answer. His eyes darted around the room. They landed on the closed en suite bathroom door. He stepped toward it and rattled the handle.

Locked.

She had to be in there, but his panic wouldn't ease.

"Maryse!"

There was still no response. He leaned against the wood. From inside, the beat of water hitting the tub suddenly came to life.

She's showering? Now?

"Answer me, sweetheart," he called, "or I might feel obligated to break down this door."

At Brooks's statement, Maryse tensed. The knife on her throat tightened. And Dee White spoke into her shoulder.

"Don't make a sound," the tiny woman warned, her voice low.

The door thumped, and Brooks's call carried through again. "Maryse, I'm going to count to three!"

"He'll do it," she whispered, careful to move even an eighth of an inch—she'd seen the slice the blade had made when it nicked the shower curtain.

"He'll go away. He thinks you're in the shower."

"He doesn't care if I'm in the shower."

There was a pause. "It's like that?"

"Yes."

Another bang. "Two!"

The knife eased just a tiny bit. "Tell him you're fine. Make him believe it."

She let out a breath, then took another and called, "Brooks?"

"Sweetheart?" His reply was puzzled. "You all right?"

"Perfect," she lied. "Just…cleaning up."

"You sure you're okay?"

Maryse forced a laugh. "Aside from the fact that I'm trying to rinse while talking to you?"

She could feel his doubt almost as strongly as she could feel the knife. "As long as you're fine."

"I'll be out soon." She felt tears sting her eyes as she misled him yet again.

"All right," he called back. "Masters is bringing some pizza."

"Sounds good."

The other side of the door went silent. For several seconds, Dee held still behind her, the knife at her throat. Then she relaxed her hold and stepped back.

"We're going to have to go out the window," she stated.

"Out?"

"Did you think we were going to stay here?"

"I—"

"You what?"

"I don't know."

Minutes earlier, Maryse had woken with fear gripping her. She's assumed it had been about Cami. About waking up in a strange place. But as she'd started to sit up, the petite woman had leaned over her. At first glance, Maryse hadn't even recognized her. The long blond ponytail was gone, and in its place a short, dark bob. The grubby clothes had been traded in, too, for a pair of pin-striped pants and a crisp blouse. The woman had dusted her face with subtle makeup and didn't look in the slightest like a career criminal.

Then she'd uttered the first threat, and Maryse knew exactly who she was dealing with. She attempted to fight back with kicks and screams. The effort had earned her a blanket in the mouth and the weapon on her neck. She hadn't had *time* to think about what the other woman wanted or what she was going to push her to do.

But leaving...

She cast a desperate look toward the door. And Dee caught it right away.

"I can get to him, too," she said. "And if that doesn't motivate you enough, then keep this in mind... I know where they're holding your daughter and I'm willing to help you get there if you don't tell Detective Small where we're going."

Maryse's attention whipped away from the door, her mind stalling, then starting. "What?"

"Camille. I know where she is. And I'll take you."

"How do I know you're not lying? Or setting a trap?"

"I'll make you a deal. I'll tell you my story on the drive, and if you don't believe me, I'll let you out and you can walk away. I give you my word. One mother to another."

"*You* have kids?"

"I did," the woman corrected.

Oh, God.

Maryse didn't like the pointed way she'd said it, and she couldn't think of a properly sympathetic reply for the woman who'd held her own daughter captive. But Dee didn't seem to want one anyway.

"Your boots are there by the sink. All you have to do is put them on and follow me. But we really only have a few minutes," she said.

A few minutes until what? Maryse wanted to ask.

But the other woman was done talking, at least for the moment. She was already tucking the knife into her boot and moving toward the window. And as she climbed onto the toilet, she didn't even look back. She just slid the window all the way open, clambered up and jumped out. Maryse waited for her to call through the opening. But the only sounds were the continuing rush of the shower and Dee's boots crunching on the ground outside.

"Dammit," she said under her breath.

It was wrong to leave Brooks. Really, really wrong. She knew it deep down in her gut. But the chance to see Camille—even if it was slim—couldn't just be put aside. She wished she had a lipstick in her pocket so she could scrawl a note across the mirror. He would understand, if he knew. Subconsciously, she dragged a hand to her pocket. Then she remembered.

Quickly, she stuck her hand inside and dragged out the passport-sized photograph of her daughter. The one that she'd grabbed from Dee's house and had been carrying around ever since as some kind of talisman. She squeezed the little photograph for a moment, examining the details of Cami's solemn face, so unlike her usual smiling self. She traced the outline of her soft, sweet cheek, then lifted the picture up and stuck it to the corner of the mirror.

Please understand, she said silently as she slipped on her boots and climbed onto the back of the toilet.

Swallowing a need to look back, she made her way up and out. She landed without much grace—one hand and one knee smacking the ground—on the rocks below the windowsill. She couldn't quite hold in a pain-filled yelp as a particularly sharp stone dug into her palm. When she lifted it to look, a bruise was already forming around a small puncture.

Dee's hand appeared in front of her face, stretched out in an ironic offer of assistance. Maryse took it anyway and let herself be helped up. She was just glad that the safe house happened to be a rancher. If she'd had to jump from a second-story window, she would've broken a few bones, she was sure.

"You okay?" the other woman wanted to know.

Maryse shot her a look. "Really?"

At least she looked contrite. "What I meant was…did you hurt yourself?"

"I'm fine."

Dee opened her mouth, closed it, then shook her head and said, "Keep to the edge of the house. I don't want your boyfriend to look out and decide to perform a rescue mission."

"All right."

She slunk along beside the diminutive woman, feeling as much like a rat as she must look like one. She kept going anyway, moving along stealthily until her foot smacked into something solid. A quick glance down made her gasp. The object in question was a boot. And the boot was attached to Masters, who was splayed out in the bushes beside the house.

Alarmed, Maryse lifted her eyes to Dee.

"Relax," said the other woman. "He's alive."

"What did you do to him?"

"Chloroform."

"What?"

"I just knocked him out. He'll have a headache, that's all. Come on."

They picked their way along the edge of the yard to the unconscious man's borrowed taxi, and Dee yanked a set of keys from her pocket, then moved to the driver's side door, where she paused.

"Last chance to back out."

Maryse met the other woman's eyes. "You just threatened to kill me, offered to take me to my daughter, and now you're giving me a chance to back out?"

"I threatened you, but I didn't threaten to *kill* you," Dee corrected. "But where I'm taking you…your life will definitely be on the line."

"Like it hasn't been on the line for the last day?"

"This is different."

"What about Brooks?"

"His presence would *guarantee* your death. So…" Dee gestured toward the car. "It's up to you."

"I'm coming."

"Good."

Dee motioned for her to climb in. Still leery—and more than a bit confused now—she followed the directions and slid into the passenger seat. Before she even got her seat belt buckled, the car was rolling out of the driveway. For several blocks, they drove in silence. But after a few minutes, Maryse couldn't keep quiet.

"Why are you helping me?" she asked.

"Do you have a cell phone?"

"Yes."

"Toss it."

"Pardon me?"

"Toss it."

"But…"

Dee's hands were practically white-knuckled on the steering wheel. "Listen. You want my help. You *need* it. And you have no reason to trust me. But if I'm going to tell you anything, I need to do it in a way that puts us both in as little danger as possible."

Maryse bit her lip, then reached into her pocket. The phone was a lifeline. But it wasn't what was going to help her get to Cami. So she rolled down the window, took a breath, then threw the slim device straight out. She pretended that the clatter as it hit the pavement didn't make her pulse spike.

"Okay," said Dee. "I'm going to talk fast because we only have a short drive before we get changed and get into character."

"Into character?"

The other woman ignored her puzzled question. "So the first thing that I should probably tell you is that my name isn't really Dee White, and I'm not a criminal."

"Who are you?"

"The important thing isn't *who* I am. It's *what*."

"What?" Maryse was starting to feel like a parrot.

"I'm a fraud investigator." Dee shook her head. "Or maybe I should say *was*. Because I sure as hell doubt I'm going to have a job when this is all said and done."

Chapter 19

Dee sped through the streets quickly, her mouth working almost as fast as the wheels beneath them, and Maryse worked to follow along with what she was saying.

"Before this, I was a bank manager for almost a decade. A few years back, though, my family was targeted. The victims of fraud. We did everything right. Filed all the reports, redid all the paperwork. But somewhere along the line, things got crossed. The person who took our identity was a bad guy, to say the least. But he was involved with some even worse people. Those people got ahold of our address, thinking it was his, and…" Dee lifted a hand to her mouth and chewed on a nail before clearing her throat and going on. "They came to the house. They killed my husband and my son. They would've killed me, too, but I happened to be out that night for a girls' night."

For the first time, Maryse softened toward the other woman. She still didn't trust her—how could she?—but Dee's carefully schooled expression made her sure that at least some of the story was true.

"I'm sorry."

"Me, too. Every day. And that's what motivated me to try and find a way to move on. To help other people."

"And that's why you became a fraud investigator?"

"Yep. I tried to go after a police job at first, but they rejected me. Told me to take some time and figure out if I was just trying to get revenge or if it was a career path I really wanted to follow," Dee said. "So I spent a year—*another* year, actually—in therapy, working through things. Nothing changed. I came back to the police. They still sent me away. So I took some courses, became certified and landed a job with a company that works right alongside the police anyway. I stayed behind the scenes for a long time. Then this opportunity came up. The hotel was suspicious of one of their employees. So they set me up at the hotel, tracking this guy."

"Greg?"

"Uh-huh. They couldn't seem to catch him in the act, and they wanted me to do it. But it was supposed to be simple. Go in, get to know him a bit, figure out what he was up to, then hand over the info to the hotel manager. Turned out to be more complicated than that. It was his brother and his sister-in-law masterminding the whole thing. Moving the stolen IDs across the border. Took me about three months to even get in tight enough that he was willing to let me know what was going on. One day, he invited me to come to a meeting. I didn't think it was going to be a big deal. I had just about everything I needed from them already, but I went along anyway because I thought they might be suspicious if I didn't. I guess we were supposed to meet the guy who handled the transport of the physical IDs—passports and driver's licenses, stuff like that—when all of a sudden this other guy shows up." Dee tapped the steering wheel and shook her head. "Caleb Nank. It turned out that Greg's brother had double-crossed him and stolen a bunch of his business. And he really did tell Greg that the kid belonged to him."

"So that story you told us at your house…"

"Was more or less true. I'm not ashamed to admit that I was in over my head. I wanted to shut it down."

"So why didn't you walk away?" Maryse wondered aloud.

"Nank. He didn't trust Greg or his brother. He *really* didn't trust the wife. Which meant he didn't trust *me*. He had us all tailed, 24/7. And one day, Greg's sister-in-law didn't come home. She'd been talking nonstop about going to the police or just plain running."

"But you don't think she did?"

"Not a chance. We couldn't prove anything, but we were all sure Nank had her permanently taken care of. You know…there's just something about the man. He's smart but cruel, and nothing gets by him. Ever."

For a second, Dee sounded almost like she admired the man. But then she shivered, and Maryse remembered that Brooks had said something similar.

The other woman swallowed, her eyes a little too bright. "I knew if I didn't want to wind up like Greg's sister-in-law, I'd either have to go into hiding or I'd have to bust Nank himself. But it was so complicated. He doesn't live there, and aside from the one visit, he never came back. Just sent his men up to collect the IDs. I didn't have any cross-border connections, and I couldn't find a way to get out without getting caught by Nank. God knows I didn't want to wind up living somewhere in police protection."

"So when did my daughter come into the equation?" Maryse made herself ask.

"About a month ago, Greg came to me and told me he had a way out for the three of us. He didn't really explain what it was. Just said it would get Nank off our backs permanently. It gave me a bad feeling from the beginning, but I wasn't expecting Greg to show up with a kid. And when he did…"

"You panicked."

"Understatement of the year. I made the guys leave Camille with me while they searched for an out. I wanted to just bring her home to you."

"But they wouldn't let you?"

"*I* wouldn't let me. If Nank didn't already know where you lived, he would now. I was sure he was still having us watched. If I sent her back, he'd just find someone else to take her again. Or worse."

Dee paused, and Maryse was sure she was thinking of her own child. Her heart squeezed, sympathy taking root, even as she tried to fight it in the name of remaining aloof.

"Thank you for trying to keep her away from him," she said softly.

"I failed," the other woman said with a headshake. "When Greg called me and said you were at the hotel, I knew we were in trouble. I sent his brother to get you."

"But he got shot."

"Yes. And then your hero dived onto the scene. I didn't know he was a cop. God. I don't even know *what* I thought. Greg was going nuts, and I just knew I had to get your kid out of there. I started to make the passports. I thought maybe if I could just take her away from the city, I could make sure she was safe. I failed again. When I was getting things ready, Nank's guys came to the house to take her. I fought them as best as I could, but they knocked me out and left me for dead. The next thing I remember is waking up out near the garden shed and seeing your cop friend there, sneaking around."

"You could've said something then."

"It was stupid not to. But I was scared," the other woman said. "I was ashamed. And defensive. I let you—another mom—down completely. Worse than that, even. And I still didn't know your guy was a cop. But once I ran out and finally calmed down, I realized I'd made an even bigger mistake in not helping you."

"So you followed us?"

"I went and got Greg from the hotel. I talked him into using his resources to track the license plate from the car you guys were in. From there, he figured out that Brooks Small was a detective. He was able to get Brooks's cell phone number and track the location. That's how we got to you. I thought our plan was just to find you and tell you everything we knew about Nank."

"Until Greg pulled a gun."

"I swear I didn't know about that. I mean, I was obviously aware that his character wasn't the best to start out with, but I didn't think he'd go around shooting people. I couldn't go to the local cops because Nank was still watching. So I contacted Rain Falls PD, where your detective works, and I begged them to pick me up. But Nank figured out that I was coming to town and he beat them to it."

Maryse leaned back against the seat and closed her eyes. She wasn't sure what to make of Dee's story. She didn't want to believe it. Not all of it, anyway. But if the woman really did know where Nank was holding Cami, she couldn't walk away. In fact, she couldn't even consider it.

She opened her eyes. "So what now?"

"Now I take you to him."

"To Nank?" Maryse's heart skittered nervously.

The other woman inclined her head once. "Nank knows you're working with Brooks because Greg told him. But the one thing we have going for us is that he doesn't know who *I* am. He still thinks I'm just an angry identity thief who was trying to rip him off."

"And he thinks you have something to prove."

"Actually…he thinks I took you at knifepoint from the safe house and that I'm taking you there now."

"Which you did. And which you are."

"Yes. But he doesn't know that I'm helping you. Which is why I need you to put on a convincing act."

"By doing what?"

"Letting me make it look real."

Maryse took several slow breaths. Then nodded. Something was off. But once again, she couldn't argue. She didn't see herself as having another choice.

Brooks paced the length of the living room for what had to be the hundredth time. He half expected to look down and see a path worn through the rug. He glanced up to the door, waiting. Masters hadn't turned up with the pizza yet, and Maryse seemed to be taking an extra-long time in the shower. In fact, he didn't know how the water couldn't be ice-cold.

He paced again. Then paused. Since knocking on the bathroom door, his stomach had been churning. Something was off but he couldn't point to what. Though he was being sarcastic before when he said he'd like to just confront Nank directly, he was really considering it now. Nank believed taking Camille settled some kind of debt between him and Maryse's dead brother. As far as Brooks knew—and he was *more* than familiar with the shady undertakings involved—keeping his business intact was the only thing that motivated the man. Sure, the guy had to have some pride. But pride was something that got in the way of success. Just like greed.

Brooks paused in front of the sea of sticky notes, staring hard at the one with Caleb Nank's name in thick black writing.

"Not you, buddy," he said aloud to the empty room, then strode back and forth past the coffee table again.

The thing that made Nank stand out in a world of prideful, greedy criminals…he didn't appear to be either. Not really. He wanted money. He had money. He held *on to* the money. His business thrived, but it didn't swell to the point of breaking. There was no overreaching, and that was the key. Nank wasn't after an empire; he was content with a slow rise and keeping what he had.

Brooks paused a second time. *Maybe that's it.*

Whatever debt Nank felt he was owed jeopardized what he had going. What could a six-year-old deaf child have to do with the man's underhanded business? Camille had been an infant when Maryse took her from the Las Vegas area. She couldn't have witnessed anything that happened.

He ran a frustrated hand over his chin. Again, he felt like he was missing some key piece.

No concrete connection between Dee and his own boss.

No concrete connection between Nank and the kid.

"C'mon," he muttered. "Give me *something.*"

As if on cue, a sharp rap that sounded from outside the room grabbed his attention. It was intrusive—more than a knock but less intense than the sound of someone trying to break in. He stilled, his eyes darting toward the bedroom. Maryse was still in there, unguarded. Unclothed, even.

The bang came again, and Brooks didn't know which direction to move. He wanted to warn her immediately, but if he could head off the intruders before they even got inside, it would be better.

Assuming you can *stop them.*

He hadn't thought to ask Masters about a weapon, or about who else might know about the safe house.

Stupid.

A third thump told him whoever was there was growing impatient. He wished he didn't have to go past the front door to get to the kitchen. There'd be more options in there for something to be used as a defensive weapon. A knife. A cleaver. Hell. He'd gladly take a pepper mill at the moment.

He swept his gaze across the room, searching quickly. Aside from the mess they'd brought in with them, it was tidy. Almost free of adornment. Then his eyes landed on the bookshelf. Lots of reading material for anyone who had to be holed up there for a while, but it wasn't the books themselves that caught his attention. It was a small, horse-shaped bookend.

Brooks strode toward the shelf and snagged the item in question. It was solid—probably brass—and fit in his palm perfectly with the legs sticking out between his fingers.

"Okay," he muttered.

Careful to keep as quiet as possible, and avoiding the windows—which were covered, but could still give him away in a silhouette—he turned his determined gait toward the knocking. He inched closer to the door, stopping only when he was near enough to reach out and touch it. He pressed his hands against the wood and peered through the peephole.

"Damn," he swore as he pulled back.

He didn't know who he'd been expecting to find, but it sure as hell hadn't been his boss. Taking a wary stance, he slid the multiple locks open and swung the door wide.

Captain Fell had his fist raised and ready for another smack on the door. When he spotted Brooks, he dropped his hand to his side. Close to his holstered weapon.

"Detective Small," he greeted in a growl. "What the hell are you doing here?"

"I feel like I should be asking you the same question," Brooks replied.

The other man's eyes found the brass horse. "You planning on poking my eyes out with that thing?"

"Not yours, specifically."

"Expecting bad news?"

"Pizza, actually."

"You want to tell me— You know what? Never mind. I'll ask later." His boss frowned, then shook his head. "Where is she?"

Brooks tensed. "Why?"

"Because she's in a mess of trouble."

"You going to be more specific?"

"You going to let me *in*?"

"I'm guessing I don't have much choice."

Captain Fell smiled a toothy smile. "Not so much. This safe house is property of the LVMPD, after all."

Brooks sighed and stepped out of the way. His boss tipped his head and slipped inside.

"Lead the way," the other man said.

He started to gesture toward the living room, but a thought made him stop. "You didn't know I was here?"

"No."

"What about Maryse?"

"Who?"

"The woman who's in a whole mess of trouble."

His boss turned his way. "What are you talking about?"

"Maryse LePrieur," Brooks said. "The person you're looking for."

"I'm looking for Deanna Whitehorse."

"Who?"

"A fugitive."

Brooks stared at his boss for a long moment. "*De*anna *White*horse."

"That's what I said."

Dee White.

Fear reared in his heart.

"She's—" His boss cut himself off. "What the hell's the matter, Small?"

He didn't bother to answer. He pushed past the other

man and bolted up the hall. He slammed into the bedroom and pounded on the bathroom door.

"Maryse!"

The water still hit the tub, but there was no answer. Why the hell hadn't he listened to his gut?

"Maryse!"

This time, he didn't wait for a reply. He drew back a few feet, lifted his boot and smashed it full force into a spot right below the doorknob. The wood heaved and gave way immediately. The door flew back and hit the wall with a resounding thump.

Empty.

"Damn, damn, damn!" Brooks hollered, kicking the door once again.

He spun back and smacked straight into Captain Fell.

"Small!" snapped the other man. "What the *hell* is going on?"

"She's gone."

"Deanna Whitehorse?"

"Maryse. And I need to go, too."

His boss slapped a hand onto his shoulder. "Back the truck up. Who's Maryse? I got an anonymous tip telling me Deanna Whitehorse would be at *this* address, willing to talk if I showed up alone. No mention of you, no mention of anyone named Maryse."

Brooks shook off the captain's grip and pushed back into the bathroom, scanning for a clue. His eyes landed on the mirror. He took three quick steps toward it, then snatched up the picture tucked into its corner.

Camille.

There was no mistaking the passport-sized photo. He spun back to his boss and held it out.

"Here."

"What is it? A picture of a little girl?"

"Evidence."

"That you're putting your prints all over?" Captain Fell's face screwed up in irritation. "Listen, Small—"

Brooks spoke over his boss's words. "No, *you* listen. I have to—"

A groan cut them both off, and they turned together. Masters stood in the bedroom door frame, one hand on his head. He nodded at Brooks, then cringed and eyed up the captain nervously.

"Hey, boss," he greeted him.

"You're involved in this, too?" Fell threw up his hands. "Of course you are. Why am I even asking?"

Masters smiled weakly. "You guys know that tiny little woman with a bad attitude? I'm pretty damned sure she knocked me out and stole my cousin's taxi."

Brooks didn't think his heart could drop any further, but it did. "She took her."

His partner and his boss answered in unison, "What?"

"Dee White. Deanna flipping Whitehorse. She took Maryse and *she* left you that message, Captain, because she knew you'd try to stop me from chasing after her. I guarantee it." He snagged the picture back. "And this is the clue Maryse left behind to tell me, in case I didn't figure it out on my own."

Realizing he sounded a bit wild and out-of-control, but not able to do anything about it—and maybe not wanting to because, so help him, if Dee brought Maryse to Nank, he'd lose it for real—he tried to shove past his visibly groggy partner. Masters's hand shot out and closed on his elbow. He tried to shake it away like he had with Fell's grip, but his partner wasn't shy about squeezing harder and holding him in place.

"C'mon, man," Masters said. "We've got holes to fill in. The captain can help us with that. Give you some insight.

Making a move without a plan and with bad information never works out."

"I'm wasting time," he growled.

"You're going to waste *more* time if you take off like this. Five minutes."

Brooks ground his teeth together. "Five minutes. But I swear to God, Captain, if you can't help me, I'll hand over my badge right now and walk straight through the door without looking back."

Finally, like he knew he couldn't win the argument, his boss lifted his hands in acquiescence.

Brooks spun, snapping over his shoulder, "Four minutes and forty-five seconds."

Chapter 20

Brooks stared at his boss, incredulity filling his mind as he turned over the revelation the other man had just provided. Captain Fell sat on the couch, looking—for the first time since Brooks had met him—old and tired. His shoulders slumped, his sharp gaze was dull, and his suit was rumpled and too big. He'd said nothing for the last few moments, and it was Brooks who finally prodded him to add something new.

"You can't be serious," he said.

Captain Fell nodded. "I am."

"You've been following a *series* of anonymous tips?"

"They've all panned out so far."

"That's…"

"Reckless?" the other man filled in. "I know."

"Insane," Brooks corrected.

"We're *required* to follow up on any credible tips," his boss reminded him.

"And log it. And inform the officers involved."

"I did. The first couple of times. They were little drug busts."

"Nank's men?"

"Nank's competition."

"It never occurred to you that it might be Nank himself, stringing you along so he could solidify his own hold over the trade?"

The captain sighed. "Of course it did. But it still got us busts, Detective."

"That's all that matters?"

"If no one is getting hurt or killed in the process. It's our job to take these guys off the street. I didn't break any laws."

"Maybe a few moral codes."

"Maybe," the other man acquiesced.

"And just so we're clear…you sent me to another country on forced leave based on one of these tips?"

"Don't make it sound like more than it is."

"More than it is?" Brooks felt his hands start to ball into fists, reminded himself that his boss's stupidity had led him to Maryse, then forced his fingers to relax. "How does this connect back to Deanna Whitehorse?"

Captain Fell shrugged. "Got a call this evening, telling us that a fugitive with that name would be coming through the airport. Got a description and a time, contacted TSA to get permission to grab her from the baggage area. Thought they changed their minds and scooped her instead. At least I did until I got the second call."

Brooks inhaled. "You're *still* being played. I'm 99.9 percent sure it was Nank's men who snagged Dee. What's she wanted for?"

"Fraud. Identity theft."

"You verified that?"

Fell gave him an annoyed look. "Of course I did. Looked her up in the database. Got arrested on some con charges a few years back."

"How many years back?"

"Why does it matter?"

Brooks shook his head, not even sure why he'd asked.

It was just the first question that popped into his head, and it seemed significant.

"It just does," he said vaguely.

"Maybe seven or eight? Can't remember the exact date."

Brooks's fists were growing tight again. Eight years ago. When Jean-Paul Kline, posing as Elias Franco, had come to him. The first time he'd heard the name Caleb Nank. It might've been a coincidence. Except something told him it wasn't. A half a dozen emotions played through him. Anger. Fear. Confusion. Something that bordered on paranoia. He forced them all aside to focus on what he needed to do right that second—get to Maryse. And a thought occurred to him then.

"Masters...the taxi... Does it have a GPS tracking system?"

"It could," his partner replied.

"Can you find out?"

"Yeah. Gonna be an awkward conversation with my cousin, though."

"I've got nothing but the utmost faith in you."

"Flattery?"

"Honesty."

Masters sighed. "All right. Give me a minute."

He slipped from the room, phone in hand, and Brooks turned back to their boss. "I need your car and your gun."

"I'd like to think you're kidding."

He shook his head and seized on the one thing he knew his boss valued most—his career. "Not even close. And I'm not above blackmailing you to get both. I'm happy to place a call to the chief and ask *him* how he feels about the Rain Falls captain running operations based on questionable anonymous tips."

"To save this woman? Maryse? Explain to me again who she is to you."

"She's…everything." It was a lame statement, and Brooks knew it.

His boss did, too, if the eyebrow raise he received as a result was any indication. "Bit of a leap."

"Bit of the truth," Masters interjected as he came back in.

Their boss turned to Brooks's partner, the eyebrow still up. "Now *you're* kidding me, right? At the moment, I'm searching for a reason *not* to suspend you and you're still going to jump in with that?"

Masters shrugged. "Love, right? What're you gonna do?"

Brooks sighed and waved off the topic. "Any luck with your cousin?"

"Good news. The taxi *is* wired. I told him we're thinking of something new for the squad cars and he gave me the password for his tracking system. All you gotta do is let me download the app for you, and it'll pinpoint the location within a block or two."

Hope squeezed through the worry, and Brooks held out his phone. "Good enough."

"You want backup?"

He shook his head. "Just because I'm letting my heart run my body doesn't mean you need to risk your life, too."

"You know it's not like that," his partner replied.

"You've got a wife and two kids at home, Masters. They need you a hell of a lot more than I do." He turned back to his boss. "Keys and gun, Captain. Please."

Fell reached into his coat reluctantly, then handed both over. "We're both going to lose our jobs if this goes south."

"It's a risk I'm willing to take."

"Sure as hell hope she's worth it."

"She is." Brooks managed a smile. "And don't worry.

If we take down Nank in the cross fire, I'll make sure you get the credit."

He tucked his reprogrammed phone into his pocket, fit the gun into his belt, then looped the key ring around his index finger. He moved toward the front door. Then paused as his gaze caught a flicker of movement on the other side of the drawn curtain. A quick peek told him that a neutral-colored SUV had pulled in behind Captain Fell's vehicle, blocking it in.

He stepped back into the living room and asked in a hushed voice, "Either of you expecting anyone?"

"Nope," said Masters, while their boss shook his head.

"Anyone know where you guys are?"

He got the same response for his second question, and he dropped a curse under his breath. "I think we've got some trouble."

Masters came to his feet immediately, fumbling for a weapon. Brooks already had his—the one he'd procured from his boss—on the ready. Accustomed to working together, the two men formed a shield around their captain.

"Think we have time to get to the back door?" Masters asked in a low voice.

Brooks shook his head. "Nank's men are smart. Probably covering it before they even try to get in. Bedrooms?"

"Three. All the windows are completely sealed."

"What about the one in the bathroom? The one that Dee and Maryse went through?"

"Too small for either of us. Maybe the captain, though…"

"Let's do it."

Captain Fell started to voice a protest, but Brooks wasn't interested in arguing.

"There's a chance for you to get out," he said. "You have to take it. And if you won't do it just because I want you to, then remember that the whole department relies on you."

With a grunt, their boss pushed to his feet. Brooks nodded at his partner, and they flanked the other man, weapons out. As a unit, they slid up the hall to the bedroom, then slipped inside. Masters stood guard at the door while Brooks climbed to the back of the toilet and peered out cautiously. The frosted glass led to a narrow space between the safe house and the house next door. A glance up and down told him it was clear, and though the front was open to the yard, the rear offered the cover of some bushes.

He ducked his head back inside, then jumped down and gestured to the window. "All right, Captain. I think you're good. You can use the shrubs to sneak from here to the neighbor's house."

"Let me guess," Fell replied. "You'd prefer if I didn't call for backup."

"Just give us a chance to get out before you do, and we'll *become* your backup."

"Unless you don't get out."

"Ten minutes. That's all I ask."

"Counterproductive," his boss muttered, but he stepped up and pushed himself out anyway.

Brooks waited, counting to thirty, sure if the men outside had caught his boss, he would've heard some sign of it. Then he slid the window shut and turned back to Masters.

"Escape plan? We need to move fast before—" A noise from out in the hall cut him off.

"Before we get ourselves cornered?" his partner finished.

"Yeah, that."

They moved together toward the bedroom door, but the sound of muffled boot steps and lowered voices already carried through. Thankfully, the intruders were moving slowly. Probably searching thoroughly while trying to go undetected.

"At least two guys inside," Brooks whispered. "No way to get out through the door."

Masters nodded at the window. "Break through?"

"Noisy as hell. We'd be lucky if even one of us made it."

"So we go out firing."

"Or we barricade ourselves in and hope our skills are better than theirs."

"Mattress and frame as a shield? Peg 'em off?"

"Yep."

It wasn't even close to a good plan.

But it's all we've got, Brooks reminded himself.

He grabbed one edge of the mattress and Masters grabbed the other. As they started to lift, Brooks's eyes strayed up. They landed on a panel above the dresser.

An attic.

"We still doing this?" his partner prodded.

He shook his head, dropped his corner of the bed and pointed up. "I've got a better idea."

It only took a few seconds to boost himself onto the dresser and push open the panel. A few more, and he was inside the low-ceilinged room. Careful to keep his weight on the support beams, he pushed back and waited for Masters to follow him. His partner came up quickly, replacing the panel as he clambered in. Just in time, too. Below them, the door squeaked open, and a rough voice trickled through the ceiling.

"I'll be damned," it said. "I think maybe they're not here at all."

A second voice joined the first, this one tinged with an accent of some kind—maybe Russian, maybe something else Slavic. Brooks couldn't have said for sure.

"Don't know how the hell that's possible," it replied. "The car's out front. Those notes are all over the damned living room. And she *said* they were here no more than ten minutes earlier."

Her.

They had to be talking about Dee White. Brooks exchanged a look with his partner. Even in the dark, he could read the other man's puzzlement. What *was* the tiny woman's deal? She clearly had an agenda. From the fraud business and Camille to tipping off the captain to setting up this intrusion... He couldn't wrap his head around her end goal. Shaking his head, he turned his attention back to the continued conversation from below.

"What should we do?" Rough Voice was asking.

There was a pause, and then Accented Guy said, "Hell if I know."

"Call her?"

"Yeah. Hang on." A moment passed, and Accented Voice launched into an explanation, presumably on the phone with Dee, then finished with "Uh-huh. Got it."

"Well?" said Rough Voice.

"She wants us to burn it down."

"What?"

"She said they're smart. Could've found somewhere to hide. At the very least, it'll smoke 'em out. At best, it'll kill 'em."

"Nank?"

"Sanctioned it."

"There goes subtlety," muttered Rough Voice.

"It's worked before," Accented Guy said.

A lick of anger made Brooks's jaw clench. He could think of only one other instance where Nank's men had been involved in an arson—the one Maryse had told him about. The one that resulted in her brother's death. He was well acquainted with how that had ended up. The victim blamed. A kid abandoned.

Not going to let that happen again.

He flicked his gaze around the attic, searching for an out. The only thing he could see were piles of insulation, grime, exposed beams and a series of exhaust vents.

The vents.

With a silent nod toward his partner, Brooks pulled his phone from his pocket and fumbled until he found the flashlight function. He dragged it in a slow arc across the ceiling. He paused at the gable. There was the biggest of all the vents.

But is it big enough?

He didn't have the space needed to stand, so he got down on his hands and knees, then picked his way over the beams as quietly as he could, still taking care to not put any of his weight on the drywall below. When he reached the vent, he grabbed ahold of the wall and pulled to his knees. A quick examination of the metal piece told him he and Masters could probably squeeze through. Barely. And first he'd have to get it open.

He turned back to his partner, who inclined his head in understanding, then reached into his pocket, pulled out a utility knife and crawled a little closer. Gratefully, Brooks took the proffered tool and set to work. The screws were in tight, but a bit of patience got the job done. There was a rubber seal under the frame, too, but the sharp knife and some strong-arming took care of that. Brooks pried the whole thing free and peered outside. The roof just below the vent was sheer, but beneath that was a wide soffit, and from there, the ground was only six feet or so farther down. He brought his head back inside just as the first whiff of smoke-scented air touched his nose.

Damn.

Rough Voice and Accent Guy would be heading outside any second, searching the escape routes.

"Too late to change our minds now," Masters said.

"Yep."

Without looking back—because Brooks knew without confirming it that his partner would follow—he used the beam overhead to support his body, then stuck his feet through the vent one at a time and pushed his way through. He made it out. He made it to the soffit. He even made it as far as kneeling down and readying himself to hang on, then drop to the ground.

As he lowered his first leg, though, a shot zinged by and slammed into the siding a few inches from his head.

He dropped a curse, then hollered a warning to Masters. It was a little too late. The other man's booted feet were already sliding through the hole in the way.

Brooks tried to yell again, but a second bullet came flying at him, cutting him off. This one came even closer to hitting him—near enough that he could feel its heat as it lodged into the exterior of the house.

"Screw it," he muttered, then let go of the soffit and let himself drop.

The ground came up quick, and there was no pretending it wasn't hard. Pain shot through Brooks's shoulder, and he rolled to his other side with a groan. He couldn't help but close his eyes for just a second, but almost as soon as he did, the sound of boots hitting pavement hit his ears, forcing his lids to lift again. The gunman—or gun*men*, if he was really unlucky—was on his way.

"Crap," he groaned, rolling again, searching for something to use to leverage himself up.

After a brief flail, he managed to grab a thick shrub. He tugged himself to his knees, then his feet, reaching for his weapon as he got his footing. He wasn't quick enough. A gun cocked, close enough that he could hear it. Even though he couldn't see who wielded it, he tucked and rolled, hoping that he'd have surprise on his side. As he hit the ground, though, he realized his effort was almost unnecessary. With a wild yell, Masters flew from above, feetfirst. Brooks stared up in surprise as his partner sailed through the air. He twisted his head to follow the other man's motion and watched as he streaked through his vision, then plowed straight into the man with the gun.

The assailant had zero reaction time. Though he'd thrown up his hands to protect himself, it did nothing to stop him from falling backward as the two-hundred-pound cop slammed into him full force. The gun flew from his hands, skittered over the sidewalk, then came to a stop on the grass.

Brooks jumped up and retrieved it, keeping it out in case one of the man's friends chose that moment to come around the side of the house. Then he turned back to Masters to see if he needed any help securing the other man. His partner had the situation well in hand. He held the man flat on the ground, a knee in his back and a wad of tissues stuffed into his mouth. Though the gunman was jerking around, he didn't stand a chance of getting free.

Masters tipped up his head. "Of all the days to leave my handcuffs at home…"

"Yeah, *that's* our biggest problem," Brooks replied with a sigh and another glance around for any more company.

"Think he'll tell us anything?"

"Doubtful."

"What do you want to do with him?"

"I want to toss him in lockup. But I guess we need something easier."

"Garden shed?" Masters nodded toward the small building at the back of the yard.

"Good enough."

His partner lifted the crook—who tried uselessly to

issue a kick—and as he did, a set of keys dropped from the man's pocket. Brooks snapped them up, thankful that at least one thing might work in their favor. He followed along as Masters dragged the shooter over the grass, and he swung open the door to the shed. A quick look inside produced a long piece of rope, which he used to secure the man's feet and hands as Masters held him still. When he was tied up tightly, they tossed him into the building and turned back to the house. A few tendrils of smoke were spiraling out of a vent on one side.

"Should we do something about that?" Masters asked.

Brooks clenched his jaw, wishing he could say no. All he wanted to do was get to Maryse. But he couldn't just let the house go up in flames, and who knew how long it would take before a neighbor noticed?

Too long, probably.

They still had to deal with the other men who were undoubtedly sitting in wait at the front of the house, too.

"Well?" his partner prodded.

"Let's move up on either side of the house," Brooks said decisively. "They'll probably be expecting us to come together. So if we divide and conquer, it might throw them off. Once we're out, we'll call fire base."

"Sounds like a plan."

Silently, the two men separated and moved to opposite corners of the house. Brooks shot Masters a final nod, then slipped around the corner. He kept himself pressed to the exterior, slinking along with practiced stealth. He reached the edge of the house quickly. There, he stopped and considered the best way to proceed. A glance down gave him an idea. He bent and retrieved a small, flat rock. Then he tossed it out. The response was immediate. Feet hit pavement, lightly but still audible. Two sets, if he wasn't mistaken.

Brooks flattened himself back against the wall, and the second he spotted a boot, he pounced. As hard as he could, he smashed his own foot down on top of the other man's, then lifted a knee and slammed it between the guy's legs before he could recover. He kept an ear out for the owner of the second set of feet, too. Obligingly, the guy's friend dropped a curse before making a move.

Brooks turned his head in the direction of the voice. It belonged to a small man in a tracksuit, who was just lifting his weapon. Instinct and training kicked in, and Brooks dropped to the ground, rolled out of immediate danger, then readied his own gun.

Masters beat him to it. His partner had slipped out from the other side of the house and moved in. He lifted his weapon up and smashed it into Tracksuit Guy's head. The gunman wobbled. His eyes rolled to the back of his head. Then he collapsed to the ground beside his friend, who was still clutching himself and groaning a little.

Brooks pushed up and brushed off his pants. "Shed?"

His partner nodded. "Yep."

"Fire department first?"

"Probably a good idea."

In minutes, they had all three men bound, gagged and stacked against one another in the little building. They'd placed a call to someone they knew at the station, who dispatched a truck without too many questions, and they'd called Captain Fell to apprise him of everything that had transpired. They were on the road—choosing Nank's men's vehicle in hopes that it'd get them that much closer to wherever Dee had taken Maryse—and trying to come up with a plan that suited them both.

"C'mon, man," Masters was saying to Brooks. "You know you could use my help."

"I know I could," Brooks agreed.

"So take it."

"No."

"We could—"

"No."

"Let me do something."

Brooks tapped the steering wheel. He hadn't even wanted his partner to get into the SUV with him, but the man had made himself comfortable in the passenger seat and refused to dislodge himself. Now they were ten minutes into following the GPS signal—which appeared to be headed for the desert—and he still hadn't found a way to get rid of his eager partner. Brooks had had no choice but to keep driving with his unwanted helper in tow. Stopping would slow them down. Staying behind would've meant getting tied up in red tape.

Red tape.

He snapped his fingers as an idea occurred to him. "Paperwork."

"What?"

"That's what I need you to do."

"Paperwork?"

"Research, to be more accurate."

"About?"

"Deanna Whitehorse."

"The woman who took your girl?"

He nodded, a now-familiar squeeze of worry tugging at his heart. "Something isn't right."

Masters narrowed his eyes. "And you want *me* to dig around?"

"Who else can I ask?" Brooks waited, knowing the other man would see the truth in his words in a moment or two.

Sure enough, his partner sighed. "Fine."

"Yeah?"

"Yeah."

Relieved, Brooks made the adjustments to his drive. He took Masters home—his partner said he'd work better from there than the station, and it was safer anyway—then cut across town to hit the highway. He tossed a glance down at the GPS tracker on his phone. Definitely desert-bound. He shoved aside fear about what that meant.

"Don't worry, Maryse," he said aloud to the empty car. "I'm on my way."

But for an experienced cop, the desert and an unwanted person usually meant only one thing.

Chapter 21

Maryse was grateful that Dee White hadn't insisted on talking through the trip. Once the other woman had given her a vague explanation about how they'd make sure Nank believed she was being transported against her will, she more or less zipped her lips. The silence gave Maryse more time to think. But the thinking wasn't all positive. Something still nagged her, just like it had since the moment Dee first opened her mouth the previous day. Maryse didn't have a natural tendency to dislike someone, and she rarely made snap judgments. In fact, her inability to assume that anyone and everyone could be up to something suspicious was what kept her from truly settling in over the last six years. She always saw the best in people, and she didn't always trust herself to see someone in a bad light.

But Dee...

Maryse stole a quick glance at the now-brunette woman. She was capable of holding down a full-time job in an upscale hotel. She was perfectly at home acting like a crazed criminal with a gun. And now she was something else entirely. None of it, though, seemed real.

She tugged on Cami's bracelet hard enough that it snapped in her hands. But even the feel of a dozen silver, heart-shaped beads in her hands couldn't distract her from the question that she kept coming back to.

So if Dee White is acting all the time...who is she underneath it?

She was so caught up in her thoughts that she didn't notice the cab was slowing down until it had almost come to a complete stop. She turned her attention out the window, trying to sort out where they were. There was nothing to see except the expanse of dry land. But Dee was already swinging open her door.

"C'mon," the other woman said. "It's hot out here, and we've got a bit of a walk."

Confused and increasingly anxious, Maryse slipped from the car, a bead falling from her hands as she hurried to catch up. Dee moved at a quick pace, seemingly with a destination in mind, even though the horizon appeared barren. After a few moments, though, the ground began to slope.

Maryse slowed, wondering how Brooks would possibly find them now. She squeezed the remaining beads in her hands.

Bread crumbs, she thought suddenly.

She'd already dropped one. Would Dee notice another?

Maryse decided to hazard it. She released a bead, tossing it behind her back. When the slope became a hill, she let go of a third one.

Dee didn't slow and she didn't turn back. Maryse wasn't quite as sure-footed, and she used it as an excuse to move slowly, dropping another little heart every few yards, careful to make sure they didn't simply roll down. As they neared the bottom, though, she lost her footing. She landed on her rear end, then slid the rest of the way down. As she hit the ground, the remaining pieces of the bracelet cascaded around her, drawing Dee's attention.

"What're these?" the other woman demanded.

Maryse was glad that she had the fall as an excuse for her flush. "My bracelet broke."

Dee narrowed her eyes. *"Yours?"*

She remembered that she'd grabbed the jewelry from the other woman's own home, and she corrected herself quickly. "Camille's. I grabbed it—"

Dee cut her off. "I know where you got it. Never mind. Just leave it there. Let's go."

Relieved, Maryse pushed to her feet, then started to walk again. But stopped as she spotted what lay in front of them. Another road, overgrown and unused. And what looked like an abandoned gas and service station. Something straight out of a serial-killer movie.

Dee turned her head over her shoulder and smiled. "Stop looking so worried. If I wanted to kill you, I would've done it by now."

Maryse didn't smile back. She just shivered and forced herself to get all the way up. Her feet dragged as she approached the run-down buildings.

Nothing good can come from this, she thought.

Dee, though, still moved confidently. She bypassed the old pumps and the store attached to the station, and she walked straight up to the service-bay door. There, she bent down, twisted the rusted handle and slid the rusty mechanism up. It groaned and scraped, but still lifted. And inside the large space sat a new-looking black sedan.

"Nank keeps these stashed here and there," Dee explained. "In case of emergency."

Maryse's throat was thick with nerves. A new wave of worried questions sprang to mind. But the most pressing one was how *Dee* knew where to look. Why was *she* aware of Nank's getaway plans? And how come she reached down so surely to retrieve a key from under the front bumper of the sedan? That wasn't just peripheral awareness. That was inside knowledge.

She fought another shiver. "Are we far from where we're going? Do we need a new car?"

Dee shook her head. "Not terribly far. But I'm not underestimating your guy. If he managed to evade Nank's men, he'll be finding a way to track that taxi."

"Nank's men are at the house?"

"Why do you think I was in such a hurry to get away from it?"

Maryse swallowed, guilt and desert heat making her head swim. "I don't know."

The petite woman shrugged, then lifted a piece of rope off the wall beside the car. "You ready?"

"You want to tie me up?"

"And I want to put you in the trunk."

"What?"

"I said we were going to make it look real."

The air was suddenly thick and heavy, and Maryse shook her head. "I can't."

"If you don't, we may never get to your daughter."

Oh, God.

She eyed the closed trunk lid. Even from the outside, it looked small. And airtight.

For Camille, she said to herself. *You can do this.*

Wishing she could do anything else, she swallowed against the tight, raw feeling in her throat, and she held out her hands. Dee seemed indifferent to her suffering. She bound her wrists, then guided her to the car, where she popped open the trunk and helped Maryse in.

"It won't be long," she promised.

But as the lid slammed shut, Maryse had a feeling even five minutes would feel like an eternity.

* * *

From its spot in the dashboard cup holder, Brooks's phone issued a beep that cut through his brooding thoughts. He cast a glance down at the electronic device. So far, it had been sending him steadily south. Straight out onto the highway for well over thirty minutes. Maybe even close to an hour. Now, though, the blip on the screen had stalled. For a second, he thought maybe the GPS had stopped working, and his heart seized. When he lifted up the phone, though, he realized that the cab must've come to a standstill. Sure enough, a message from the tracking app popped onto the screen, telling him the tracked object had been idle for more than five minutes.

Does it mean Maryse and Dee have reached their destination? Or is it something more sinister? Brooks shook his head. *Don't even consider it.*

His foot still insisted on pushing down a little harder on the gas pedal. As the speedometer climbed, his cell beeped again, this time with an incoming call.

Masters.

Trying to sound cheerful—and failing to succeed even a little—he pressed the speakerphone button. "Small."

"Bad news," his partner announced without preamble.

"Tell me."

"Neither Deanna Whitehorse nor Dee White really exist."

"What do you mean?"

"Both names are aliases."

"The captain did say she was wanted in connection with fraud."

"Yeah. She's unlocked an expert level of fraud, I think. The aliases are pretty solid, which is why no one caught on. Like, if I wasn't specifically looking into her, I'd never have noticed. Passports, driver's licenses, everything looks completely legit. Dee White is an upstanding Canadian citizen, who didn't even exist until thirteen months ago. Then bam, there she is. Deanna Whitehorse is the same. A year ago, she was arrested on a Nank bust. Didn't have a record, made bail, never showed up for pretrial. But guess what? She only started to exist a few years ago, too. Three, to be exact. Valid Social Security, valid driver's license."

"And before that?"

"Well, I plugged in a bunch of variations of the name and came up with another match. Anna White."

"Let me guess… She had a short life span, too?"

"Uh-huh," Masters agreed. "Sure did. Her identity was on the scene for about two years. Got picked up as a witness on—get this—a Nank-related incident."

Brooks swore, then asked, "What about fingerprints?"

"Exactly where I went next. Weren't any on file for Dee or Deanna. Anna, on the other hand, had a set. But because she was a witness…"

"No one bothered to run a check for a match."

"Exactly."

"But *you* did."

"Yep. And Anna White has the very same prints as a woman named Anne Black."

"Is Anne Black a real person?"

"Think so. Married name, but seems legit. Eleven years ago, Anne's husband—Saul—was set to be arrested on an identity-theft charge. He was a dude with a pretty damned colorful history. Worked with a fraud unit for years. Then they caught him stealing info from his cases. Got fired, served some time. He met Anne through one of those write-to-the-prisoners programs. When he got out, the two of them got married. Set up shop here and there over the years, always seeming legit. Then some teenager got busted for a fake ID and rolled on them. Some kind of bust was set up.

Things went badly. There was a standoff. Both Saul and his and Anne's kid got killed in the cross fire."

Brooks's stomach churned. "There was a kid?"

Masters's voice was suitably solemn. "Yeah, man. Unfortunately, there was."

"Was Anne Black charged in any of it?"

"Nope. Couldn't find anything that connected her to the fake identity ring—which was huge, by the way. Practically a passport production facility in their basement. It was under lock and key, though. Anne was reportedly unaware of its existence. Thinking that's probably not true."

"Probably not," Brooks agreed. "Any thoughts on how this connects back to Maryse?"

"Not yet. But I'm going to dig around a bit more. Head up to the station and see what I can figure out."

"Good. You check in on the captain?"

"He's fine. Seething. But alive."

"All right. Call me if you come up with anything."

"Will do."

The phone went dead, and Brooks turned his attention back to the barren landscape in front of him. His mind, though, stayed on the details his partner had just provided. There was no doubt that this was the connection he'd been looking for. He just had to figure out exactly what it was.

With frustration just about drowning out his worry, he stomped on the gas again. The little blip on the GPS tracker still hadn't moved, and if he was estimating correctly, he had less than thirty minutes to go before he reached it.

Underneath Maryse's body—which had been shaking uncontrollably since the moment the trunk closed—the car finally rolled to a stop. For a second, the engine continued to hum. Then it cut out completely, and the lid popped open. She wished she wasn't so relieved to see Dee's face, but she couldn't stop the feeling, and when the other woman reached down to help her out, she took the assistance gratefully, gulping in a breath of air as she did.

She wanted to cry. And stretch. And run. Instead, she made herself stay planted to the ground and took a slow look around as her eyes adjusted to the light.

"What is this place?" she asked.

But before the question was even all the way out, she spotted a sign.

People With Paper, it read.

Caleb Nank's front. Her brother's ex-employer. And the front for all the bad dealings.

Dee noted her recognition. "You know the company?"

"Brooks mentioned it," Maryse replied cautiously, not wanting to say anything about Jean-Paul.

"There's no need to be coy about it. Your detective is familiar with Nank's enterprises. He told me at the house in Laval, remember?"

"Right."

Something in the other woman's smile made her want to flee, but she forced her feet to stay planted. She inhaled to steady her nerves, and a pulpy scent filled her nose. She looked around for the source of the smell, but all she could see was the back of a squat warehouse.

"This is just a small piece of the operation," Dee explained. "A holding station for the boxes before they get shipped to the local companies. Cheaper to buy and build in the desert. No moisture to wreck the paper."

"So this is an *actual* paper company?"

"Some of it is. On the surface, anyway. There's a mill in Northern Nevada and about five of these warehouses." Dee grabbed ahold of her bound hands and tugged. "I'm sorry about this."

"Sorry about wh—"

A rough shove sent Maryse to the dry, dusty ground before she could finish. Startled, she tried to draw in a breath and instead got a lungful of dirt. Coughing and choking, she rolled to her side. The move earned her a kick in the ribs that was hard enough to make her cry out. A second kick turned the cry into a sob. Tears formed in her eyes and trickled down. She crawled over the ground, but Dee's foot landed solidly on her ankle, sending a shooting pain up her leg and forcing her to stop. As a deep throb bloomed out from the point of impact, she blinked up at Dee, who now stood over her with an angry scowl on her face.

"Have to make it look real in case anyone's watching."

Maryse braced herself for a third kick. But it didn't come. Instead, Dee reached down and pulled her back to her feet, then gave her another shove, this time just hard enough to make her stumble forward.

"C'mon," the other woman said, pushing her toward a set of metal doors. "We don't want to keep Nank waiting."

Maryse did as she was told, hurrying across the dirt, her ankle protesting the whole way. Genuine fear—both of Nank and the woman who was able to so casually deliver a beating in the name of pretense—made her feet move fast. When they reached the doors, Dee grabbed her hands again, then stepped up and rapped on the metal. Her touch was confident and it sounded like code.

Tap-tap.

Tap-tap.

Tap.

Sure enough, there was a ten-second pause, and then an answer came from the other side in an identical pattern. When it was done, Dee reached up again, and this time she delivered two quick bangs. Then she pulled Maryse back, and the doors swung open. Two men stood on the other side. Each was dressed in an identical gray suit. They were both young and visibly fit, and neither looked pleased to see them. As one shifted to let them go by, Maryse spotted a gun—large, black and frightening—on his hip. She couldn't fight a shiver.

"Gave her a pretty good beating," the gunman said, just shy of smug.

"She was being uncooperative," Dee replied indifferently.

"Better you than us," the other man added. "I wouldn't want to hit a girl."

Now Dee smiled. "And that's why you're just a doorman."

Two spots of color formed in the guard's cheeks, but he didn't retaliate. Dee smiled even wider, then guided Maryse up the dimly lit corridor, not speaking until they reached a second set of doors at the end.

"Your brother did that job," she said.

Maryse just about fell over. "What?"

"Jean-Paul," Dee replied. "He was a guard like those guys back there."

"You knew him?"

"Yes. Good kid."

A lump formed in her throat, thinking about him. Maybe he *was* a good kid. Or at least not overly bad. Sometimes, it was hard for her to separate the path he'd taken from the one he'd been on when they were growing up. It was something she'd tried hard to reconcile over the last six years. The revelation provided by Brooks—that Jean-Paul had been a confidential informant—helped. Still.

Six years.

It was such a long time.

Wait.

Maryse's feet dug into the tiled ground.

"You *knew* him?" she repeated.

"I just said I did."

"When he worked for Nank?"

"Yes."

"But that was six years ago."

"Yes."

Maryse's mouth was growing steadily drier, her pulse increasing quickly. "Didn't you tell me in the car that you just met Nank?"

"I don't think I said that specifically." Dee's hands closed on the rope that held her. "Let's keep moving."

"And if I say no?"

"Where are you going to go?"

The other woman was right. If Maryse thought she'd had no choice before, she knew it for sure now. Dee held every single card. From the knife, to the location, to whatever secrets she carried in her head, she had everything. All Maryse could do was hope that she was at least telling the truth about taking her to Camille. She stepped along, her mind and body both protesting. Dee pushed her through the swinging doors, which led to a small staircase. At the top of those was a third door, this one made of tinted glass. They moved through it, too, and Maryse found herself staring through an equally darkened sheet of glass. The panel was just one piece of a completely enclosed walkway that spanned the length of the warehouse. Below it were hundreds—maybe thousands—of boxes and a dozen or so employees moving through the open spaces, checking things off on clipboards as they inspected the cardboard containers.

Dee moved her forward again and said, "They're legitimate workers, mostly. Ninety percent. Good pay. Decent benefits. Hard to fault that."

"And the other ten percent?" Maryse asked.

"They know a little more, so their pay and benefits are even better."

"And *you*?"

"Let me introduce to you Nank himself."

They'd stopped now, and they stood in front of a final door. Maryse's head spun, anxiety spiking and making her chest squeeze.

You can do this, she said to herself. *Go in there and ask for your daughter back. Beg if you have to.*

The sweat was already starting to drip down her face, the dirt from her tumble outside following it. So when Dee opened the door, and Maryse inched forward, it was in near blindness. Being sightless did nothing to ease the building tension in her rib cage. She wanted to turn and run. She had to force each step. As she moved into the room—an office, she noted vaguely—she used the memory of Cami's sweet face to keep herself from simply freezing to the spot. But as she made herself glance around, made herself look at the heavy desk and wide-backed office chair, confusion took the place of fear.

"There's no one in here," she said.

Dee moved around her to lock the door, then smiled and seated herself at the desk, speaking in a conspiratorial tone. "*We're* in here."

"I don't understand."

The other woman glanced around like someone might be listening, making Maryse wonder if she was more than a little crazy. There was no one in sight. In fact, there was almost *nothing* in sight. No filing cabinets, no intercom system. Just the desk, chair and the computer.

"It's me," Dee said.

"What?"

"I took Camille, Maryse."

"Why?" She heard the desperation in her voice, but she couldn't curb it. "You were a mother! You told me!"

"That's right. I *was*. But your brother took that from me."

"My brother is dead!"

"No one knows that better than I do."

"You killed him?"

"Yes. And I thought it would be enough."

Maryse's head was spinning, trying to make sense of what the other woman was saying. But she just couldn't. Her brother had taken motherhood from Dee White? How?

"Camille isn't your daughter," she whispered.

"No."

Thank God.

For a second, she sagged with relief. But it was short-lived. Then anger took over. This woman had killed her brother. Taken her daughter. Told her a hundred little lies and made her feel sympathetic.

Without thinking, Maryse lunged forward. She forgot about her tied hands and her injured ankle. She forgot that she needed Dee alive so she could get her daughter back. She just wanted to hurt her, to give her a tiny taste of the pain she'd been enduring for the last day and a half. She'd never felt such a terrible fury. And giving in to the urge to channel it destructively brought her down.

She fell forward. Her chin smacked the desk. For a second, the world blurred. Then it disappeared.

Chapter 22

Brooks spotted the yellow taxi on the horizon, and his fingers clenched. There was nothing nearby, and even from a distance, he could see that the doors were wide-open. He glanced up and down the dusty road, searching. It was fruitless.

Where are they?

His foot was pressed to the floor now, trying to close the final distance between himself and the cab as quickly as possible. The car groaned a protest underneath him. Thankfully, though, it kept moving. The bland scenery whipped by, and in under two minutes, he reached his destination. He slammed on the brakes, pushed the car into Park, then leaped from the vehicle. He stopped just short of hollering Maryse's name into the empty air.

There was no sign of her, or of Dee White/Anne Black. Obviously, they'd left on foot, but the dust and the wind meant no prints on the ground. He scanned and scanned, then scanned again. He still came up with nothing.

"What the hell do I do now?" he muttered.

He wasn't used to being without a clue. He didn't like the feeling one bit. With a muted growl, he turned back to his car, thinking maybe he could call Masters for an update. As he spun, something shimmered just a few feet away.

Automatically, he stepped toward it. Then he bent down and lifted it from the ground.

It's a heart. A little silver one.

Why did it look familiar?

Then he remembered.

"Camille's bracelet."

Hope building, he fanned his gaze out. There, in the distance, another bit of silver glinted.

Thank God.

Quickly, he moved back to the car and gathered up his phone and his gun. Then he set out to follow the trail left behind by his very clever woman. The second bead brought him to a hill. The next few led him down it, then to a steep ridge. As he leaned over it, he spotted the rest of the silver trinkets, a set of narrow tire tracks and an abandoned gas station. For a second, he just stared down at it. Then he shook his head and pulled out his phone. He was surprised to see that he had full service.

He dialed Masters, who answered on the first ring. "Good news or bad?"

"Good. I hope. You make it to the station?"

"Yeah, I'm here."

"Think you can run a location for me?"

"Sure. What location?"

"Mine."

"You that lost, Small?"

"Ha-ha. I'm in the middle of the desert, Masters, but I've got better reception than I get in my living room. Can you find out where the cell tower is and what else is in the area?"

"Yeah. Hang on."

Brooks waited with as much patience as he could muster. His eyes followed the overgrown road in front of the station. The tire tracks ran alongside it, but he imagined that a little farther up, they'd move directly onto the road. Where did it go? He ran his hand over his chin, racking his brain for an idea. One stretch of desert looked essentially the same as another.

"Small?" Masters's voice brought him back to the moment.

"I'm here."

"You're not going to believe this."

"What?"

"You're about five miles from a brand-spanking-new storage facility for People With Paper."

"Of course I am," Brooks muttered. "Which way?"

"What're you near?"

"A gas station."

He heard the telltale tap of the keyboard before his partner spoke again.

"Okay," the other man said. "I've got it. You can see a road running along in front of the station?"

"Yep."

"Drive west for five miles, then—"

"I'm on foot."

"Well. Damn."

"Yeah."

The keyboard clacked again.

"Actually," Masters said, "you're in luck. If you were driving, you'd have to go back and forth for about fifteen miles. On foot, you can cut west for a couple miles, where you'll find the cell tower that's giving you that great service. From there, you move south. A mile and a quarter'll bring you directly to the road that leads to the warehouse."

"Perfect," he replied. "Anything else on the Anne Black front?"

"Nothing yet, man. Sorry."

"Well. You know where to find me. Literally."

"Sure do."

Brooks clicked the phone off and stood in the sand for a second. It was hot and dry, and he was sure he'd need hydration if he planned on walking over three miles. He tapped his phone against his thigh, then moved toward the gas station. A quick search led him from the broken front door to the falling-apart shop. Inside, he threw his gaze around in search of water. The shelves were bare, the fridges long cold and decidedly empty. A quick check of the bathroom told him that the water had been shut off, too.

"Dammit."

He was about to give up when he spotted the swinging door behind the desk.

Worth a shot.

He slid behind the counter and pushed through to the service bay. As he did, he immediately realized it'd been used more recently than any other part of the station. The scent of fresh gas filled his nostrils, and as his eyes adjusted to the dimmer light, he saw why. Gas cans lined one wall. Tools hung from another. And in a corner, he spotted an old vending machine. Though it wasn't functioning, the side hung open.

Hopeful, he stepped toward it. Luck went his way. In the very bottom of the far corner of the machine, he found a full sealed bottle of cola. He pulled it free, tucked it into the rear of his waistband beside his weapon, then strode back out into the sun.

Shooting a glare at the blink-inducing blaze, he positioned himself to the south. "All right, sweetheart. Whatever you're doing, sit tight. I'm on my way."

Consciousness hit Maryse like a tidal wave of cold water. One moment, she was oblivious to the world around her, and the next, a hundred sensations assaulted her senses.

She could smell paper. And sweat. She could hear ringing. But she thought that might be in her head. She could feel a throb in her temple. And a tiny hand in her own.

A tiny hand.

Maryse's eyes flew open. For a long moment, she thought she was dreaming. Blue eyes—just the same shade as her own—fixed on her, while a shock of untidy blond hair tickled her shoulder.

Camille.

She tried to say her daughter's name, but all that came out was a croak. She closed her eyes again, thinking that when she opened them, the wishful image of Cami's face would be gone. But when she was done counting to ten and she forced her lids up, the blue-eyed blonde still knelt beside her, and the warm hand still clasped her own.

This time, she managed to speak. "Sweet pea?"

Her daughter collapsed back onto her knees, her face filled with a relief that was heartbreaking. Her hands flew through the air in a flow of long, disjointed language.

Mommy. You're okay. I'm so tired and hungry, and I miss Bunny-Bun-Bun but the lady told me you were gone. I thought she meant gone like dead, but she wouldn't answer me when I asked. I don't think she knows how to sign. The lady who doesn't know how to sign told me you were gone. Why would she tell me you were gone? Why were mom *and* gone *the only two words she could make? Why did she bring me here? I was in a room before. But if you were gone—*

Ignoring the ache in her head, Maryse cut her daughter off by pulling her close. She hugged her as tightly as she could, and she didn't bother to fight the tears that filled her eyes, then spilled over. Finally, Cami made a small, squeaky noise—a rarity for her at all—and Maryse let her wriggle free. Then she pulled back to examine her daughter more closely.

Are you hurt? she asked, even though she couldn't see any sign of outward suffering.

I wasn't until you squeezed me.

In spite of everything, Marsye laughed. *That didn't hurt.*

Camille's nose wrinkled up. *How do you know?*

I just do. Because I'm your mom.

That's not a reason.

It is today. Did the lady who couldn't sign hurt you?

No. She made me eat porridge. Cami added a face, emphasizing her disgust.

The very normal reaction in an anything-but-normal scenario made Maryse's heart ache. She reached out for another hug, wishing she could hold on to her daughter for a whole lot longer. But she needed to find a way out. From wherever they were.

She leaned back again, this time to survey their surroundings. Above them, a steel-framed bulb provided the only light, basking the small room in a yellow glow. And it *was* small. No more than a ten-by-ten square, and stacked with boxes of what looked like computer paper.

Where are we? Cami asked.

Maryse shook her head. They had to be somewhere inside the storage facility. She pushed her hands into the concrete ground, then stood up and looked around. Right away, she spotted a door. But before she could even step toward it, Cami tugged her hand, then shook her head.

Locked, the little girl told her.

"Dammit," she swore, then shot her daughter an apologetic look and shrugged. *Sorry.*

When we get home, you owe the swear jar a dollar.

Yes. I do.

Maryse moved around the room, but other than the

locked door, she saw no way of getting out. What had been going through Dee's mind when she brought them in here? Why bother reuniting them if it was going to be like this? Not that she wanted to undo the chance to see Camille, but she couldn't come up with an answer that made sense.

Absently, she tapped one of the boxes. It made a hollow sound rather than a thick, full one. It piqued her curiosity, and she lifted the lid. What she saw inside made her frown. It wasn't a stack of paper at all. Instead, it was a single file folder with a name and a photo on the outside.

Maryse lifted it out, and Cami tugged at her shirt.

What is it? her daughter wanted to know.

Maryse shrugged. *I'm not sure.*

But as she lifted out the folder, she got an idea of what it might be. A complete identity. Quickly, she moved on to the next box. Then the next. In each, she found the same thing. A picture and a name. A list of ID numbers.

Her mouth went dry as she formed a conclusion. *These files aren't just stolen identities. They're entire lives.*

What she was dealing with—what Dee White dealt *in*— was so much more than simple fraud.

"People with paper," she muttered, understanding the horrifying play on words.

Maryse let the lid she held slip from her fingers. She and Camille didn't just need to get out. They needed to get out *now*. Feeling desperate but not wanting to show it, she moved toward the door slowly and studied it. Maybe her six-year-old daughter couldn't get it open. But she was a grown woman. One who'd just been through hell to get where she was at that moment, and she wasn't about to give up. Her eyes traveled the length of the door in search of a weakness. The handle was seamless. The frame was snug and allowed no light to pass through.

But the hinges.

She didn't realize she'd signed the phrase until Camille tugged her shirt again and repeated it. *The hinges?*

Maryse nodded. It was implausible. A little crazy, even. The door was metal and heavy looking, and there probably wouldn't be anything subtle about their attempted escape. But it was the only option she could come up with. She stepped close, eyeing the screws. *Flatheads.* Her eyes flicked around the room again. Finding a screwdriver was out of the question. The paper clips in the boxes were too flimsy to be of any use. Then her gaze landed on Camille. Around her neck hung the familiar MedicAlert charm. Stainless steel and emblazoned with the word *DEAF* on the back.

Can Mommy borrow that? Maryse signed.

For the hinges?

Yes.

Okay.

She turned around and lifted her hair up obediently, and Maryse placed a quick kiss on the back of her neck before unfastening the clasp. She slid the charm off quickly, then moved to the door. When she pressed the little piece of metal to the screw head and it fit perfectly, she wanted to cry with relief. But freeing the hinges didn't prove to be easy work. Loosening the first one made her hands ache. The second set them afire. And the third resulted in a fast-forming blister. But she fought through pain, seizing on every bit of adrenaline her body had to work off.

You have to do this, she said to herself. *Or you'll both die. You'll never see Brooks again. He'll never meet Camille, and she'll never get to use his slide.*

Now the tears came for a different reason. Still she pushed through. Where she'd previously held on to her daughter's image to give her strength, she now used Brooks's face. His worried hazel eyes. His soft but firm lips. The strength in his jaw. She recalled each one perfectly as she worked.

And the way he made her feel. That was cemented in her mind, too. When she was with him, she felt like she could rely on someone other than herself. Like she wasn't alone in the world. Like she had a match.

Like I'm loved. The thought was so startling that she just about dropped the charm. *Loved? Really?*

Carefully, she tested out the idea. Under any other circumstance, it might've been far-fetched. But the way Brooks looked at her spoke volumes. The warmth and tenderness in his eyes, his commitment to helping her rescue Camille… All of it fit. And the bright bloom in her own heart matched.

Loved, she thought again, a little more firmly. *And maybe* in *love, too.*

The admission was enough of a distraction that she almost didn't notice that she'd freed two complete sets of hinges now. And opening the one at the top wouldn't even be necessary. Holding the door—which wasn't quite as heavy as she'd assumed—she pushed it open and ducked down to peer out into the hall. Empty. Satisfied that they were safe for the moment, she turned and gestured for Cami to slip through. Her daughter bit her lip nervously, then nodded and did as she was asked. Then, being careful not to simply drop the door down, Maryse bent and followed her.

Almost home free, she thought, grabbing her daughter's hand.

But they only made it two triumphant steps before a gun clicked from the dark hall in front of them, freezing Maryse—and by extension Cami as well—to the spot. And a soft almost-indistinguishable yelp was the only warning she had before her daughter was snatched from her grasp.

Brooks stood just behind a large sign in front of the squat building. He had no doubt that Maryse was being held inside. The People With Paper sign out front was an ominous reminder of who owned it. So for the last few minutes, he'd been doing what he did best. Watching. Assessing. Deciding what the best course of action would be. He took a large sip of his warm, nearly empty soda and studied the various entrances.

The front wasn't an option. Too obvious. The back might've been good, but his experience with criminals told him that was probably the most closely guarded way in and out. So that left the side door. Which was where he'd been focusing his attention.

Three men.

That was how many he'd counted coming in and out. One brought out a garbage can. Another came for a smoke. The third was still there now, leaning up against the wall with a book in his hand. None of them had looked particularly dangerous. Certainly none were armed that he could see. Most important, they hadn't used a key to get back inside.

He took another sip and waited a little longer. Five minutes passed. Then the third man closed his book and slipped it into his coat pocket before going back inside, too.

"All right, door number three," Brooks said as he set down the empty can. "You're up."

He started to slink forward, but before he could get one foot in front of the other, his phone chimed in his pocket. A glance at the call display told him it was Masters, so he tapped the button and answered.

"Small."

"Are you there?"

"If by 'there,' you mean at the paper place, then yeah."

"I've got some info for you. And you're not going to like it."

"In a bit of a rush here, Masters."

"Remember when I said that some kid turned in Anne Black's husband?"

"Kid with a fake ID, yeah."

"It wasn't just some kid, Small. It was Jean-Paul Kline."

Maryse's brother.

Masters kept talking, saying he'd looked up the name and found out about his connection to the arson six years ago. That his sister had been his next of kin, but that she'd never been found. That her name was Maryse, and that it wasn't a coincidence, was it? Brooks, though, had gone still. Everywhere but his hand and his mind. The former tightened so hard on the phone that he was surprised it didn't shatter. The second worked in overdrive to put together the events.

A teenage Jean-Paul turned on Saul Black.

The bust led to Saul's death. And the death of his son. Of *Anne's* son.

Brooks remembered what Maryse had said about her brother going through a particularly rough patch when he was eighteen. Probably right around the time. The guilt would've been overwhelming.

Then…fast-forward a few years. Jean-Paul has a child of his own. A child Anne feels is owed to her.

"Holy hell," he muttered.

"Small?"

"Masters, I need a connection between Nank and Anne Black."

"Didn't you hear anything I just told you?"

"No."

His partner swore, then said, "They're the same person."

"What?"

"I was sitting there, staring at the name when it hit me. Caleb Nank. If you rearrange the letters, they make her name, too. Caleb Nank is her ultimate pseudonym."

Brooks's eyes whipped to the building. Maryse—the

woman he was damned sure he was in love with—was trapped in there with the slipperiest criminal he'd encountered in twelve years of police work. And the criminal in question had a personal vendetta against Maryse's daughter.

He slammed his phone off, dropped it into his pocket and hit the ground at a dead run.

Maryse shook with fear, her eyes darting between her daughter and the petite woman with a gun.

Dee smiled, cold and dark. "I take it you found my girls. One of them was her mother, you know."

Maryse knew without being told that she was talking about the stack of boxed-up identities in the room behind her. And she wished she was impervious to the bait. But she wasn't. Especially not with her daughter's life hanging in the balance. She stared at the other woman, waiting for the smug explanation she knew had to be coming.

"He was working for me then, even though he hadn't figured it out yet," Dee said with a shrug. "And I was content to leave it that way. I'd already been waiting for five years, so what was another bit of time? He was trying hard to stay straight. Really thought his gig with People With Paper would pan out. Figured out quickly that it wouldn't, though. I didn't even realize until it was too late. He'd already gone to your detective. He thought he was smart. He thought he could *out*smart me. Pretty obvious in the end that he wasn't quite so clever."

Maryse drew in a breath, still not making complete sense of what the other woman was saying, but knowing she had to keep her talking. "But it wasn't enough, you said before. You killed Jean-Paul. I'm guessing his girlfriend died in the fire, too. But it didn't make you feel any better."

"For a little while, it did. I thought I got all three of them. That I destroyed his family the way he destroyed mine."

"What happened?"

"I found out that *she* lived." Dee gestured toward Cami, who stood wide-eyed and still.

"How?"

"Dumb luck. I'd been trying to find ways to move my girls across the border. I started feeling around for a place to set up shop. I was in Laval. You were in Laval. Shopping, maybe, I don't know. I saw your daughter and *bam*. I just knew. She looks exactly like her father. And I knew that was what I'd been missing. *She* was what I needed."

Maryse blinked. "Who the hell are you?"

The answer came from behind her instead of from in front of her. "She's Caleb Nank."

Brooks.

God, she was relieved to hear his voice. And terrified by what he'd said.

"Or Anne Black. Or Dee. Or maybe Deanna," he added. "Depending on who you ask."

And suddenly it all clicked. Nank and Dee were the same person. Maryse couldn't fight a gasp. Brooks's hand landed on her shoulder, but his reassurance did little to ease the frightened thump of her heart.

"Why'd you send me to Laval, Anne?" he asked.

She shrugged. "I was hoping you'd get yourself killed. You're a sucker for anything related to the Nank case."

"Couldn't just walk up and kill me?"

"I could've. But where's the fun in that? I *like* being in charge, Detective Small. I like pulling the strings and pretending I'm on the sidelines when I'm really the ringmaster."

"The long con."

"More or less."

"Like with Jean-Paul. You held him responsible for your

son's death and you were perfectly happy to drag out his punishment."

"He *is* responsible. He turned us in. Turned Saul in. If he'd just kept his mouth shut…"

"So now what?" Brooks asked, and Maryse tensed, waiting for an answer she knew she wouldn't like.

"Depends," Dee replied. "Do you want things to be hard? Or easy?"

She missed the rest of the interaction because her eyes were drawn to her daughter, who was gesturing in ASL. Tiny motions, almost unreadable.

The man behind you?

Maryse tipped her head just enough. *Yes.*

He says he loves you.

She swallowed, her heart aching so badly it burned. *Yes.*

Do you love him?

Yes?

Weird.

Maryse fought the tiniest smile. *Yes.*

He talks funny. He wants us to count to three and then lie on the floor.

He does?

Yes.

Then we probably should. Ready?

A small nod.

One, Maryse signed.

Two, added her daughter.

"Three," Brooks whispered.

Maryse hit the ground, watching to make sure Cami did the same. As they landed, Brooks's arm came up. The flash of metal warned her of what was about to come, and she reached across the floor to drag her daughter closer. The shot reverberated through the hall, and she didn't have to look up to see that Brooks had met his mark. Dee—Anne

Black—fell backward, and the big cop strode forward, his weapon still raised.

Maryse sat up and drew Cami into her arms, careful to keep the carnage out of sight. She opened her mouth, but whatever she was about to say was drowned out as a noisy, too-close *thump* filled the air.

A helicopter?

She tossed a worried look at Brooks, but he just shot her a smile in return.

"Masters," he yelled over the noise.

And in minutes, the building was teeming with cops. Then with paramedics. A hundred voices flooded through, and though she clung to Cami, she quickly lost sight of Brooks. Before she could find him again, she found herself wrapped in a blanket, seated beside her daughter in one of the helicopters. Cami was already asleep, but Maryse was too wired to even think about resting. All she wanted was to see Brooks. To get some more answers and to hear *him* explain all the bits and pieces. But the sea of people was too thick, the hum of movement too overwhelming. Just as panic set in, his warm, familiar body slammed into the seat across from her. His knees brushed her, and he reached out to touch her face.

"Your brother was a hero, sweetheart," he said.

She nodded. That much, she'd picked up on. He'd tried to do the right thing. He'd succeeded in saving Camille. And for that, Maryse would be thankful forever.

"Is it really over?" she asked, her voice raw.

"Over-ish," he said.

"What?"

He bent forward and brushed his lips across hers before answering. "I don't want to say *over*, because I have a whole hell of a lot of more work to do. Questions to answer, lists to cross off. It's gonna be a while before all of this calms down."

A twinge of disappointment hit her. "Oh."

"But one thing's for sure," he added. "Camille and you won't be separated. I made damned sure of *that*."

There weren't enough words to express her gratitude for the reassurance, so she settled for the simplest. "Thank you."

Brooks leaned back as the helicopter whirred to life. But he wasn't done talking yet. His hands flashed.

There's another thing that makes me pretty sure it's not over. That funny little person on your lap did give you my message, right?

Maryse's face warmed. *To count to three and drop?*

That, Brooks replied. *And the other bit. No big deal. Just that I love you.*

Now her whole body heated. *She did.*

And?

And I love you, too.

See? he signed. *Not over. Just beginning.*

And for the first time in six years, Maryse wasn't worried about what the next day would bring.

* * * * *

If you loved this suspenseful story, don't miss the exciting first book in Melinda Di Lorenzo's brand-new series, coming in September 2017!

And don't forget her previous books:
WORTH THE RISK
LAST CHANCE HERO
Available now from Harlequin Romantic Suspense!

"You overheard enough to realize that he'd make me fire you."

"Oh, I know that," he heartily agreed. "What I don't know is why you wouldn't want to fire me." Was it possible— Could she be as attracted to him as he was to her? He'd caught her glances whenever he went without a shirt. Had he just imagined her interest?

"So do you want me to fire you?" she asked.

"No." And it wasn't just because he still wanted to search for those rooms. It was because of her—because he wanted to keep spending his days with her. "I told you that I need this job."

"You don't need this job," she said, as her dark eyes narrowed slightly with suspicion. "With your skills, you can do anything you want to do."

"Really?" he asked.

"Yes," she said. "Your injury is not holding you back at all."

It was, though. If he didn't have the scars and the missing eye, he might have done what he wanted to do sooner. "So you really think I can do anything I want?"

She sighed slightly, as if she was getting annoyed with him. "Yes, I do."

So he reached up and slid one arm around her waist to draw her tightly against him. Then he cupped the back of her head in his free hand and lowered her face to his.

And he kissed her.

Her lips were as silky as her skin and her hair. He brushed his softly across them.

She gasped, and her breath whispered across his skin. With her palms against his chest, she pushed him back but not completely away. His arm was still looped around her waist. "What are you doing?" she asked.

"You told me I can do anything I want," he reminded her, and his voice was gruff with the desire overwhelming him. "This is what I want to do—what I've wanted to do for a long time." Ever since that first night he'd heard her scream and found her in the basement with her pepper spray and indomitable spirit.

Her lips curved into a slight smile. "I didn't mean this…"

But she didn't protest when he tugged her back against him and kissed her again. Instead she kissed him, too, her lips moving against his, parting as her tongue slipped out and into his mouth.

Don't miss
THE COLTON MARINE by Lisa Childs,
available July 2017 wherever
Harlequin® Romantic Suspense books
and ebooks are sold.

www.Harlequin.com

Turn your love of reading into
rewards you'll love with

Harlequin My Rewards

**Join for FREE today at
www.HarlequinMyRewards.com**

Earn **FREE BOOKS** of your choice.

Experience **EXCLUSIVE OFFERS** and contests.

Enjoy **BOOK RECOMMENDATIONS**
selected just for you.

PLUS! Sign up now
and get **500** points
right away!

Earn **FREE** REWARDS
HarlequinMyRewards.com
Join Today!

MYR16R